**"I guess I better go check on Sundance,"
Dylan said. "He probably needs a walk."**

Dylan was looking skyward instead of at the floor, which he must have memorized by now with all the time he'd spent looking at it.

"And I need to get the desserts out to the barn for the other guests," Georgina said.

He didn't respond, simply held his gaze on the ceiling. It wasn't until he looked back down—directly at her this time, with a nervous smile and shake of his head— that she realized why. He'd been standing under the mistletoe.

Good thing she didn't buy into all that nonsense, although for a fleeting moment she imagined she could. With the right man, of course.

Not that he was thinking that way about her. His slipping out from under the mistletoe pretty much confirmed it. At least they seemed to agree on that much. Still, no use taking chances.

*Note to self: Avoid the foyer.*

Dear Reader,

I bet we all know the disappointment when our dreams and schemes don't go as planned. Then there are those times when the broken ones result in something more wonderful than we could have ever imagined.

In *The Cowboy's Holiday Plan*—the fifth book in my Destiny Springs, Wyoming series—the hero and heroine experience both when tasked with co-planning his famous father's nuptials.

Their visions for weddings—and for living, in general—clash. Georgina believes it is a woman's most special day. And someday, it will be her turn. In the meantime, being a professional wedding planner fits her better than a custom-made gown. For Dylan, his wedding was the worst day of his life. It's something he vows never to repeat. But as their attempts at co-planning fall hopelessly apart, Dylan and Georgina drift closer together.

I hope all your dreams and schemes come true. But if they don't, may the broken ones end up gifting you with something even more special in the end.

Warmest wishes,

*Susan Breeden*

# THE COWBOY'S HOLIDAY PLAN

## SUSAN BREEDEN

**HEARTWARMING**

**H Harlequin®**
**HEARTWARMING™**

ISBN-13: 978-1-335-46019-6

The Cowboy's Holiday Plan

Harlequin Enterprises ULC
22 Adelaide St. West, 41st Floor
Toronto, Ontario M5H 4E3, Canada
www.Harlequin.com

Printed in U.S.A.

**Recycling programs for this product may not exist in your area.**

**Susan Breeden** is a native Texan who currently lives in Houston, where she works as a technical writer/editor for the aerospace industry. In the wee hours of morning and again at night, you will find her playing matchmaker for the heroes and heroines in her novels. She also enjoys walks with her bossy German shepherd, decluttering and organizing her closet, and trying out new chili con queso recipes. For information on Susan's upcoming books, visit susanbreeden.com.

### Books by Susan Breeden

### Harlequin Heartwarming

### *Destiny Springs, Wyoming*

*The Bull Rider's Secret Son*
*Her Kind of Cowboy*
*The Cowboy's Rodeo Redemption*
*And Cowboy Makes Three*

Visit the Author Profile page
at Harlequin.com for more titles.

For all my friends and family
who not only put up with me and my unconventional
schedule, but who love me in spite of it.

A very special thanks to my agent, Cori Deyoe, and
my Harlequin editor, Dana Grimaldi. I couldn't have
written the Destiny Springs, Wyoming series without
such amazing support and guidance!

# *CHAPTER ONE*

"YOU'D BETTER WATCH OUT, MAX," Georgina Goodwin admonished.

The little redheaded cutie had appeared at some point and was staring up as she positioned the final decoration onto the bottom of the chandelier in the foyer of the Hideaway B and B.

Unfortunately, her words triggered another thought—*You'd better not cry*—which could too easily grow into an earworm. Last thing she wanted was a Christmas song stuck in her head.

What she had really meant to say was that he shouldn't stand so close to people on ladders. Thankfully, her work was done. When she returned to solid ground, she brushed a tendril of hair out of her eyes with the back of her hand, then wiped her palms on her pink sweatpants and looked up at her handiwork. Even though she wasn't a fan of this holiday or tradition—quite the understatement—it was going to be fun to see how the B and B guests reacted. Fortunately, she was immune to the plant's alleged powers.

"Watch out for what?" Max asked.

"The mistletoe." She pointed to the culprit. "When you're standing under it, someone can steal a kiss."

The six-year-old's eyes opened wide with what she guessed was fear as he looked up again, then back at her as if hoping for some sign that she was teasing.

She bit her lip as the little boy's mom snuck up behind him, wrangled him into a hug despite her very pregnant belly and proceeded to smother him with kisses as he attempted to finagle out of her grip while giggling uncontrollably.

Finally. A bit of brightness amid the gloom of this particular season. The smile that Max had just put on his mommy's face spread just as fast and wide as the holiday spirit had in Destiny Springs, Wyoming, once Thanksgiving had wrapped up. And that was saying something. This place was Christmas on steroids, with all the festivities and decorations.

Not only was Becca Sayers the coolest boss in town, she was also a terrific mom to Max and the best friend ever to Georgina's little sister, Hailey. The list could go on and on. Come to think of it, both of those ladies had married their perfect match. And Georgina had helped make her younger sister's wedding special, if not as extravagant as she thought Hailey deserved. Then there was Faye, their older sister, who'd eloped. Unimaginable, in Georgina's opinion.

Pachelbel's Canon in D Major suddenly popped into her head, temporarily blocking out the country crooning of Montgomery Legend that she'd decided to play in the background instead of depressing Christmas songs. But this tune invited in even worse thoughts. Although she loved her job here at the B and B, she missed her full-time career as a wedding planner.

Soon enough, Penny galloped in on her three legs. The rescue labradoodle tried to get in on the hugging action, but she only served to break up their party. Except...the dog didn't have any snow on her fur or paws. Georgina could've sworn Penny had been outside with Becca's husband, Cody.

She walked over to the window, where the bundled-up cowboy was still talking on his cell and pacing the length of the patio, while a dog frolicked in the snow. Upon closer inspection, that canine definitely had four legs. And longer, straighter fur. Possibly a golden retriever.

She swiveled back around to catch Max and Penny now running down the hall and Becca checking out the vase of pale pink roses Georgina had placed on a table.

"Did y'all get another pup?" Georgina asked.

"Not a chance," Becca said.

"Then who's outside with Cody?"

"That's what I need to talk to you about. It isn't Cody."

Georgina turned again to the window for yet another look. He was wearing a black Stetson like the former bull rider always wore, and he looked to be about the same build. Perhaps a bit taller and leaner, now that she was looking more closely. But his head remained down as he continued to talk on his cell phone so she couldn't see his face. She'd just assumed it was Cody.

She turned back to Becca, who looked beyond nervous with the way she was wringing her hands. The woman had been doing a lot of that lately. She was due in January and wasn't relinquishing nearly enough duties to Georgina. But there was nothing to worry about. She was pretty sure she could fill in the blanks.

"Let me guess. The gentleman outside is staying at the B and B and brought his dog, which means I'll have some extra duties."

Becca took a deep breath. "Exactly. But not the duties you might expect. And you can say no to the biggest one. Please understand that before I ask."

Georgina cocked her head and waited. She was out of guesses, and frankly, this was starting to make her nervous as well. She usually wasn't given the right of refusal. Besides, she'd never say no to Becca anyway. The woman had given her a job after Georgina's partner at their high-profile wedding-planning service had kicked her to the curb for "lacking originality," which was ridiculous. And professionally devastating.

"Mom and Monty want to get married before the baby arrives."

That was fast. Georgina knew that Becca's mom, Rose, and country-music star Montgomery Legend were engaged, but they seemed to otherwise be taking their relationship slowly and keeping things very quiet and private. Maybe that was what was causing Becca to be so nervous. Totally understandable.

"That's terrific!" Georgina said, if only to comfort her boss, who was already overwhelmed.

"It can be. With your help." Becca bit her lip and forced a squeamish smile.

Georgina's breath caught in her throat. Was Becca about to "pop the question" she'd been hoping to hear from someone—anyone—for almost a year?

"Meaning…?" No use jumping to conclusions. She'd been disappointed enough for one lifetime.

"Will you help plan their wedding?"

"Yes!" Georgina wasted no time giving Becca a hug, careful not to crush her precious cargo in the process. She then pulled away. "I'll handle everything, so don't you worry."

All of a sudden, the full magnitude of it set in. A celebrity wedding would put Georgina back on the map. The guest list, along with the exposure, would open doors that remained bolted shut to most planners.

"Not everything," Becca said.

At that, Georgina deflated. She'd gotten a bit ahead of herself. Of course there could be other people involved. But she'd bet they didn't have the kind of experience and vendor connections she had.

Georgina straightened. "Understood. Just let me know what you need me to do. Remember, I'm used to handling everything when it comes to nuptials, so use me. Please."

"Actually, I won't be involved at all. But Monty's son will be."

"Is he a wedding planner, by chance?" Georgina asked. Hopefully not. That way she could certainly make this project her own.

"No. He's a rodeo announcer. And he's the gentleman pacing the porch. I told him I hadn't talked to you about it yet, and he was giving his dad one last opportunity to provide any input. He'll be staying here for a couple of weeks."

"Before we bring him in, is there anything else you need to talk to me about?" Georgina asked. This was turning into an emotional roller coaster, which was happening more and more as Becca reached her due date. Understandable, with everything on the woman's mind. Might as well get the whole ride over with at once, if possible.

"Maybe just one thing." Becca nodded sideways at the pink flowers.

"I know. They're not Christmassy, but I couldn't help myself. The florist was about to throw these away to make room for more poinsettias." Which, on second thought, was exactly what she was supposed to get in the first place. *Oops.*

Becca didn't say a word. She simply stared at the blooms, many of which were torn and on the verge of withering. To Georgina, they were so much prettier than the new ones that were flawless. But she was in the minority on that opinion.

"That's fine. They can stay. After all, you're doing me a *huge* favor." Becca opened the front door and waved to Georgina's co-planner for the next two weeks, who sounded like he was wrapping up the call to his dad.

*That voice!* No wonder he'd gone into rodeo announcing. It was even deeper than Montgomery Legend's, whose music was still piping through the downstairs instead of the Christmas music that Georgina had been instructed to play. Becca had yet to point that out. Considering this new information, maybe it would work in her favor.

The golden retriever took the lead and bolted through the front door, nearly knocking Becca down in the process. The full-grown pup immediately summed up Georgina as an animal lover and total pushover, running over to her for some pets and hugs.

The pup's owner finally came inside, removed his Stetson and shook out his hair, then gave Becca a huge smile and a hug. He paused in his tracks, tilted his head and squinted.

"The music is a nice touch," he said.

Georgina liked the guy already.

Becca cocked her head to match his angle. "Yes, it is. I hadn't noticed until you pointed it out, Dylan." She then cast a knowing look to Georgina, who simply shrugged.

Looked like she already had an ally in this stranger. That was a good sign. No reason why this shouldn't go smoothly. He then turned his attention toward Georgina, only briefly making eye contact before looking down at his golden retriever, who seemed to adore her.

"Sundance. Leave the nice lady alone, please," he said.

The dog did as told and ran back to his owner, his entire backside wagging the whole way. In the process, Georgina got a better look at the man's face. It suited the voice. His almost-black hair was straight but a bit shaggy after spending who knew how long beneath that cowboy hat. He looked like he could use a shave, with the slightest bit of stubble. He was, indeed, taller than the former bull rider she'd first mistaken him for, but he lacked Cody's confident swagger.

Becca closed the space between them.

"Georgina, this is Dylan James. Dylan, Georgina Goodwin. I've filled both of you in on the situation, and I have zero doubt you'll come up with something special for my mom and Monty," Becca said, adding an extra big smile for her soon-to-be stepbrother.

Georgina, for one, had a very good feeling about it. An even better one when he finally looked directly at with her with those Nikko Blue Hydrangea–colored eyes.

*Something old, something new, something borrowed...*

Hopefully, that saying was a powerful enough earworm to cast out "Santa Claus Is Coming to Town."

But then his expression changed. The smile faded, along with the enthusiasm. Either she looked worse than she thought or he was having second thoughts about having a co-planner. Or both.

"Nice to meet you, Dylan." She extended her hand, because he wasn't taking any initiative.

He put his cowboy hat back on, then shook her hand.

Cordial enough, but not very encouraging.

Dylan turned back to Becca. "I better get Sundance situated and get unpacked. Maybe Georgina and I can open up the discussion after I get settled in."

Georgina's back stiffened. His demeanor not only changed, he was speaking as if she wasn't even in the room. The initial warm-and-fuzzy turned into something a little cooler and much scratchier. Yet when he looked at her again, he offered up a warm smile. Confusing. Perhaps he was simply as unsure about this arrangement as she was.

"Maybe you two could meet in an hour or so and start with a decision on a wedding date. Give Georgina a fair chance to wrap her mind around all of this, since I just sprung it on her," Becca said.

How long had Becca been holding out on her? And why? Maybe she was her boss's last resort rather than her first choice.

No matter. Becca would not regret this decision. Georgina was going to make absolute sure of it.

"That's a great suggestion. We're serving coffee and dessert in the barn in about an hour. How about we meet there? It will be a 'date' date," Georgina said, hopefully in a way that didn't make this working relationship even more awkward than it had to be.

Dylan glanced at her for a brief moment and nodded. That was better than nothing, but still strange. He collected a large piece of luggage and a backpack from the patio, and rallied Sundance to his side. He paused, then nodded toward the pink roses and murmured, "Pretty."

"Yes, they are," Becca said, then looked at her and shrugged.

Georgina wasn't sure how to interpret that. Was her boss shrugging because the compliment caught her off guard? Or did she also pick up on the fact that their new guest was barely acknowledging Georgina and wasn't sure what to make of it? Either way, Georgina had a feeling Dylan wasn't completely on board with co-planning a wedding with anyone. And for some reason, especially not with her.

Becca led the way up the stairs to show Dylan to his room, leaving Georgina in their dust. Utterly thrilled at the possibilities before her, yet hopelessly confused. Either this was going to be the best opportunity for her to breathe life back into her wedding-planning career…

Or it would put an end to it altogether.

"How old do I look, Sundance? Because I felt like a ten-year-old down there," Dylan said as soon as he closed the door to his room and locked it behind him.

Not because he expected his dog to answer, but because he had to find out if any words could come out of his mouth. His persistent stutter, which had been nowhere around when talking to Becca, had come on that quickly with... *Georgina, is it?* As soon as Becca made the introductions, he felt the words logjam in the back of his throat and her name flew right out of his brain.

He wasn't sure what he'd been expecting when it came to working with a professional wedding planner. But it sure wasn't a blond, brown-eyed vision in a pink sweatsuit and tennis shoes.

Dylan laughed and shook his head as he hefted his suitcase onto the soft denim bedspread. Yep, he was in the right place. Becca had said she was putting him in the Denim Room, and it didn't disappoint. Meanwhile, Sundance had made himself comfortable on an oversized acid-washed denim chair before Dylan had a chance to drape a sheet over it. If he didn't take care of this situation, the chair would be wearing a fur coat when they left in two weeks. Becca assured him that the bedspread was washable, so that would be an easy fix.

"Up!" He patted the mattress, and Sundance jumped off the chair and onto the bed, where he curled up on his usual side. Dylan promptly covered the other tempting surfaces in the room with the extra sheets he'd requested, then opened the denim curtains to an expanse of bluegrass blanketed in white, with snowcaps overseeing it all in the distance.

The multicolored lights strung along the rooftop had been a warm greeting on such a frigid day. Once he'd stepped inside the B and B, he'd been greeted by the smell of pine and vanilla and apple pie.

*Christmas.* There was no day more special.

This year, however, the entire month would be extra special. He'd been honored when his dad had trusted him to plan the wedding. Seemed Dylan had finally convinced the man that he was a grown-up, capable of handling whatever life tossed him. Beating the odds and succeeding at rodeo announcing must have done the trick.

But then his dad's fiancée, Rose Haring, had to throw a wrench into it by lining up some "professional help" in the form of a wedding planner.

As much as Dylan wanted to prove that he could do this all by himself, a part of him had been relieved. The more he researched what would be involved—even with a small wedding—the more he was convinced it wasn't something just anyone could do.

Enter Georgina, who'd rendered him temporarily speechless.

The last thing he needed was any challenge to his focus. Not this close to the Fort Worth

Charity New Year's Rodeo for ovarian cancer. The announcing gig promised to put him on the map and secure a place on the roster of regular announcers. But that was a secondary benefit of doing the gig. Maybe it was too late to save his own mom, but other folks shouldn't have to lose theirs.

Dylan sat beside his half-unpacked suitcase and shook his head, then made a decision that he was pretty sure his mom would have approved of. He would provide the wedding planner with his short list of non-negotiables—a Christmas Day wedding with family and dearest friends only—and let her decide the rest. His dad and Rose wanted to be surprised, after all. He'd given the man one last chance to make any special requests, which was a futile effort. And his future stepmother wasn't any more forthcoming with Becca apparently.

Dylan wouldn't mind being surprised too. The million-dollar question now was would his voice cooperate for this hopefully one-and-only meeting?

"I guess we're about to find out."

He finished hanging his clothes in the closet and arranging his toiletries on the small bathroom sink counter. That was when he realized he'd forgotten his razor. He took a quick shower, which felt good after the three-hour flight from

Dallas, followed by another hour of drive time. He brushed his teeth and changed into some fresh clothes. That would have to do.

Sundance jumped off the bed as if he were going along. Dylan would love to have him there for emotional support and to help ward off any stuttering, but he didn't want to take Sundance into the barn where food was being served, even though Becca had given him permission. Or he shouldn't, in case it would make some folks uncomfortable.

Well, perhaps he *could* get away without the formalities here. Some places let him. *Places that know I'm Montgomery Legend's son.*

Yep. Doors just flew open for him sometimes. Problem was certain ones he wanted to open for himself. The most important being his career opportunities. If word got around about his identity, that would all change. And he'd never know whether he got the gigs on his own merit.

He grabbed a pen and notepad—the only things that might possibly get him through this meeting without a hitch. If the words wouldn't come out while he was looking at her, he could usually get them to flow if he focused on something other than the source of stress. He hated to resort to that because it came across as rude, but this situation was what it was.

That was the beauty of rodeo announcing. He

watched and reported on what he loved most, and no one was looking at him. If someone did happen to glance his way, Sundance would steal their attention.

Dylan made his way downstairs, past the parlor. His father's music was still playing, which nourished his resolve to do a good job on this. He made his way through the kitchen to the back door, which Becca had said would lead down a path to the barn.

A few people were headed the same way, and a couple were leaving just as he entered.

He spotted Georgina immediately. She was flitting back and forth between the coffee station and a separate table where a tray of desserts, along with plates and forks and napkins, were stacked.

She looked up, smiled and waved, then pointed at a small table in the far corner with two chairs facing each other. The community table would have been better for his nerves. They could sit side by side on the long bench, and he wouldn't have to look directly at her.

Then again, he wouldn't *get* to look at her either.

*Oh boy.* That was a thought he didn't need to have.

The table she'd pointed to wasn't exactly empty, however. There were books and magazines on weddings splayed across its surface. She was awfully prepared for someone who'd had this task sprung on her about an hour ago. But that made him more confident in trusting her with most of the decisions.

He set down his pen and notepad and walked over to the coffee station. As the mug was filling, Georgina tore herself away from one of the other guests and approached him.

"How about a homemade apple-pie square to go with that?" she asked.

He smiled and remained focused on adding some cream and sugar to the mug. Then stirred and stirred, willing a simple word to come out.

"Sure," he said, then looked at her again.

Georgina's smile wavered just a little. Yes, he knew his response was a little too short and didn't rise to her level of enthusiasm. But it was better than appearing to ignore her completely.

"Th-thanks," he managed to say without too much impediment, which seemed to perk her up a bit.

"I'll meet you at the table. We have so much to talk about. I know you probably have lots of ideas. This is so exciting!"

He nodded. It was all he could manage. So much for this being a "date" date. At least he could use Sundance as an excuse, if not a crutch.

Wasn't fair to leave him alone in a strange room, by himself, for too long.

Yet her enthusiasm was encouraging. In fact, he was breathing a little easier already.

He chose the chair facing the wall and started jotting something down on his notepad as she placed the apple pie square, fork and napkin next to him.

She went back and retrieved another mug of coffee for herself, then settled into the chair across from him.

He finished jotting down *Christmas Wedding*, for lack of much else, then looked up. She was taking a sip of coffee while stealing a glance at his notepad. He turned it around for her with one hand while taking a sip of coffee with the other.

She immediately shook her head. "New Year's Day wedding."

Well, this was getting off to a bad start. He took a deep breath, then pulled the plate in front of him and spoke as he focused on cutting the perfect-sized bite of the apple slice square.

"No can do. I have plans that day." He looked up as the words hit and took a bite of the dessert, if only to keep from having to say more. This wedding day wasn't about him. He had his dad's full support to choose the rodeo over the wedding. But Dylan didn't want to choose between honoring his mom by participating in the fundraiser and celebrating his dad's new future.

She squinted. "Why Christmas?"

He looked down and carved out another bite from the square. A bigger one that would take longer to chew. If only he had a little more time to chew on his response to her question.

"Why not?" he asked, then looked up and placed the bite in his mouth.

"I don't want their special day to compete with what a lot of folks think is the most important day of the year. Besides, at this juncture, all the guests may have trouble making it."

All the guests? Although she did have a valid point about Christmas, a big guest list was the worst thing she could suggest. This couldn't be a large wedding, for several reasons. First and foremost, his dad wouldn't want it, even though he didn't specifically say so. Secondly, Dylan had accomplished so much as *Dylan James* and hoped to eventually be "the voice" of a top rodeo—without the benefit of his famous father's name or connections. The fewer guests, the less chance of anyone putting two and two together and "outing" him. Sure, his being Monty's son was old news to his side of the family, but when it came to Rose's side, news like that was more likely to spread.

Looked like his brilliant idea to hand the planning over to her had been a very bad one. That meant only one thing: He'd have to spend even more one-on-one time with her until they could iron out both the date and the guest list. And no telling what other details he wasn't considering. Unless he could talk Becca into letting him handle the planning by himself. Even he knew that wasn't a great idea, but he didn't have a better one.

Dylan dared to look up at Georgina. She'd propped her elbows on the table and was resting her chin on her clasped hands. A wisp of blond hair had fallen across one of her eyes, but it didn't seem to distract her. She raised her brows as if waiting for a response or counteroffer. Her determination both scared and intrigued him.

Their "date" date was turning out to be a disaster, which meant they would need at least one more, because talking about *anything* right now wasn't an option. The prospect of spending even more time with Georgina than originally anticipated left him completely tongue-tied. This was going to be a challenge, on more levels than one. *Story of my life.*

This time, however, he was kind of looking forward to it.

# *CHAPTER TWO*

BECCA SNATCHED A strawberry out from under Georgina just as she was about to slice it.

"You're going to have your hands full in less than a month. You might just need all those fingers. And I don't think our guests would appreciate one of them in their breakfast fruit bowl," Georgina said. "Besides, shouldn't you still be asleep?"

"I couldn't find a comfortable position last night. I'll fall asleep standing up a little later, if I'm not already asleep as we speak," Becca joked as she eased onto one of the barstools. An equally risky choice, with the way the thing wobbled beneath her oddly distributed weight.

But Georgina wasn't laughing. She had something she needed to talk with her boss about—and in a big hurry. She hadn't given Becca a progress report on her initial meeting with her wedding co-planner, and she wasn't looking forward to it.

"I'm sorry you couldn't sleep, but I'm glad

you're up. I need to talk to you about Dylan. We didn't have a very productive meeting yesterday."

Becca shifted and sighed. "I know. He told me *all* about it."

At that, Georgina stopped cutting. She collected some sliced strawberries and put them in a bowl. From there, she retrieved some whipping cream from the refrigerator and added a healthy dollop to the top before placing the bowl and a fork in front of Becca.

"You mean he can actually talk?" Georgina asked.

Becca nodded while chewing and swallowing a rather large bite. "Of course! Why would you even say such a thing? We had a long conversation, in fact. You talked to him too. He said so."

If her boss hadn't been sitting right there, Georgina would have thrown the knife into the sink and her hands into the air. Dylan really didn't like her—for some reason. It wasn't just her own lack of sleep talking. If this was going to work, she'd have to be completely honest with Becca about her concerns.

"I did almost all the talking. It won't be easy for us to work together," she said.

Becca looked at her. Unfazed. She loaded up her fork but paused. "He feels the same way."

Georgina could practically feel her jaw drop but tried not to let it show. She hoped the guests were hungry for strawberries, because she was probably going to slice the whole lot before this conversation was over.

"Since he was so chatty to you, did he say why? Except that we couldn't agree on a wedding date. At least I provided a reason for not supporting a Christmas wedding—a good one."

Yet not wanting Rose and Monty to share their wedding day with that particular holiday wasn't the only reason, of course. But no one needed to know how she felt about sharing her birthday with Christmas every year. How she'd missed out on the kind of parties other children were given. Even her Sweet Sixteen came and went with minimal fanfare. Sure, she got an extra gift, wrapped in actual birthday paper, but her day was otherwise too tangled up in all the tinsel and ornaments and endless strings of lights.

Wouldn't matter anyway. Besides, she wasn't a child.

"He mentioned the wedding date disagreement, yes," Becca said.

"It's a common debate with such events. No reason for him to go behind my back and talk to you about this."

"Yeah. That's the wrong thing for a person to do. *Ahem*."

Okay, so she was doing the same thing. But wasn't she hired to be Rose's advocate by Becca herself? To make sure her mom got a dream wedding? Becca had confided in her that Rose didn't have a proper ceremony the first time. They'd married at the courthouse, with strangers as witnesses and a single daffodil stem as a bouquet. Wouldn't take much to improve upon that for her second marriage, which would also be Rose's last, judging by the love the couple shared for each other. All the more reason to make it *extra* special.

"If you don't want to do this, you don't have to," Becca said. "I wasn't sure how you'd feel about taking on so much. I can work with Dylan. That's what I would have done anyway, if it wasn't for this little person kicking and screaming inside me."

"Or I could handle the whole wedding myself."

"I have to be honest—Dylan extended the same offer," Becca said.

Georgina could feel her cheeks turning pink. Not that she was mad. They'd gotten off on the wrong foot somehow, but she was a professional. One that was not going to step aside. Instead, she was going to fight even harder for it.

"You know I can do this much better and more efficiently than someone who has probably never planned a wedding before. Not only that, I *really* want to. Does he?"

"I know you want this and that you're the best

choice. That's why I asked you to be involved. But Monty asked Dylan himself. It's not my place to 'fire' him."

"Then your mom and Monty might be getting two separate ceremonies, because neither of us seem to be willing to budge on the date. Maybe we could simply ask the bride and groom to make that decision. It's their day, after all."

"I did ask Mom. Last night. And she asked Monty."

"And?"

"You'll laugh if I tell you what solution she suggested," Becca said.

"Good! I could use a good laugh. And an even better solution."

Georgina waited. And waited. Becca seemed lost in thought, then a smile tugged at her lips.

A knock on the doorframe interrupted what Georgina hoped would be a helpful suggestion. And there he stood. The topic of their discussion and the current bane of her existence.

"Good morning, ladies," he said, looking to Becca first, then to her.

That deep smooth voice tamed her frustration, even though nothing had been solved. He held on to the leash as Sundance tugged toward a plate of breakfast sausage that Georgina had set out to cook.

"You're up early," she said, forcing a smile. At least she couldn't be accused of not being cordial.

He looked down at Sundance. "Yep. Someone needs to go outside. Thought I'd grab a cup of coffee when I come back in. If that's okay with you, Becca."

Georgina didn't even try to hide that she was rolling her eyes. He wasn't looking at her anyway. But Becca was, and she simply shook her head in admonishment while Dylan looked a little confused.

*Good.*

Furthermore, if he wasn't going to look at her, she'd stop looking at him. Georgina turned her attention back to preparing breakfast.

Becca eased off the barstool. "We'll have some for you when y'all get through with your walk. And I'll need you to hang around if I'm not back when you return. We all need to have a little chat."

Dylan tipped his hat and made a quick exit.

As soon as his bootsteps faded, Georgina turned back around and put a hand on her hip.

Becca pursed her lips and squinted at Georgina as she proceeded to pull a fresh mug from the cabinet. No doubt she was about to reprimand her employee for the whole eye-roll thing.

"I see what you mean. He didn't even look at you," Becca said instead.

A wave of relief swept over her. "So I wasn't imagining it."

"Until you turned around, that is. Then he watched you chop strawberries as if it were a rodeo performance."

"Even weirder," Georgina said.

"You must make him nervous," Becca said with a resolute tone.

"What? Why?"

"Have you seen yourself?"

"As a matter of fact, I have. And I look as tired as I feel most times."

She didn't state the obvious—that she was barely bothering with makeup these days, and her hair was impossible to handle outside the confines of a French twist. And Becca shouldn't even get her started on the extra weight she'd put on since taking over all the cooking at the B and B. Whoever came up with the concept of sweatpants was her hero or heroine.

Judging by the knowing smile on Becca's face, her boss clearly wasn't buying any of Georgina's excuses—spoken or unspoken.

Becca turned and headed out of the kitchen.

*Don't leave me alone with him.*

"Where are you going and when will you be back?" Now she was the one who was nervous. Maybe she'd gotten a good look at herself, but she'd gotten a better look at him. Difficult not to look.

Becca paused. "Just down the hall. And I'll return with the perfect solution."

THE EARLY-MORNING weather was more frigid than usual. Even Sundance was eager to get back inside, where the fireplace in the parlor was already roaring and coffee was brewing in the kitchen.

But something else was brewing as well. Something not nearly as pleasant.

Dylan was tempted to circle the property one last time and endure the cold if it meant Becca would be there when he went back inside. They'd talked last night, and she promised to speak with Georgina about letting him take the reins on the project. A small wedding he could manage. He'd planned to do that in the first place. Besides, with the pressure off, he might even be able to talk to Georgina without the words getting stuck to the roof of his mouth.

Sundance tugged him toward the door, and he gave in. Once inside, they went directly to the fireplace, where the full-grown pup found a nice spot on which to curl up while Dylan warmed his hands. He could hear Georgina in the kitchen, but there wasn't any talking.

His timing turned out to be perfect, because the little redheaded boy he'd met yesterday came running down the hall while staying flush against the wall in the foyer for some reason. Kids were so cute. Max was still in his purple flannel pajamas and was hugging a matching purple stuffed animal of some kind—a bull or longhorn. He ran to the kitchen without even saying hello, although Dylan was quite sure that if the little boy had noticed Sundance, he wouldn't have been in such a hurry.

Becca was trailing far behind, holding her swollen tummy from underneath with every step and pausing in front of the fire.

"I spoke with Georgina. You probably already gathered that," she said.

"And?"

"She voiced the same concerns as you did, but she still wants to be involved. In fact, she offered to handle the whole thing. If you want."

Dylan blew out a long breath. That couldn't happen, although he'd dared to entertain the possibility. But that was before they'd discussed the date and before she mentioned "all the guests."

"I take that as a no. But don't worry. I have the perfect solution. Follow me," Becca said.

He grabbed Sundance's leash and brought him along. He was going to need all the support he could get.

The kitchen seemed brighter than when he left. Must have had something to do with the precious little boy. Dylan would've liked to have started a family by now, but in retrospect, it was a good thing that he and his ex-wife never had kids. He and his ex were total opposites, and while it was part of the attraction initially, the reality was they weren't suited for each other. For his ex-wife, socializing was fun. For him, it was work—mainly, just to get the words out when talking with strangers. However, people he knew and trusted? No problem at all. It was almost as if his stutter had never existed.

"Okay, kids. And by that, I mean you two," Becca said, pointing at Georgina, then Dylan. "I heard both sides of the story, and it sounds like the only solution is to take my mom's advice and bring in a tiebreaker."

Max raised his hand and jumped up and down. "That's me!"

At that, he and Georgina exchanged looks. No words needed.

"That's right," Becca said. "So let's all sit, and Max will render a verdict. That will go for any future decisions where the wedding planners can't agree. Georgina, could you hand me the calendar, please?"

She retrieved one from a drawer and placed it on the table. Becca opened it up to December and positioned the grid in front of Max.

"See these squares right here, cowboy? I need

for you to pick a day between now and the first week of the new year." Becca marked the parameters with her fingers.

Max seemed to study the boxes, then pointed to tomorrow's box and looked up at his mommy.

"Okay, then! It's settled. The wedding will be tomorrow," Becca said. "Is everyone still on board, or will I have to plan it myself?"

*Is she serious?*

Georgina looked as deflated as he felt. Again, there were no words needed to express the fact that tomorrow wouldn't be the least bit doable.

"That's a romantic idea, Max. But I'm not sure we could secure a location by then," Georgina said.

"They can lope so they won't need a location," Max said.

"Elope?" Dylan clarified.

"Yep. Miss Hailey has some horses and a trail, so they can go horseback riding and come back married," Max said.

"Hailey's my sister," Georgina said. She was looking at Dylan now. "She runs Sunrise Stables and offers trail rides. Revived a Destiny Springs tradition. Max assists by telling the true story about how our grandparents eloped on one of the early rides."

He wanted to say that sounded quite romantic, but his voice wasn't cooperating.

Fortunately, Becca threw in her two cents. "That's a beautiful idea, Max, but it might be too cold. She isn't scheduling regular rides at the moment anyway. Do any of these other boxes look good?"

Max clutched his stuffed bull and studied the calendar through a deep yawn. It was quite a responsibility for the little guy, especially so early in the morning.

Becca brushed the hair out of his eyes and kissed him on the forehead. "Why don't you go back to bed and sleep on it. You can put on your decision-making hat and pick out a date later."

"I don't have one of those," Max said with the saddest little face.

"You can wear your purple cowboy hat instead," she said.

"Purple, huh?" Dylan asked. "That's one of my favorite colors."

"Mine too!" Max practically screamed.

That put a smile back on the little boy's face. Nothing worse than an unhappy child.

"We'll reconvene in the parlor after breakfast, when we all have a full tummy. How does that sound to everyone?"

Seemed neither he nor Georgina had a choice but to reconvene, unless one of them would go ahead and give in. Sure wasn't going to be him. He halfway suspected that had been Becca's plan all along by bringing in Max as a tiebreaker. To force him and Georgina to reach an agreement between themselves. Like adults would do. But he did have one request.

"Can we meet after lunch? Say, around one? I have something I need to do first."

No objections were voiced. Becca stood and took Max's hand, leading him back down the hall to his room and leaving him and Georgina alone.

This time, she was the quiet one. He wasn't sure what to say either, but he knew what he needed to do. He needed a little more time to accomplish it, however. And that was to either win the little decision-maker over or win Georgina over.

Or hopefully both.

# CHAPTER THREE

DYLAN SCRAPED HIS boots across the welcome mat to knock off the snow, then opened the front door of the B and B.

The coast was clear. He even had a few minutes to spare before the dreaded reconvening.

The whole house smelled of cookies. He smiled and nodded as an elderly couple slowly made their way down the stairs, holding on to the railing and taking each step with intention. They commented how much they liked the music that was still piping through the downstairs from somewhere—his dad's songs. They had no idea that the music legend's son was standing right there, watching as the man made his wife stop beneath the mistletoe hanging from the chandelier, then surprised her with a kiss.

Dylan smiled and bit his lip as they passed by him. That was the way a relationship should be, and not just during the honeymoon phase.

He wouldn't be standing there at all if he hadn't needed to see one person in particular prior to the group meeting Becca had called. Problem was Dylan wasn't quite sure where to find that little boy.

In the meantime, he removed a package of mint gum from the plastic bag he was carrying. Another thing that helped with his anxiety at times. He slipped it into his leather jacket pocket, then tucked the bag and its remaining contents beneath his arm. Unfortunately, he didn't have time to wrap the gift he'd picked up at the drugstore. Kind of surprised they had what he was looking for—make that something reasonably close.

Dylan peeked into the kitchen, where Georgina was busy baking. A person could get very spoiled over the next two weeks, with all the homemade desserts and tea that were served in the barn every afternoon. He watched as she pulled something out of the oven, inserted a toothpick into its contents, then returned it to the heat and set a timer. After that, she turned her attention to a stack of dishes. No doubt she'd be occupied for a little while longer.

He pivoted and returned to the parlor, then surveyed the place, not sure where to begin looking...until he heard the sound of nails on the hardwood floor, followed by the pattering of tiny feet.

The three-legged labradoodle nearly knocked

him down, and Max was doing a commendable job of trying to keep up.

"Max! Stay inside," Becca called from down the hallway.

Dylan swooped him up just in time, as Max was reaching for the doorknob. In the process of saving the day, Dylan dropped the plastic bag onto the ground. He set the little boy back down, retrieved the bag and presented it.

"I had to run to the drugstore, and I came across something you might need this afternoon," Dylan said.

Max took the bag, looking up at him as if wanting approval.

"Go ahead. Open it. What's inside won't bite."

Max slowly opened the bag, and his little face lit up. "Wow! It's a hat, and it's purple!"

More like a blueish-purple knit cap, with one bossy matching fur ball on top. The little boy pulled it out of the bag.

"It's a decision-making hat. I remembered you didn't have one," Dylan said.

Max started to put it on, but the tag was getting in the way. Dylan managed to yank it free without the whole hat unraveling.

By the time Dylan looked up again, Becca was standing there. He probably should've asked permission or given her a heads-up that he'd gotten Max a gift, but time was of the essence.

"He said he needed one, and I happened to see it at the drugstore, so…"

Becca crossed her arms and gave him a raised brow look that said, *I'm onto you*. Before he even tried to come up with an explanation that didn't sound as devious as he felt about it, her husband walked in, removed his Stetson and shook it off.

"Not in the foyer! You'll get the floor all wet," she admonished.

Cody Sayers barely glanced at Dylan before rushing over to his wife and giving her the sweetest kiss.

"No, sir. You're not going to kiss your way out of this one," Becca said.

He pointed up to the mistletoe she was standing under. Once again, Dylan felt invisible. But in the best possible way. Then it struck him how he wished he really were invisible. Cody had been a champion bull rider, so he had plenty of connections. And he was about to have one more reluctant one. Hopefully, the guy wouldn't someday out him as being Montgomery Legend's son.

"Dylan, this is my husband, Cody. Y'all are both rodeo pros."

*Oh, I know who you are.* Just about anyone involved with the rodeo did.

Cody extended his hand. "Becca told me all about you. Where are you announcing next?"

"Fort Worth," Dylan said, not offering more than that.

"Where the West begins. I love that city," Cody said.

Dylan retrieved the pack of gum he'd tucked into his pocket, popped a piece into his mouth and offered some to both Cody and Becca.

Fortunately, Max reappeared and practically jumped into his daddy's arms.

"What have we here?" Cody tugged on the beanie's pom-pom.

"It's my decision-making hat," Max said.

"And what decisions are we making today?" Cody asked.

"He's helping Georgina and Dylan with Mom and Monty's wedding," Becca said.

"I get to pick the day," Max bragged.

"Well, that's the most important part, isn't it?" Cody said. "Gotta make sure the bride and groom are there at the same time."

Max nodded, and the fuzzy ornament flopped around, which was beyond adorable.

"You're welcome to join us," Becca said to her husband, adding a grin.

Cody set Max down and shook his head. "Oh, no. I've already done my part by introducing the happy couple."

Dylan remembered the story. His dad had recited it enough times, about how Cody had asked him for a favor—to come to Destiny Springs and have dinner with him, Becca, Max and Rose—so that Cody could win over his then ex-mother-in-law and win Becca back. But his dad had fallen in love with Rose in the process.

"Yeah. Th-thanks for doing that," Dylan offered.

Neither Cody nor Becca so much as blinked at the pause, but he chewed his gum a little harder anyway.

"Anytime. Let me know when you're announcing in the area, and I'll come out to support you," Cody said, extending his hand.

Dylan tried to match Cody's grip, which had probably softened since the man had been away from the rodeo for nearly a year. Gripping a rosined bull rope for dear life was a lot different than raising a family and helping run a B and B, which the bull rider somehow made look easy.

At that, Cody left him and Becca alone in the foyer, the hands of the clock now showing exactly one o'clock.

"You and Max get situated in the parlor. I'll fetch the other team member." Becca got halfway to the kitchen before stopping, seemingly a bit winded. "Georgina! We're ready for you."

"Be there in a few minutes!"

Becca joined them in the parlor before Dylan had a chance to subtly make his case about having a Christmas wedding. Hopefully little Max would take the gift into consideration, as underhanded as his tactic was beginning to feel.

Georgina came out of the kitchen, all smiles and holding a tray. He frankly didn't care what was on it. He'd spent his lunchtime shopping for an acceptable bribe, and he was starving.

She stopped in her tracks. "Max, your hat is adorable!"

"Mr. Dylan gave it to me. It's a decision hat."

Georgina looked at him and raised a brow. She set the tray on the table. So that was the cause of the house smelling so good. Homemade cookies with chocolate kisses in the center. His mom used to make them for him all the time. Before she got too sick.

"Those are my favorites! Can I have one?" Max asked.

"Of course you can! I made them *just* for you," she said, speaking to the decision-maker first while handing the little boy a couple of napkins. All she served Dylan was a sly smile.

He couldn't help but smile in return. Devious minds must think alike. Their unspoken conversations were fun. At least, for him they were. Even though they'd clashed right from the start, he felt drawn to her. It was safe to assume everyone probably did.

"Wow, thanks!" Max grabbed the nearest cookie.

Instead of biting into it, he placed it on a napkin and gave it to his mommy.

"That's so sweet of you," Becca said.

Dylan couldn't disagree. Next, Max put another one on a napkin and handed it to Georgina, then gave a third one to him. Finally, he took one for himself.

Georgina stood. "I'll get us all some milk, if that's okay with everyone. Trust me, no other beverage will do with these."

Dylan stood as well. "I'll help you carry th-the glasses."

Georgina blinked and cocked her head, almost imperceptibly. He simply smiled and chewed his gum a little harder.

"That's a nice offer. I'll take you up on it," she said.

He followed her into the kitchen and watched as she filled three glasses and one plastic cup.

Better look at her while he had a chance, because he wouldn't be able to if this whole tie-breaker experience was going to mean they'd be working together after all. Agreeing on a wedding date would be only the beginning.

As nervous and tongue-tied as he felt around Georgina—and no matter how much he wanted to learn more about her—he still needed to keep some guardrails in place regarding the wedding itself.

As far as the two of them went, he'd be willing to let his personal guardrails down.

Just a little.

"YOUR BRIBE WAS BETTER." There, she said it.

Georgina finished pouring the milk. She was rather glad Dylan had offered to help carry the glasses, because she was dying to call out his action for what it was.

It also unburdened her of her guilt over having baked a special bribe of her own for Max. Besides, she'd been thinking about the whole situation. A Christmas wedding wouldn't be the end of the world. In fact, it might even help rebuild her business, with all the social media tie-ins she could do in the future around this time of year.

A well-rounded portfolio was a good thing, even though she wouldn't get the guest list she wanted for the couple. And, admittedly, for herself. If she did, that would end up being the best birthday gift ever, although it wasn't as if she'd get to celebrate it anyway.

But if Max chose New Year's Day, all the better. That was, if Dylan could change his plans. What could be more important than your dad's wedding, for goodness' sake? It would be for a very good cause, after all. It wasn't every day that people fell in love and it stuck. Plus that day would not only give the invited guests a better opportunity to attend, she'd have much more time to dedicate to the ceremony itself. And that was the biggest reward.

Dylan didn't ask for clarification on her quip about the bribe, but why would he need to? In fact, he was back to *not* looking at her again. Part of her was rather hoping Becca was right about him being nervous around her.

Together, they carried the milk to the parlor, where the cookie tray was nearly half-empty. Max was wiping his chocolatey hands on a napkin but totally neglecting his equally chocolatey face. Becca, on the other hand, looked miserable. Not too much longer of a wait—end of the first or beginning of the second week in January. Another thing to consider when planning the ceremony: a comfortable chair for the mommy-to-be. Georgina might have to help Becca shop for an outfit as well. The to-do list for this wedding kept getting longer.

"So, Max, our dilemma is that we still need to decide on a date for the wedding. Dylan wants a Christmas Day ceremony. I want New Year's Day," Georgina said.

His eyes opened wide. "Y'all are getting married? I thought it was Grandma and her boyfriend getting married."

Georgina giggled under her breath. Dylan's laugh wasn't as subtle.

"Sorry, Max, I wasn't clear. You're right— it's for your grandma and Monty's special day. Which do you think they'd like best? New Year's Day?" Georgina asked, adding a thumbs-up gesture. Dylan didn't seem amused.

"Or a Christmas Day wedding?" He jumped in, adding a double thumbs-up.

"We also need to take into consideration the rehearsal dinner," Becca added. "But I can handle those details. We'll keep it simple."

"A Christmas wedding will distract from all the fun of the holiday! I mean, what if Santa is running late in delivering the packages and any children would have to wait until that evening to open them?" Georgina asked their little decision-maker.

That got Max's full attention. He even paused before taking a bite of yet another cookie. It caught Dylan's attention too, except he wasn't so much as smiling. Maybe that was too low for her to stoop in her attempt to win. But the more she looked at Max's silly purple hat with the fur ball on top, the more determined she felt.

"New Year's Day isn't good for me, but I don't have to be there. Dad's okay with that," Dylan said. He was looking down at his hands rather than at Max. In fact, the statement felt more directed at her. "I'm announcing at a charity rodeo in Fort Worth. For ovarian-cancer research. That's what my mom had."

Georgina's heart sank right then and there. Why hadn't he said that in the first place?

She shook her head. "Then New Year's Day is definitely out, Max. If you choose Christmas, we'll make it perfect."

Somehow.

At that, Dylan looked at her, but still no smile. She could only imagine how hard his father's decision to remarry might've been for him. And here she was making it even harder.

"There are more days, aren't there?" Max asked.

"Of course," Becca said. "I think Dylan and Georgina both wanted a special day for Grandma and Monty, though. But such options are limited."

All eyes were on Max as he seemed to think about it a little too seriously. In the meantime, Becca had somehow gotten up from the chair, retrieved a calendar and set it down in front of him.

Georgina almost started laughing at the absurdity of what they were doing by letting a six-year-old make the decision. But she and Dylan had been acting even more like children than Max, and Mama Becca obviously realized it, or else she wouldn't have been putting everyone through this.

Max pointed to one of the squares, smearing

chocolate on the calendar in the process. That was as good as putting it in ink.

"New Year's Eve." Becca leaned in and confirmed. "Does that work for everyone?"

Georgina nodded.

Dylan inhaled a deep breath. "It'll be tight, travel-wise, but I can manage."

"And how about the rehearsal dinner? Pick a square for that one too, please, sir. Before the wedding," Becca said.

Another serious moment for Max. "This one, next to Christmas, because that's what Mr. Dylan wants."

"Christmas Eve," Becca said.

"Perfect," Georgina and Dylan said in unison. And to think it took a child to make such a logical compromise.

Becca started to stand again, and Dylan quickly rose to assist.

"I think it's time for at least two of us to take a nap," she said. "What do you think, Max? You worked hard today. You've earned it. Plus you'll need your energy, because I have a feeling these two are going to need your help with lots of other things."

Max nodded, and the four of them headed out to the foyer. Becca and Max said their goodbyes and made their way down the hall, leaving Georgina alone with Dylan.

He turned to her. "I guess the next question is the place," he said.

"You choose."

At that, he looked at her, shook his head and looked down again. "I'm not as familiar with Destiny Springs as you are. I'll need your help."

"Dylan, I'm sorry about the whole New Year's Day confusion. If I'd known—"

"It's okay. Really. I didn't bring it up to make you feel bad. Wasn't going to mention it because the wedding isn't about me. It's an important event, though. For more than one reason."

"I think your dad would agree it's the right thing to do, to honor your mom."

He finally looked up and half smiled. She'd take it. Hopefully their next task, and the ones that were going to follow, would go more smoothly, because she was rather glad Max had picked New Year's Eve. Gave her a little time to get to know this man better. She just might have to figure out a way to make him more comfortable around her.

"I guess I'd better go check on Sundance. He probably needs a long walk, now that it's warmed up a bit," he said, looking skyward this time instead of at the floor, which he must have memorized by now with all the time he'd spent looking at it.

"And I need to get the desserts out to the barn

for the other guests. Some of them get there early so they don't miss out."

Dylan didn't respond. He simply held his gaze on the ceiling. It wasn't until he looked back down—directly at her this time, and with those blue eyes while serving up a nervous smile and shake of the head——that she realized why. He'd been standing directly under the mistletoe.

Good thing she didn't buy into all that nonsense, although for a fleeting moment she imagined she could. With the right man, of course.

Something made her think that perhaps he totally bought into it, what with his apparent love of Christmas. Not that he was thinking about giving her a kiss. The way he slipped out from under the mistletoe once he realized pretty much confirmed it. At least they seemed to agree on that much. Still, no use taking chances.

*Note to self: Avoid the foyer.*

# CHAPTER FOUR

"YOU SHOULD HAVE let me help you wrap those gifts," Georgina said.

Her pregnant boss stood in front of the Christmas tree—its branches strained from the weight of all the balls and decorations, and a silly-looking reindeer head stared down from its apex. Still in her nightgown, Becca looked at Georgina and sighed.

"I didn't put them there," Becca said, anxiety etched across her face.

Georgina could have been looking in a mirror. She'd sacrificed sleep in favor of researching wedding venues, now that the date had been decided. But it did pay off in one way. She'd found the perfect place: Elk Lodge, fifty miles north of Destiny Springs but reasonably on the way to and from Jackson Hole, where the groom-to-be lived and, very likely, some friends and family.

She was even able to hold one of the event rooms and a block of guest suites. Not nearly enough to accommodate even one hundred guests, but the venue was the classiest around.

The lodge was willing to hold it for only twenty-four hours, which meant Georgina would have to get Dylan's blessing as soon as possible today. That should be a breeze compared to the whole wedding date debate. There were other hotels and motels nearby to accommodate the remainder of her anticipated guest list. Those, too, she'd need to go ahead and reserve, which meant yet another negotiation she wasn't looking forward to.

But first things first.

Georgina closed the gap and pulled Becca in for a reassuring side hug. The smallest of things seemed to stress her boss out. Apparently, even things that should otherwise bring joy.

"So...who are the gifts from?" Georgina asked.

"Santa." The confident declaration was followed by the deepest sigh to date.

Now Georgina was really worried. She knelt and examined the tag on one of the boxes: *To Max, with love. From Santa.*

"Maybe Cody is moonlighting as the jolly old fella." Seemed like the only reasonable explanation.

"I'd otherwise agree. But this has happened every year at the B and B since I refurbished and reopened it, and before Cody and I reunited.

Santa leaves at least one package, every few days or so, starting about two weeks before Christmas. It's even become a rumor around town, with a few folks claiming to have spotted him leaving the house in full regalia."

Georgina hadn't been around Destiny Springs during Christmas before. She'd always been busy planning weddings in other cities. Whoever this person was, he or she did a knock-out wrapping job. They even neatly squared the corners, used invisible tape and attached flawlessly fluffy bows.

If only Santa would put a birthday gift or two beneath the tree for those who were born on Christmas. That way they'd know they hadn't been totally forgotten.

But once again, she wasn't a child. The past should no longer sting. She was just grateful that Becca wasn't due until after Christmas, sparing yet another child from having to share his or her birthday with a day that was even more special.

"Any theories as to who it could really be?" Georgina asked.

Becca nodded. "Yes. Vern."

That made sense. Vern Fraser certainly looked the part, down to the white whiskers he liked to wear year-round. And he'd been in Destiny Springs forever.

"I'm going to fix you some warm milk. Then

I want you to go back to bed for a couple more hours. I've got breakfast under control." Georgina turned on her heels and nodded toward the kitchen.

Becca followed and positioned herself, once again, on one of the barstools. It teetered beneath the weight.

"Vern should be here any minute with the egg delivery. Let's just ask him and promise to keep it a secret from everyone else," Georgina said as she poured some milk into a mug and placed it in the microwave.

"I already have. He denies it, of course. Even offered to take a lie-detector test."

"How many other people have a key to the front door?"

"The guests have one, but they turn them in at checkout. Your sister has one too," Becca said. "To be honest, it's kind of fun not knowing."

Maybe for Becca, but the curiosity was going to bug Georgina. No way it was Hailey. Her gifts always looked like a four-year-old had wrapped them. But a guest could have made a duplicate key at some point. That would be impossible to track down.

"I think you were right the first time. It is Santa. He does go down the chimney to make his deliveries, and you have one of those, so..." Georgina said, adding a smile and a wink.

Becca rolled her eyes. "Nice try."

"I'm serious!" she said, offering up a grin.

The microwave dinged. Georgina retrieved the milk and placed it in front of Becca.

"It may be a little warm, so be careful. I understand why you don't really want to know. It would take the fun out of it," Georgina said, although she wasn't speaking for herself. The whole tradition wasn't magical for her, although she sort of envied those who could enjoy it.

As if he'd been summoned, Vern tapped at the side door and peered through the glass pane, his breath frosting up the panel.

Becca started to slide off the barstool.

"Oh, no, you don't! I'll get that." Georgina rushed over to open the door.

Vern walked over to the counter and set down the crate of eggs he donated to the B and B on a regular basis from his ranch. Such a thoughtful and selfless gesture. *Like the real Santa would do.* Now that Becca had planted the idea in her brain, it was impossible for Georgina to look away. The red thermal shirt that peeked out beneath his overcoat only fed her curiosity.

"Whew! I think I'm gonna need some thicker gloves this winter." Vern slipped them off and placed them on the edge of the kitchen counter. He opened the cabinet, grabbed a mug and started to pour himself a cup of coffee.

Georgina shook her head and stepped in. She'd always been more proactive in pouring a cup for him, after all he did for the B and B. But this whole town rumor suddenly had her flustered.

She eased the mug from his hand, poured some coffee and handed it back. "Maybe your little helpers can knit you a thicker pair for Christmas. In the meantime, warm your hands around this, Santa."

Vern looked at Georgina and at Becca, then back at Georgina.

"Let me guess. The jolly old fella made a delivery, and Becca has you convinced it was me," he said.

"I'm not convinced, but let's face it. You are the generous type. And you kinda look the part," Becca said.

"Which makes me a little too obvious of a choice, don't ya think?" Vern said.

The man had a point.

"Besides, there's an easy way to find out. Install a nanny cam. I'll even set it up. We'll catch the guy or gal red-handed," Vern continued.

"Well, I was planning on installing one for safety reasons at the beginning of the year anyway. Cody and I agreed it would be helpful for keeping an eye on Max's whereabouts while we're busy with the baby, since he likes to venture outside without permission," Becca said, adding a weary sigh.

By contrast, Georgina felt a jolt of adrenaline.

"I bet Miller's Electronics carries 'em. If so, I can grab one when I go down to the square in a bit and set it up for you this afternoon," Vern said.

Georgina and Becca looked at each other. Disappointment registered in her boss's eyes. Ultimately, this was her boss's decision, so she wasn't going to push.

After giving it several moments of thought, Becca rendered her verdict. "Okay. But I'm not going to even glance at any footage until after Christmas, although you're welcome to do so, Georgina. And I only want to know if it's the real Santa," Becca teased.

"Deal! I'll be the checker and keeper of the secret," Georgina said while softly clapping her hands and resisting the urge to jump up and down.

"How about you two go find a place for that nanny cam while I work on breakfast," she said to Vern and Becca, who had finished her glass of warm milk and was now yawning.

As soon as they exited the kitchen, another set of footsteps—and paw steps—were making their way down the stairs. From her place in the kitchen, Georgina could hear Becca introducing

Dylan to Vern. Sundance let out a bark to introduce himself as well. Soon enough, the foot- and paw steps headed her direction.

"I smell coffee," Dylan said, popping his head in and looking at the counter after briefly acknowledging her.

"Freshly made," she said. "You heading out for a walk?"

He simply nodded. He was barely bundled up. Just jeans, boots, a flannel shirt and a short leather jacket. At least he was wearing a hat, but he really did need a pair of gloves.

She was almost getting used to his silent responses, but not in a good way. Still, she had to find a way to stay positive through their planning, because this wedding was going to put her back on the map. She could feel it.

"Stop back in when you and Sundance finish your walk, and I'll pour you a cup. I have some *great* news about a venue for the wedding. But we have to act fast," she said.

Dylan knelt and gave Sundance a brisk petting.

"Only if you promise that the coffee is caffeinated and the venue is cozy," he said, focusing on the golden retriever instead, which was annoying.

She came so close to making a snarky remark. Something along the lines of *Let me know what you and Sundance decide*. But then the underlying implication of his comment sunk in.

*Cozy?* The lodge wasn't exactly that. For the most part, it was rather large and airy and rambling. Besides, *cozy* usually didn't accommodate many guests.

He finally looked up and gave her a smile, which did nothing to buoy that sinking feeling. They hadn't discussed the guest list, and she'd just assumed it would be at least a medium-sized wedding with a semiformal dress code. Could've been much larger if she'd had more time to plan.

"I'll whip up some breakfast to go with your coffee," she offered, because this might not be as short of a conversation as she'd thought.

"I'm not a big breakfast person. But if you have any apple pie left over…" Dylan finally looked up, his eyes reflecting hope rather than humor.

*So the man has a sweet tooth.* Good information to have, because it was looking like Max wasn't the only man she needed to win over. Fortunately, sweets were her specialty.

Unfortunately, she didn't have any apple pie left. But she did have something she could heat up—a recipe she'd been experimenting with last night and that she was going to try out on the guests today. The only thing missing was some dulce de leche on the top, because there was no such thing as too sweet.

And she was going to need all the help she could get.

ALL IT TOOK was one inhale of whatever delicious caramel-scented thing Georgina was making in the kitchen for Dylan to know he was about to be in deep trouble—in a few ways.

First, his resolve was severely weakened by desserts. If they had as much trouble agreeing on a venue as they had on a wedding date, he very well might agree to something he didn't want for his dad or himself if he wasn't careful.

Second, sweets were the magic key to opening his heart just enough to let someone inside. He and Sundance hadn't been gone long enough for even the best pastry chef and mind reader to combine his favorite tastes and smells, yet Georgina had somehow accomplished it.

Dylan was also at a disadvantage in another way. He hadn't exactly done his due diligence on coming up with a cozy venue. Except was there any other kind in Destiny Springs? She, on the other hand, obviously had.

Oddly enough, he was going to give that some thought last night. Maybe talk to Cody and see if he had any suggestions. But a late-night call from the rodeo PR folks in Fort Worth meant a slight change of plans. They needed some recorded promos ASAP for a national fundraising push. Meaning he'd need to make a quick trip to Texas in a few days. He might have to trust

Georgina with some decisions after all, and that had him a bit rattled.

As soon as he reached the kitchen, Sundance galloped over to something on the floor, and the lapping sound commenced.

Georgina must've put down a water bowl while they were gone, which was awfully sweet of her.

She paused her task whipping something around in a bowl, looked down at the happy pup and then at him. "I thought Sundance might be thirsty. I hope that was okay."

More than okay. It further reassured him that she could handle all those details he couldn't begin to think of. But there was something else about the gesture that felt…cozy. It had something to do with the way she anticipated his four-legged child's needs.

Something beeped. She promptly set down the bowl, retrieved a mug from the microwave and handed it to him.

"Thought your hands might be freezing cold since you weren't wearing gloves, so I warmed up the mug along with the coffee. You may need to set it down over there and let it cool for a few minutes." She pointed to a small breakfast table, where two places had been set.

Meanwhile, Sundance had finished drinking, but only after splashing water everywhere.

He took the opportunity to pull a few paper

towels from the holder at the far end of the bar and proceeded to clean up the water spills.

"Don't worry. I can do that when I finish up with this dulce de leche drizzle for your breakfast," she said.

She was definitely speaking his language. His resolve to stand firm on a small venue was melting as fast as sugar glaze on a hot-out-of-the-fryer doughnut.

He finished cleaning up the mess anyway. "I'll put Sundance in my room since you're preparing food in here. Doubt the guests would appreciate fur in their breakfast. He's a champion shedder."

Georgina resumed whisking.

"It wouldn't bother me. I grew up with cats who refused to stay off our kitchen counters. And it's a daily struggle to keep Penny out of the kitchen here. But you make a good point," she said.

By the time he returned, Georgina had added a sugar and creamer set to the middle of the table.

"Have a seat," she said in a warm, cheery tone, which failed to put him at ease for some reason.

After all, the woman in front of him, who was now cutting into something that smelled beyond delicious, could be his arch nemesis in this whole process because this entire scenario felt a little too good to be true. From the sweets...to the warmed-up coffee mug…to anticipating Sundance's needs with the water.

Georgina placed the most delicious-looking dessert in front of him. Definitely not the apple pie from yesterday, but possibly even better.

His hand ached to pick up the fork and dive right in, but it would be rude not to wait. So he wrapped both hands around the warm mug instead and watched as she drizzled the dulce de leche on top, making the shape of a heart—although he wasn't convinced it was intentional.

"There's dulce de leche inside the sopaipilla cheesecake bars as well. And I have plenty left over to put in your coffee. Wanna try?"

"Sure," he managed to say. He watched as she poured, amazed at how a woman could make a simple pink long-sleeved T-shirt and gray sweatpants look so good.

"Now stir it in," she instructed as she returned the pan to the back burner of the stovetop and sat in the chair across from him.

One sip and he knew he'd never again be happy with coffee prepared any other way.

She took a sip from her own mug and launched right in. "You mentioned something about cozy. The place I was thinking about for the wedding has a roaring fireplace in the lobby, with cozy chairs and sofas. It's also on the way to Jackson Hole but closer to Destiny Springs."

"Sounds good so far." What was the catch?

"Since I was able to secure only twelve rooms, the Elk Lodge can accommodate about twenty-four people, assuming there will be two people to a room. But I checked, and there are other nearby motels along the route, so I'm not overly concerned."

*Elk Lodge?* Nothing cozy about it.

His words were stuck in his throat, and it had nothing to do with the bite of dessert he'd just taken. He was having trouble swallowing what she was proposing. Even twenty-four people were about fourteen too many. And she was thinking even more?

He finished swallowing and looked at her.

Once again, her eyes were laser focused on him. Like a cat on a mouse.

He resisted the urge to squirm in his seat and reached for the napkin on his lap instead. "T-t-twenty-four guests. Plus more?"

This was going from bad to worse. But she didn't even blink. She simply took another sip of her coffee.

"That's not a lot. Trust me. We need to nail down the number, or a reasonable range, ASAP. With relatives and close friends and any important business associates, not to mention spouses and plus-ones, that number could easily triple."

That was when it struck him. He was in way

over his head in this planning. And he could drown in the negotiations. He hadn't even thought how quickly the number could multiply or how tricky a guest list could be. But he did know that keeping it down to strictly family would contain it. At least, that was what he'd assumed. Now he wasn't so sure.

He took another bite while formulating his words, which were multiplying in his head but not in any order. No way he could articulate his thoughts in this moment with any level of sensitivity and explanation.

"I was thinking a barn wedding, with family and only best friends," he said. It was all he could manage at the moment, because he didn't otherwise want his silence to be interpreted that he agreed with her. He looked up in time to see a glimpse of disappointment in her eyes, followed by her brilliant ability to change her expression back to one of optimism.

"Barn weddings are certainly popular. And most around here can accommodate more than family only. But a wedding at the lodge would be more special. And much cozier, because some of these barns can only get so warm in Destiny Springs in the winter. You probably picked up on that already," she said.

He wanted to argue that they could bring in extra heaters. And that the ceremony wouldn't be all that long, and that most folks could bundle up a little more for that portion.

But at least there was a hint of cooperation. Just like there was a hint of his favorite spice in this dessert.

"Is that nutmeg I taste?" he asked as he dissected the remainder of the dessert with his fork as if looking for something he couldn't possibly see.

"Wow. Most folks wouldn't have picked up on that," she said. "Will you be my taste tester while you're here? We're going to have to decide on the wedding cakes at some point anyway, and I'm planning to make those myself."

At that, he laughed. But then the obvious occurred to him. She wasn't only trying to sweet-talk him into agreeing to the lodge as a venue, she was seizing on his weakness like she had with Max and the cookies.

"I'll give it some thought," he said.

Becca wandered back in. "Vern will be back over this afternoon."

"I told you it wasn't him," Georgina said. "But I'm glad you're here. Looks like Dylan and I may need Max to step in again, if you can spare him for a few minutes. We have a timely decision to make."

"He's helping Cody with something at the moment. But… I have an idea. I don't want him in the house this afternoon while Vern is installing the camera, because he'll want to see the footage. Max is way too curious for his own good right now."

Becca glanced over in Dylan's direction. "I'm installing a nanny cam in the foyer for security purposes. But also for Georgina, who wants to know who has been leaving presents under the tree from 'Santa.' Whoever it is has been doing it since I moved in! Can you believe it?"

"Oh, wow," Dylan commented. That was interesting.

"Max can help me in the kitchen," Georgina piped up. "I need a taste tester for some wedding cake recipes. I offered the job to someone who shall remain unnamed, *ahem*. But Dylan wants to give it some thought," Georgina said, raising a brow and casting a stern look his way.

Sure, volunteering to spend more time with Georgina was risky, in more ways than one it seemed. But having her ply Max with sweets while he wasn't there could be much worse.

"Oh, I'm not turnin' down that job," he said.

Georgina's brow softened. "Good. But Max can still assist me with dessert in the barn while Vern is here. He's much too young to know the truth about Santa."

She wasn't giving up, was she?

"Or maybe we're too old to accept that Santa might exist," Dylan chimed in.

They both looked at him.

"You still believe?" Georgina asked.

"I sure do," he said. "But just in case, I'll take Max to look at Christmas decorations in the square this afternoon. That way there will be no danger of him somehow running back to the house and seeing the spy camera installation."

Georgina squinted at him. The gloves, it seemed, were off.

"Dylan, that's brilliant! Thank you so much," Becca said. "Georgina, you go with them. Cody and I can handle the afternoon tea and dessert. That way you two can talk with Max together, and he can break whatever ties he needs to."

"Christmas decorations, huh?" Georgina said in a rather curious way. No doubt she'd already seen them, but the whole *bah humbug* tone sounded pretty strong. What was that all about?

So much for handing the reins over to Georgina. She was clearly set on a big event.

He never imagined planning a wedding could be so complicated. He hadn't even picked out his own tuxedo for his wedding. Maybe if he'd been directly involved in the planning, like he was with this one, the outcome would have been different. His ex-wife had basically sent out all three hundred invitations without taking into consideration his feelings on the matter. Nearly five hundred pairs of eyes watched him freeze when reciting the vows. Watched as he ruined his bride's dream wedding—something she clearly hadn't anticipated even though he'd tried to warn her of the possibility. But she ignored the signs. And he ignored the huge red flag.

At least they didn't witness how he was punished for it every day after that. And at least Georgina was playing fair and listening, if not wholeheartedly agreeing.

No matter. They needed Max's assistance with this decision anyway. Whatever the little boy decided, Dylan would abide by. But he would have to make sure Max wore his special purple hat again for this and hopefully remember who gifted it to him.

And Dylan would have to wear something to protect his heart.

# CHAPTER FIVE

DYLAN WAS BEGINNING to detect a theme: pink.

Even though Georgina was wearing jeans and boots this time instead of sweatpants, her signature color could still be seen in the form of a fuzzy turtleneck peeking out beneath a black knee-length puffer.

She was walking a few steps behind Max, Sundance and himself as they navigated the pop-up booths and decorations. The square had everything imaginable. Even Christmas balloons.

The crowds were almost unmanageable, however, so he remained hyperaware of her proximity.

"Oh, wait! I want to stop at this booth," she said, threatening to disappear within the throngs of shoppers. Thankfully, her destination was right there: a vendor selling flowers and wreaths. Meanwhile, Sundance had managed to seek out the food vendors and was tugging Max in the direction of the hamburgers.

Perhaps bringing Sundance along for this outing wasn't the brightest idea. But Max had insisted.

Dylan took possession of the leash with one hand and Max's hand in the other, and reeled them all back to the flower stand.

Georgina looked up with a pained smile as they approached, and the words that were going to so easily flow stopped short.

"Sorry! I got distracted," she said.

*By pink*. Now he understood. She was admiring some pink roses that looked as though they'd seen better days.

"I was visualizing roses for Monty and Rose's wedding. If that's not too corny. What do you think? Maybe white ones? Or an assortment, although sticking with one color is more elegant," she said.

Dylan's first thought was that his mom's favorite flowers were yellow roses, so that color was definitely out, because that would be especially hard on his dad. The man had always brought home any single yellow rose he came across, and the thing would stay in the vase on his mother's dressing table until it turned crispy brown.

"I like it," he managed to say without stumbling over his words while looking into her hopeful eyes. That was a good sign. He then turned to Max, who didn't seem interested in the least. "Hey, cowboy, what color roses do you think we should get? Anything but yellow."

The little boy finally looked up. "Purple," he said, decisively.

"I'll see what the florist can do," Georgina said. "We might be limited by what's available. Plus we haven't even decided where it will be held, and that might determine the quantity."

He hadn't even thought of that.

"I'm fine with pink," he offered. Maybe if he gave her an easy win, she'd be more open to giving him one down the line.

Georgina seemed to contemplate it as she looked admiringly at one rose in particular— the most damaged one in the bunch.

She let out a heavy exhale, her frosty breath creating an ethereal cloud.

"White would be the safest bet. That way when we get together with the bride and groom tomorrow to help them pick out their wedding attire, we won't need to worry about coordinating their outfits with the flowers and we can go any direction with other decorations."

*Wait...* "W-w-what?" he asked.

So much for not stumbling.

Georgina didn't even blink. Quite the opposite. Her eyes widened. "I thought Becca was going to tell you—Rose and Monty will be in town tomorrow. They want to get their wedding outfits in Destiny Springs, since this is where they met.

And they want to support the local businesses. How sweet is that?"

Although it was a bit of an initial gut punch, it actually could turn out to be a good thing. He could force his dad's input on the guest list, which he was pretty sure would carry some weight. The man liked to keep special occasions such as his own birthday, Thanksgiving and Christmas close knit. Dylan was pretty sure his father would feel the same way about this wedding, which was the main reason he intended to push for that.

"Very sweet," he said, looking straight ahead and without a hitch. In fact, the day was looking up. He might find his voice in this after all. "Let's go over there to the tent with the heaters. Get some hot chocolate and choose a venue."

Max and Sundance were both getting antsy by that point. And everyone looked awfully cold.

Once they located an empty table for three, Dylan was ready to dive right in and defend his position to their little tiebreaker. But first things first. He pulled out some Milk-Bones for Sundance.

"Max, how about you do the honors. I know you have lots of experience with this since you have a pup of your own."

While Sundance gently accepted a treat from the boy, Dylan stood. "Hot chocolate for everyone?"

Max didn't miss a beat. "Yaaasss! Extra marsh-mallows."

"Noted. And for you?" he said, a beat before glancing at Georgina.

"Sugar-free, if they have it. Please," she said.

Nothing wrong with wanting to cut back on sugar. That would mean more left in the world for him, because there was no way he'd ever give that up.

"And if they don't? Maybe tea or coffee?" he asked.

"No way. Regular hot chocolate is fine," she said.

*Smart woman.* Not much could compare, in his opinion.

With that, he left the three others alone. As he stood in line at a self-serve station, looking back periodically to check on them, he caught Georgina glancing up and smiling a couple of times. He tried not to read too much into it. Maybe she was checking to make sure he stayed in her field of vision. Or that he wasn't watching her try to influence Max into choosing her lodge venue over Dylan's local barn suggestion.

After the third time their eyes met, he smiled and winked, hopefully sending an unspoken message that he was watching her every move as well. And if she was up to something, he wasn't going to let her get away with it.

Yet seeing Max, Sundance and Georgina all

sitting around a table together, like a family, triggered something instead of suspicion in him. Something he'd all but given up on. Strange, because he didn't know her well enough to envision himself with her. Most of what he'd seen so far were red flags, to boot.

Well, maybe not red. But definitely a proceed-with-caution shade of pink.

He managed to get back to the table without spilling any of the drinks. She didn't even ask if they'd had sugar-free after all.

"So. We're gathered here today…" Dylan started to say, then squeezed his eyes shut. Freudian slip?

"To finalize the plan to hold the wedding at the Elk Lodge," Georgina said, finishing his sentence and topping it off with a smile.

"Or in a lovely Destiny Springs barn. You know, continue the theme of supporting the locals. Unless you two reached a conclusion while I was gone. In which case, I would get to choose the guest list," he said on a whim.

All was fair in love and war, right?

He didn't have to be looking at her to know her reaction. The sound of her nearly choking on the hot chocolate told him the punchline to their unspoken joke had landed.

"We didn't agree on those conditions," she said.

Dylan finally looked at her, then grinned and

winked again, which got a smile out of her. Little did she know he wasn't entirely joking.

He looked down at the little boy, who was more interested in petting Sundance than anything either adult had to say.

"Why the Elk Lodge?" he asked. "You told me a little about your reasons, but Max probably wants to hear."

"It's a special day. Okay, maybe it's more for the bride. But I know for a fact that Rose didn't have a proper wedding the first time around. And judging by the way she looks at Monty, she doesn't intend to ever have another. Location is more important than it may seem."

"Are you also visualizing a string quartet? And a long aisle to walk down?"

There. He blurted out what few details he remembered about his own wedding. He also remembered the long train on his ex-wife's gown. Each step she took as she walked down that aisle increased his anxiety. The violin music created a nauseous mix of fear and panic in his gut. All eyes were on him at first, while he waited. Then on her, and ultimately back on them standing together as beads of sweat formed on his forehead and his mouth turned so dry he could barely swallow.

He had loved her, once, although he couldn't really count the reasons why.

"Don't be silly. Lodges don't have long aisles," Georgina said, thankfully snapping him out of his memories and back to the square, with all the beautiful decorations.

The relief was immediate and palpable. *What were we talking about?*

"You forgot the most important part," she teased. "The professional videographer and a big screen at the front so the folks in the balcony can see the *I do*s. Lights, camera, romance!"

Thankfully, she added a playful wink. Otherwise, he was going to have an internal meltdown right then and there.

"I didn't know lodges had balconies, but it's a cute idea," he said, hoping she'd see some truth within the sarcasm.

"Thanks. But nothing that dramatic for Rose. Besides, I'm saving the best ideas for my own wedding."

There it was. A deep-red-colored flag emerging from all the pink ones. And just in time, because he was enjoying their banter a little too much.

His back straightened. "What are your thoughts, Max? Barn wedding?" Dylan gave two thumbs up.

"Or ceremony at the Elk Lodge, where they have a big fireplace and they let you make s'mores in it," she said.

"Not fair," Dylan said, casting her the sternest glance as he could muster.

"They should get married at my house," Max said. "'Cause it has a fireplace, and we can make s'mores in it too, if it's okay with Mommy."

Dylan and Georgina looked at each other. That wasn't a bad idea. It would be too cold for an outdoor wedding, and none of the rooms inside were large enough to accommodate too many guests at once. Dylan was pretty sure his future stepsister and stepbrother-in-law would be open to it.

"Actually, that would be perfect, Max. Becca is closing the Hideaway for the holidays, so all the rooms will be available," she continued.

"Then the venue is settled," Dylan said, although he wasn't feeling so good about it anymore. She was the professional planner. No doubt she'd find a way to accommodate a lot more people.

Max returned his attention to Sundance, gifting him with the final Milk-Bone. Just as well. Dylan, for one, needed to get back to the Denim Room and close the door behind him. That was the best way to practice the scripts for the promos he'd be recording in a couple of days in Fort Worth. He'd planned to do that tomorrow, but now it looked as though he'd be accompanying his dad to who-knows-where instead to pick out a wedding outfit.

As they sipped the remainder of their respective hot chocolates in relative silence, something occurred to him.

"You mentioned that Rose didn't have a big wedding the first time." Instead of looking at her, he reached for a napkin and wiped away what felt to be a marshmallow mustache from his upper lip.

"No. They were married at a courthouse." The way Georgina looked away was quite telling. Although he really did respect her career, did it matter where a couple got married as long as they had each other?

"Did she have a happy marriage, do you know?" he asked.

That perked Georgina back up. "She had one of those 'dream marriages.' Doesn't happen for everyone that way even once. But it looks like she's about to have a second one."

He wanted to say that he'd had a wedding that could put the royals to shame and look how well that worked out. But this wasn't about him.

"So it didn't start with some big, fancy ceremony, yet somehow it turned out okay?" he asked, avoiding her eyes once again, when he wished he could look directly into them to see whether his point was received. But he did look just in time to see her enthusiasm deflate as quickly as one of those balloons they'd passed by.

And he was holding the pin.

*Ouch.*

The point he made about the ceremony not having any effect on the long-term happiness of a couple felt like a hammer had been taken to all of her meticulously framed thoughts and feelings.

Not that it was illogical. She simply hadn't stopped to really think about it in those terms before. Much less stopped to consider that a wedding might make no difference at all. Her philosophy had always been that the ceremony set the tone for the entire marriage.

But what really smarted was his obvious distaste for weddings in general. Planning them wasn't only what Georgina did for a living, it was sewn into the fabric of her soul.

Good information to have moving forward, however. She'd let herself get distracted enough already. She sure didn't want to become interested in a man who didn't respect what she did— or was trying desperately to succeed at again.

Fortunately, in this situation, her knowledge was a huge advantage. She was more determined than ever to end up with an impressive guest list. How to do that, exactly, she wasn't sure.

*Unless I can talk to Monty privately, and find out if he agrees with me…*

"About the wedding garments for the bride and groom. We should probably get on the same page about it since the two of them are relinquishing all control," she said.

Sundance was now sandwiched between Dylan and Max, who were both holding the leash and petting the pup. Georgina felt like a loose, dangling thread.

Dylan nodded. "My dad's easygoing."

"Whew! Then I won't have any problems. You, however, may have a harder time of it with Rose."

The way he glanced at her, then looked away and exhaled suggested he was trying to process this little dash of spice she'd thrown into the batter at the last minute by switching their roles.

"What do you mean?" he asked.

"I thought it would be fun to accompany your dad to Kavanaugh's Clothing and Whatnot so you get a chance to bond with your future stepmother and stepsister. Not to mention, I'm sure they'd appreciate a man's opinion. They're meeting with Jess, the owner of Western Wear with Heart. She and her co-owner will be creating a one-of-a-kind wedding dress for the bride. And they're a new company in town, so such a prestigious job will boost their business."

Dylan visibly inhaled a deep breath and turned his attention to the cup in front of him. No doubt he wasn't prepared for that. *She* wasn't even prepared, but it occurred to her that this would be an opportunity to discuss the guest list and preferred wedding size with the groom himself.

"I'm not an expert on bridal gowns. I wouldn't know where to begin to advise," he said.

"Which is why you and I will talk more about it in the morning. In the meantime, I'll put together some rough guidelines as far as style and formality level, just so the bride and groom don't end up being mismatched," she said.

She'd already envisioned the whole thing, even though she'd leave it up to Rose and Monty to decide how they ultimately wanted to express themselves.

In fact, she was feeling a little mischievous again. Dylan was smart. She'd already figured that out. Hopefully not smart enough—or suspicious enough—to figure out what she was up to now. But hey, since he thought weddings were so unimportant and inconsequential, he had no reason to worry, because at least one of them needed to care enough to make it special.

Things were definitely looking up. Except for the weather. The sky was skewing scary dark, and a few of the booths started closing when the wind picked up. Some people began leaving, while others decided to take their chances. With the sun behind the heavy clouds, the temperature quickly plummeted.

"We'd better head back," Dylan said. He stood

and collected the empty cups before she could take care of it and threw them into the nearest trash can.

They all stood and began a brisk walk toward the truck. Then Dylan stopped in his tracks and looked around as if he'd forgotten something.

"Sundance and I will meet you and Max at the truck," he said.

"Is everything okay?" she asked.

He nodded. "Yep. I just want to pick up a few things, but y'all should go ahead and get in the truck and turn on the heater. I'll be there in less than ten minutes."

Dylan handed her the keys and sprinted away before even Max had a chance to speak. No doubt, he'd want to tag along with Dylan and Sundance instead. But this was a smart idea.

Georgina took the little boy's hand. "C'mon, cowboy. Let's go get warm."

Max kept looking back as they made their way to the truck. She was looking back too. Didn't want Dylan and Sundance to be caught if the sky fell through.

The truck warmed up quickly, but the minutes ticked by slowly, until the ten-minute mark had come and gone. If she hadn't been so worried, and frankly curious—and if Max hadn't been with her—she'd already be on a search-and-rescue mission.

Unfortunately, she didn't even make good use of the opportunity to have a captive audience with Max. She now had a bad feeling he'd end up being the tiebreaker when it came to the guest list, and this would have been an ideal time to introduce her case. But that didn't feel right either.

Dylan finally appeared, carrying a rather large, unmarked paper sack. He opened the door to the cab first and helped Sundance get situated next to Max, ushering in a bitter-cold breeze. Then he climbed into the driver's side, leaving the paper bag on his lap and rubbing his hands in front of the heater.

And leaving them all in suspense. Especially Sundance, who wouldn't stop whimpering and fidgeting.

Finally, he reached into the bag and pulled out a doggie treat. A bully stick, it seemed. And gave it to Sundance.

"I saw a pet booth. Couldn't resist," he said while digging back into the sack. "I think there's something in here for you too, Max."

The little boy sat up straighter and wiggled in his car seat.

This time, Dylan pulled out a huge purple Christmas ball ornament and a crafty-looking paint set that also included glue and glitter.

"Oh, wow!" Max said, treating the ball with as much care as his little hands could muster.

"Purple is a very important color at Christmas. It signifies royalty, spirituality and imagination. You can paint on any message and make it a special ornament that you can put on the tree every year," Dylan said.

He practically squealed. "Can I write the names of all my best friends and Mommy and Daddy and Penny on it?"

"You sure can. Do I need to go back and get another ball, though? I have a feeling you have lots of people you love and who love you."

Max shrugged. "It's too cold, but we can come back tomorrow and get another one if we need to."

"Maybe we can," Dylan said with a bit of a laugh.

In that moment, Georgina believed he meant every word. What a thoughtful gift for a little boy he barely knew. And how amazing he would be with his own children someday.

"Thanks, Mr. Dylan," Max said.

Dylan smiled. "You're welcome, cowboy."

She was about to tell him what a nice thing he'd done, but before she could speak, he reached in again and pulled out a giant cookie. A snickerdoodle.

"Had to get something for me. Couldn't resist." He looked at her while taking a bite. He winked, then closed his eyes and savored.

Georgina felt her eyes narrowing to a squint, even though she didn't want to let him see how much he was getting to her. Why did she all of a sudden feel like she was six years old again, dealing with one of the little boys who had learned to tease little girls so efficiently? Pushing their buttons well into adulthood? Like now.

After a long, silent pause, Dylan set the remainder of the cookie down, then brushed off his hands and reached into the bag.

"Santa didn't forget you," he said as he pulled out a single pink rose. Looked like the one she'd gravitated to when they first got there. Aside from being torn around it edges, it now looked frostbitten. And more beautiful than ever.

He looked into her eyes as he presented it, which made her breath hitch.

"You shouldn't have done that," she managed to say.

And she meant it. He really shouldn't have, because that iron resolve she'd mustered was withering away.

*But I'm kind of glad you did.*

# *CHAPTER SIX*

"AHA! DON'T YOU dare move, Santa. You've been caught red-handed," Georgina called out as she made her way down the stairs and into the parlor.

Cody glanced up from the huge wrapped package he'd been busy repositioning by the Christmas tree. As he stood, his eyes settled on the single pink rose she was holding. She'd yet to find a vase small and pretty enough for the flower that Dylan had gifted her, but she hadn't looked in the kitchen. The water glass she'd kept it in overnight in her room wasn't anywhere near acceptable.

"Is that for me?" he asked.

"Maybe. If you can answer a question," she said.

"Hypothetically, if I confess to being Santa, will you make me some of those snowball cookies instead of the rose?"

"I'll make some for you anyway. But that wasn't the question I was going to ask."

"I'm listening," Cody said as he turned his

attention back to the new packages beneath the tree. Three of them, by her estimation. Their Secret Santa would've had to have made a few trips.

"Go ahead and finish up first," she said, because where would she even begin?

Unfortunately, it was a question that only Dylan would be able to answer anyway, even though Cody could offer a male perspective. Specifically, did Dylan get her that rose just because he got everyone else a gift? Or was the flower more of a romantic gesture because roses couldn't help but be?

*Could he feel that little niggle of something too?*

Or was the rose a bribe in their future negotiations? She sure didn't detect any strings attached to its stem. Her and Dylan's ride back from the square had been dominated by Max, who chatted up a storm in the back seat about the guest list itself. How they should invite Penny, his labradoodle, and how she could be Sundance's date. And how Miss Hailey's cat should come, and Miss Ellie's cat too.

Georgina had to smile. He wasn't leaving anyone out. Even though she hadn't worked at the B and B all that long, she'd witnessed Max grow and develop strong bonds with all the folks at the neighboring ranches, like Ellie Cassidy and her grandson, Austin. For the first time, she felt the pull to start a family sooner rather than later.

She'd been so lost in her thoughts about the rose, she just now realized that one very big, unrelated question could already be answered.

"Don't wake Becca up, but you have to get her phone for me. The nanny cam footage will be on it. And you can officially clear your name," she teased.

"I already looked at it," Cody said.

"Oh! I thought I was the only one interested in finding out. It's Vern, isn't it?"

"I have to admit I'm mildly curious. I really just didn't want Becca to accidently see it. But there's still no way to know. This little guy was blocking it." He picked up one of Max's teddy bears from a side table.

"I wonder if someone placed it there. Someone who knows about the camera," she offered.

Cody blew out a breath. "I doubt it. Max leaves his stuffed friends all around the house. We should probably move the camera to a higher position anyway. I have a feeling Santa isn't done delivering packages. But I must have come close to catching him this morning, because there was ice just inside the door. I already cleaned it up so any early risers wouldn't slip and fall."

"Wow. And I slept a little later than usual. Talk about unfortunate timing."

*Overslept* was a better word for it. She'd been up for hours on her computer, putting together some design options and wording for the invitations and trying to come up with theme options as well. And, admittedly, admiring the rose and feeling so hopeful and hopeless, all at the same time.

"Well, if Santa keeps this up, we might need a bigger tree to put them under," Georgina said.

"Or let Max go ahead and open some in advance. I'm not sure how much longer I can tell him no."

Understandable. The former bull-riding champ was a relatively new father to his six-year-old son. At least that Destiny Springs rumor about who was Max's biological father had been resolved. Becca had kept that secret from her ex-but-now-forever husband—and everyone else except Georgina's sister Hailey—for six years. Hopefully, the whole Santa scenario would have an equally satisfying resolution.

"How about some coffee?" she asked. She needed to get this rose in a vase anyway, before Dylan came down and saw her holding it. She could set her watch to his morning walks with Sundance.

"I beat you to it," Cody said. "What were you going to ask me anyway?"

Georgina sighed. "It was nothing. Don't worry about it."

She started to head to the kitchen, but that familiar patter of little feet came barreling down the hallway. Max's hair was disheveled, and he couldn't have looked any cuter holding his stuffed bull.

His little eyes widened when he saw the newest packages.

Like clockwork, Dylan made his way down the stairs, but without his pup. A sudden pit formed in her stomach. No way he'd go for a walk on his own.

"G'mornin', everyone," he said, glancing only briefly at Georgina.

At least she had the good sense to hide the rose behind her back.

"Mornin', future stepbrother-in-law," Cody said.

Max didn't even bother to look up from examining the new packages, lifting and shaking the two that he was able to pick up. Not that anyone could blame him.

"Max, how about you grab your coat and boots, and we'll drive around while Mommy's still asleep. See if any of the other ranches have Christmas decorations," Cody said.

That was enough to get the little boy's attention. He jetted back down the hallway as fast as he could.

His father turned to face both of them. "While I have him out of the house, do you two mind repositioning the camera? We'll be gone about an hour tops."

Georgina and Dylan looked at each other.

"Sure," she said, although she'd at least have to get some coffee in her first, to wake up a little.

Dylan looked at Cody. "Georgina and I have some wedding planning to do anyway. Might as well get started on it now."

Cody took a deep, serious breath and nodded, as if this was a covert mission that they all had to get right.

"Sounds good," Georgina agreed. "Although today's planning should be simple. I think we need to agree on colors and a theme, if any. And the design and wording of the invitation."

She was certain the conversation would be a breeze. Right up until Cody left the two of them alone again and Dylan could barely seem to bring himself to look at her.

"Is everything okay with Sundance?" she asked.

Judging by his upbeat demeanor, she had assumed it was. But still, his pattern of walking the pup had been broken this morning. And broken patterns were always unsettling.

"Oh! Yeah, he's terrific," Dylan said, making brief eye contact before deferring to the packages beneath the tree. "He needed to go outside a little earlier than usual. I put him back in the room and went ahead and gave him breakfast. Came back down as fast as I could to clean up the mess he and I tracked back in. Didn't want anyone to slip and fall, but it looks like someone else has taken care of it."

At least the theory that Santa had tracked in the snow was put to rest. Unfortunately, it also raised more questions than it answered. But would that have been so difficult to say while looking at her directly? She'd received a tiny sample of what that felt like yesterday. And she'd liked it.

She gripped the stem of the rose she was still holding behind her back. Its single thorn threatened to pierce her palm.

Moments later, Cody and Max reappeared. The cowboy winked and nodded at both of them before he and Max disappeared through the front door, closing it behind him.

"Why don't you scout out a new place for the camera, and I'll pour us some coffee," she said to Dylan. That would give her at least a few minutes to collect her thoughts. And her feelings, because as much as she was trying to read something meaningful into the gift of the rose, this not-looking-her-in-the-eye thing kept throwing ice on it.

He glanced at her, nodded and commenced "scouting."

"Should I add anything to your coffee? Cream? Sugar? Dulce de leche?" she asked.

"The last one. Thanks, Georgina. And I've been thinking about what you said about the guest list. We should probably go ahead and make a decision on that too."

"Well, our little tiebreaker won't be here to help, but we can certainly talk some more about it," she said, stopping short of promising anything, because unless Dylan agreed to a reasonably sized guest list, they weren't going to solve that issue this morning. Besides, she needed a chance to talk with Monty about it first.

"Before we do anything else, even before we have coffee, there is one other important thing," he said, his tone now a little too serious.

In the silence that followed, her stomach dropped to her feet at what he might say. Especially after the way he'd not initially told her about his mom's death from ovarian cancer and about the New Year's Day rodeo benefit. Hopefully, it wasn't something equally saddening or she might just have to cave to his demands for a small wedding. And she wasn't quite ready to do that.

"I'm listening," she said.

A mischievous smile crossed his lips. Like the cat who got the cream.

"You might want to put that rose in some water."

TALK ABOUT A lucky break.

By being given the task of finding the perfect camera location and remounting it, Dylan was spared from having to look at Georgina directly while saying what he needed to say. It wasn't getting any easier to do both.

Honesty was always the best policy, although not always the smartest one. But she'd been sensitive to the whole New Year's Day dilemma, once he spoke the truth. Perhaps she would be equally sympathetic and cooperative about the guest list with a little more reasoning.

Georgina emerged from the kitchen with the mugs and handed him one. He took a sip, and not a moment too soon. Just the right amount of dulce de leche stirred in.

He pointed to the top of a hutch. "That would be a good place. The way the mount is constructed, we could angle it down and toward the tree."

She took a sip of her own coffee, then cocked her head and put her free hand on her hip.

"My only concern is that it might not capture enough of Santa's face."

She had a point. He walked back over to the tree and scoured the landscape in front of him.

"How about on the second shelf?" he asked.

Georgina shifted a couple of the knickknacks around, then took a step back.

"That should work as long as we can somewhat camouflage it. Don't want Max to somehow spot it and start asking questions."

He walked back over and stood a little closer than intended, but she didn't step away. Nor did he want to. She smelled like vanilla, which made him wonder what delicious dessert she'd be whipping up for everyone later. Dylan hadn't forgotten that she asked him to be her taste tester for new recipes. No way he'd turn down that offer.

As they worked together to move a few more things around, she asked the question he was dreading—even though it was his idea. "What is it you wanted to say about the guest list?"

"Nothing that will likely surprise you. I'd like to keep it small. I guess I never fully explained why."

"Yeah, I've been thinking about that too. Maybe between the two of us we can extract some kind of preference out of the stubborn bride and groom this afternoon," she said.

"What is Rose like?" he asked. She was going

to be his stepmom, after all. His dad had nothing but praise for her, but perhaps Georgina could offer a more objective analysis.

"She's an older version of Becca, except perhaps a tad more serious at times. They're super close, so don't make either of them mad."

At that, he finally summoned the nerve to look at Georgina. But she wasn't looking back. Instead, it looked as though she was trying to contain a smile but doing a pitiful job of it.

"So you were saying…?" she asked.

*Avoiding saying* was more like it.

He began finagling the clips that Vern had used to initially mount the nanny cam while summoning the courage to speak.

"There's a reason why I go by Dylan James instead of Dylan Legend," he said while repositioning the camera and securing the clips onto the portable mount configuration.

"I figured it was your professional name, although I have to admit if I were you, I would take advantage of your real one."

Dylan had figured that much about Georgina but privately hoped he was wrong. No denying the truth of it now. Not that he blamed her, because everyone he'd ever met expressed the same sentiment, more or less.

"I want to make it on my own talent. That's important to me."

"I'd say you have. And I have so much respect for that. Everyone else will too, whenever the truth finally comes out."

Sounded like she meant it, which was validating. At the same time, he maintained hope that it wasn't a matter of *when* but rather a matter of *if*.

"I've worked hard to make sure it never happens. All it would take is one viral story, and I would be exposed. But I suppose if it ever does, I could take the easy road to bigger success," he said, forcing a smile.

"Would that be such a bad thing?" she asked.

*Yes.*

"If it comes out now, people might think I planned it that way. To give me a leg-up for the rotation in Fort Worth. Couldn't fault 'em for assuming that much. If it comes out later on, folks might also conclude that my dad has been helping me the whole time," he said as he finished positioning the clips—and saying his piece.

Or at least part of it. There was no way he'd choke out the full story about how he'd battled with, and all but conquered, his stutter. Not with her standing so close and looking right at him. That confession had always seemed to change the way people responded to him, as though he needed to be handled with kid gloves from that point on.

He definitely did not.

"You did a great job with the camera. As soon as Becca gets up, we can check her phone and make sure it's at the best angle," Georgina said.

"Th-thanks," he barely eked out.

She picked up the mug he'd set down and handed it back to him. It had cooled just enough for him to take a couple of generous gulps. Not that caffeine would calm his nerves.

"We could make all the guests sign nondisclosures regarding the attendees and details about the wedding planners," she offered. "That way, we'd have full social media control and could leave Dylan James Legend out of it completely."

At that, he laughed.

"You think I'm kidding? I've done it before on high-profile weddings. Remember when the actress Olivia Bennett married that famous NFL quarterback? What was his name?"

"Sampson Thomas?"

"Yes! You remembered. I'm impressed."

"Rodeo isn't the only sport I like," he said. "So why did people have to sign something?"

At that, she looked at him. "I can't tell you. I signed one too, as one of the wedding planners."

He took a step back and looked at her. "Now I'm the one who's impressed."

Although he knew she was trying to tame his fears, the last thing he wanted to do was turn this into some big legal ordeal and have people fear uttering a word. It was supposed to be a joyous day.

Georgina looked straight ahead, and her smile faded. "Don't be. My business partner decided shortly thereafter that he didn't want to work with me anymore. Said I was 'unoriginal.'"

"He told you that?"

She took another long sip of coffee, then shook her head, not blinking even once but fixated on some point in front of her. If he wasn't mistaken, her eyes had suddenly dampened.

"No, he didn't. I had to hear it from other people. I should've made him sign a nondisclosure about our partnership, because after that, I couldn't get any clients."

*Until now.*

"It's like I'm invisible," she continued, then looked at him.

Dylan gulped. He'd never imagined such an upbeat, outgoing woman had a vulnerable side, and he wasn't quite sure what to do, except to be completely honest.

He wanted to say that he trusted her opinion as a wedding planner, but he'd yet to prove it to her. They'd butted heads on everything so far. And it wasn't over yet. But there was one thing that seemed perfectly safe to do.

"I'd love for you to decide on the colors and theme and invitation design—without my input.

I trust you. You're not invisible. *I* see you," he said, his voice never wavering.

"Is that so? Funny you say that," she said while offering up an unexpected smirk. "Not sure if you realize it, but you rarely look at me when you talk. What's that all about?"

The air escaped his lungs. He figured she'd noticed but was kinda hoping he was wrong. He'd never imagined she'd ask why. That was a depth of honesty he wasn't quite ready to plunge into.

"I'm just teasing. Sort of," she said, mercifully letting him off the hook.

At least, for now.

But the first question he didn't even have to think about. Yes, he saw her. Even more clearly now.

Question was did she *hear* him?

# CHAPTER SEVEN

DYLAN WASN'T SURE what to expect, but it certainly wasn't this.

"Buck Stops, huh?" he said as he climbed out of the truck and dropped boots on the soil of Nash Buchanan's sprawling Wyoming ranch. It was about the furthest cry from a bridal shop that he could think of. Not that he'd so much as imagined one.

He quickly circled around to the passenger side and offered a hand to his soon-to-be stepmom. "Please watch your step, Rose."

Ordinarily, he wouldn't want to come across as if he thought she was feeble. She was probably a couple of decades from needing any assistance. But she'd decided to wear some pretty ivory-colored heels—the ones she'd explained on the way over as being those she planned to wear with her wedding outfit.

Unless there was more to this ranch than met the eye, Dylan had to wonder if they had any dresses to try on at all. Seemed like the further he and Georgina got into this whole wedding-planning situation, the less he understood about it.

Dylan made sure Becca and her precious bundle got out of the cab safely as well. He had to admit he was pretty excited about having a "little sister."

Worked out well that they were both "only" children. They had something in common, right out of the gate.

In the distance, a cowboy jumped off his perch from one of the fences. Beyond that, three young girls were riding horses. The cowboy said something to the older-looking one, then headed toward the truck, taking long strides and closing the gap in record time.

"You must be Dylan Legend. Nash Buchanan," the man said as they exchanged a hearty handshake.

Hearing his legal last name made Dylan wince a little, but he tried not to let it show. Maybe Nash didn't travel in rodeo circles, although there was no doubt he was a rancher. Quite a spread he had here.

Nash swooped in and gave Becca a long but gentle hug, followed by a more reserved one for Rose before pulling away.

"Go on in. Door's unlocked. Jess is ready for you ladies," Nash said, then caught himself. "And gentleman. Sorry about that." He leaned into

Dylan and whispered, "If you need an escape, you're welcome to join me and the girls out here."

Dylan wasn't sure whether that was a good offer or one he'd best avoid. The less he got to know the locals, the less chance of word getting around that he was his father's son.

"I heard that, Nash," Becca said. "And it's totally up to Dylan, although I really want as much bonding time as I can get with my new big brother. Besides, if y'all start talking rodeo, he may forget that Mom and I are even here."

"Rodeo, huh? Which sport?" he asked.

Dylan shifted his weight. "Announcing, actually."

Nash raised his brows and nodded, then squinted and stared as if trying to place him.

"Definitely sneak away, then. Would love to chat with you," he said, his expression softening. The rancher tipped his hat and swiveled around, but not before saying, "Y'all have fun!"

Rose, Becca and Dylan went inside. Becca knew just where to lead them…to a room at the end of the hall. Tacked onto the door was a makeshift sign that read: *Western Wear with Heart.*

She tapped on the doorframe, which seemed to startle their hostess. Jess looked up from some sketches she was holding, set them down on a table in front of her and walked over to Becca and Rose. Another set of mutual hugs were exchanged. That was one thing about this town—people were very friendly.

When Jess finally got around to Dylan, he extended his hand. But she pulled him in instead.

"I'm glad you decided to join us. Georgina wasn't sure you'd be willing to play along. It's good to get another man's opinion. Nash already gave me his. Besides, you're more aware of the tone y'all are going with," Jess said.

He wanted to say, *You mean I had a choice about coming?* But even as a joke, that sounded rude. Besides, if the rugged cowboy outside was willing to throw in his two cents on such an important decision for the bride, then Dylan was more than happy to "play along."

And yes, they had agreed on a theme. Make that he let Georgina dictate it: Fresh start, with classic undertones. Neutral white or ivory base. Old school with a modern twist. How that would translate into a dress, he wasn't so sure.

Jess picked up the sketches and stacked them on an easel, as if this were a formal presentation or some such. "This first sketch is a two-piece suit. A Western-style, dramatically cropped ivory blazer with long matching silk maxi skirt. This is just the silhouette. Dorothy, my co-owner, and I will add some embellishments. Pearls, rhinestones, piping. That sort of thing."

Dylan looked to Rose to gauge her expression,

but she simply had a pleasant smile on her face that didn't waver.

"That would look so beautiful on you, Mom," Becca said.

"This next option is an empire-waisted sleeveless jumpsuit with wide, flowing chiffon legs. A bit more youthful and casual, but we can fancy it up with some embellishments as well. And add a faux-fur stole or cape if she gets cold. It would be very Halston-ish."

Whatever that meant. This was turning out to be a much harder task than he had anticipated. He couldn't even decide which one he liked best between the two he'd seen so far.

"That is gorgeous, Mom. So very 'you,'" Becca chimed in. This time she raised a tissue, dabbed at the corners of her eyes and squeezed her mom's hand.

Rose remained pleasantly stoic. The two seemed less alike that Georgina had indicated.

"And finally, the third option, although we can always sketch out more. This one is a full-length ivory satin dress with a deep cowl neck in the back. Much more Audrey Hepburn–ish. I'll show you another sketch, along with my recommended accessory."

Now that name was familiar.

Jess lifted that sketch to reveal an additional view of the dress. It did indeed reveal what she'd described, in great detail, with the addition of a long string of pearls, tied in a knot mid-back, as if the jewelry was on backward.

Becca started sobbing unapologetically. Rose put her arm around her daughter to comfort her. At that moment, he realized that if he didn't get outside to that arena, he might start bawling too. The last dress was his favorite.

Truth be told, they all fit the theme, because the parameters were so loosely defined. In the end, he had to trust his gut on this one. And the tears being shed from the others confirmed it.

"I like the last one the best. It will be perfect. Dad is gonna love it," he said, rendering his verdict.

No verbal responses, but plenty of nods.

"For the wedding, I agree. It will be," Rose said. "But…"

"But what, Mom?"

"I do love the jumpsuit. It would be perfect for the dinner we're planning with Monty's original Proud River bandmates when they come to Jackson Hole for Christmas to chat about their reunion tour next year. The tour will be later in the year—after the baby is born, of course. Monty doesn't want to miss those first few months, so much of the planning is on hold."

*What?* How did he not know about this? But yes, he remembered the gentlemen well. As he should. They were at all his birthday parties in lieu of friends his own age.

"Oh! We should invite them to the wedding," Becca suggested. "Imagine the photos and the great PR the band could get out of it. Kind of a teaser for the reunion."

"I *love* that idea!" Rose said.

*No!* Dylan froze. Even though Georgina wasn't anywhere around, it seemed as though her spirit was.

"But they may already have plans," Rose continued. "This whole wedding is so spur of the moment. I know I said I wouldn't get involved in the planning or decisions, and whatever you decide is fine with us, Dylan. But perhaps mention the whole band thing to Georgina. Y'all are getting together tonight to compare notes, right?"

"Yes, ma'am." At least, to the second part. Adding high-visibility folks to the guest list, and then promoting it, was going the wrong direction fast. Except he did need to know one other thing. Something that might help him justify conveniently forgetting to mention it to Georgina at all.

"How large of a wedding would you like?" he asked.

Rose shook her head. "No, sir. I've already said enough. Monty and I want to be surprised. I can tell you, though, that my side of the family is quite small. I don't have that many people to invite. Maybe ten? Becca can pull that information together for you."

At least Rose's confirmation on that part, along with the small number, gave Dylan a little hope that he could rein this in with Georgina. He didn't know diddly squat about wedding etiquette, but it didn't seem right for the groom to have disproportionately more guests than the bride.

In fact, it took him back in time to his own wedding. How their guest list read as a Who's Who. He'd been asked his opinion, and he argued it, although she didn't seem to listen to a word he said.

In the end, he let her decide. The fact that she disregarded his stated feelings should have been the mother of all red flags. Hopefully, he wasn't going to relive a similar experience with Georgina. This time the final decision could affect his career, making the stakes arguably higher.

"You can leave now, Dylan. I need to take Rose's measurements and get these two outfits started," Jess said.

He wasn't about to complain.

"I'll go see what Nash is up to," he said, then put his Stetson back on and headed down the hall and out the door.

As he approached the arena, he recognized the barrels and their configuration. More than that, he recognized one of the riders: Taylor Simms.

He'd guest-announced at one of the rodeos in Montana where she had taken first place. Maybe that was why Nash squinted at him funny. Maybe they'd all been there at the same time.

He hefted himself up on the fence next to Nash.

"I'm guessing at least one of these girls is yours and Jess's," Dylan said.

Nash kept his eye trained on the smaller girl, who was taking the barrels at impressive speed for her size.

"They're all mine now. I brought the twins to the marriage. Jess brought Taylor," Nash said. "You announced in Montana recently. You may remember her."

"I did. And I do."

Nash nodded and smiled, just like a proud father.

"I remember you now as well. You have a golden retriever. I guess I was thrown by the different last name, when Jess told me you were tagging along with the gals today."

"James is my middle name. I still go by it, professionally."

"Sounds like there's a story there somewhere. But I'm a strong believer in not prying. Can't say the same for some other folks in Destiny Springs."

Which was exactly why he wanted to get in and out of there as quickly as possible.

"Not much of a story, really. I just don't want to let my good fortune in having a famous dad keep me from making a name for myself the hard way. My dad worked his way from playing guitar and singing in my grandparents' garage to headlining at top rodeos. I want to follow in those earlier footsteps rather than the ones he's already forged."

Nash nodded but kept his eye on the little barrel racer in front of him.

"You, my friend, are an inspiration. So, how did you get roped into planning a wedding?"

Dylan had to laugh. He believed his dad had developed faith in him, but to leave Dylan to make such a decision must've seemed risky to the man.

"I guess I'm a pushover for romance," he said, although the words escaped his mouth before he could edit them.

"How is it working with Georgina?" Nash asked.

"Challenging, in a good way." *Fun. Thrilling. Terrifying.* "How long have you known her?"

Nash blew out a long breath. "Less than a year. But she's turned some heads in town. And she seems super sweet. If you like that sort of thing. Really good at planning weddings."

The cowboy couldn't have had any idea how right he was. Sweets were Dylan's weakness, and

Georgina was definitely that—even when she stood her ground.

"Don't get me wrong—being asked to help with the wedding is an honor, but I'm craving something to balance it out. I don't have any announcing gigs until New Year's Day."

Nash gave him a good long look.

"How would you feel about announcing at a small ranch rodeo this week? Instead of charging an entry fee or admission, we're asking folks to bring unwrapped Christmas toys for some of the less-fortunate kiddos in the area—Toys for Little Wranglers."

Now, that was a good idea. Made him think of Max and all his toys. Then it reminded him of something else.

"Wish I could give you some of the gifts that have appeared under the tree at the B and B, but they're not mine to give. Seems Santa makes multiple stops leading up to Christmas," Dylan said.

Nash laughed. "I thought that was only a rumor. I pretty much grew up here, but that story didn't start circulating until Becca opened the B and B. She told me it was happening, but I thought she was just pulling my leg."

"No, it's for real. Vern Fraser even set up a nanny cam to try to catch Santa in the act."

Nash nodded. "I always suspected Vern, but I guess I was wrong."

They sat in silence while two of the three little girls took turns doing drills around the barrels. Made him want to contribute something to it, if only he had a microphone.

"Think about the ranch rodeo," Nash finally said. "We've had a couple of fellas volunteer. My ranch hand, Parker, has the voice for it, but not the vocabulary. It may be a small production, but we want it to be a serious one."

"It's for a good cause," Dylan said. It would elevate his visibility, as long as they used *Dylan James* instead of *Legend*.

Nash gave him a reassuring smile, as if he understood what Dylan was thinking. Then the cowboy said the magic words.

"Georgina would be mighty impressed. It's one of her favorite charities."

Exactly what he didn't want to think about, but it seemed he was helpless against it. Even though his banter was fun and light-hearted, announcing was serious work. Serious for the competitors too. Impressing Georgina would be like having a little sweetness mixed in.

"You have yourself a deal."

THE LAST THING Georgina ever imagined doing was standing by while one the greatest country music singers of all time was getting a pair of black trousers tailored. At Kavanaugh's Clothing and Whatnot in Destiny Springs, Wyoming, of all places.

The pants looked good. Not as formal as a tuxedo, but not jeans either. Should work fine with a white button-down and one of the black blazers that Ethan, the owner, had pulled.

Unfortunately, the ensemble didn't do justice to her vision. Of course, that would've been something along the lines of a Saint Laurent double-breasted tuxedo. The good news was Ethan promised to tailor any item to perfection. A terrific fit could make a less-formal garment really shine.

Jackson Hole wasn't that far away. They could've made it there and back in a day and gone to one of her favorite spots for men's formal wear. Or even raided Monty's closet, since a full-on formal black-tie wedding had been ruled out. But it was sweet, and actually quite special, that Monty and Rose both wanted to support local businesses in this endeavor.

That said, the couple's preference for staying local would have been good information to have earlier, when she was pushing for the Elk Lodge. But that was the risk with couples who wanted to be "surprised."

"I'm a big fan, Mr. Legend. Especially of your

earlier work," Ethan said as he proceeded to adjust and pin the hem.

In Georgina's opinion, Ethan should've known not to make this any more uncomfortable than it had to be for Monty. Not to mention it was a bit of a back-handed compliment, wasn't it?

Thankfully, Monty let out a hearty chuckle in response. "That's mighty kind of you to say, son."

"Where are the ties?" Georgina asked.

Ethan pointed to the counter. "Over there. On the whirly thing."

While Ethan was busy fanboying, Georgina might as well select some accessory options. The current ensemble needed something to make it look polished.

But Kavanaugh's offered only three ties, and they were all...*strange*. Much too bold and colorful. She was thinking more along the lines of a simple black bowtie or a solid-color regular tie that wasn't as fat as the ones on the whirly thing. Yet there was one very cool alternative. A bolo tie, with a black cord, silver hardware and turquoise stone.

She lifted it from the adjacent spinner and walked back over to Monty and Ethan, the latter of whom was attempting to sing the lyrics to one of Monty's most popular songs while the country legend humored him by smiling and nodding.

The two of them had also selected a blazer.

Once Ethan had finished making some marks, Monty pushed back his shoulders and checked himself out in the mirror, doing all sorts of movements to make sure it hadn't been pinned too tightly.

"Looks sharp, Ethan. What do you think, Georgina?" Monty said.

"You look very handsome, but something is missing." Repositioning herself in front of Monty, she showed him the bolo tie. Then she proceeded to raise it over his head but stopped short. "May I?"

He dipped low enough to accommodate the request, and Ethan stepped in to help tuck the back and sides of the cord underneath the collar.

Monty looked in the mirror and smiled. "You're brilliant, Georgina. I think Rose will like what she sees."

"No doubt in my mind," Ethan said.

It warmed her heart to hear such words from a groom. She'd been around plenty who'd had a serious case of the jitters. Or worse, felt pressured into getting married too soon, if at all. The words they spoke when they thought she wasn't listening were colder than frostbitten feet.

No, what was even worse than missing out on a beautiful wedding was having a reluctant groom or bride. Definitely wasn't going to be the issue with Rose and Monty.

"I think we should celebrate. Let me buy you a cup of coffee at the diner. You too, Ethan," Monty said.

The young man shook his head. "I'll have to take a rain check. I'm alone in the store today. But congratulations! Send me a photo of you and Rose in y'all's fancy duds."

Monty nodded, then whispered to Georgina, "Let's put him on the guest list."

"Actually, that's one of the things we need to talk about. Over that cup of coffee you offered."

Monty finished removing the bolo tie and handed it to Ethan, who treated it as though it were the Hope Diamond. "I'll wrap this up for you, sir."

Another chuckle. "Please. Call me Monty."

"Yes, sir," Ethan said.

Georgina managed to stifle a snort. Sure, they were in the presence of country music royalty, but Monty was so easygoing and humble, it felt like she'd known him for ages.

It also made her wonder what life must have been like for Dylan, growing up in his father's expansive shadow. For the first time, she understood how Dylan might have wanted to succeed without Monty's connections. Admittedly, when he first said that, she thought he was being ridiculous.

Still, the lengths he seemed to go to in order

to avoid being associated with his father seemed a little unnecessary. He'd clearly proven his talent. Otherwise he wouldn't be getting announcing gigs.

Georgina and Monty said their goodbyes to Ethan and then tailgated to the diner, where Monty's appearance caused a few whispers and stares as they headed to some barstools in the back, next to the soda fountain.

Fortunately, the waitress didn't seem starstruck as she took their order.

"Two coffees. And do you have any strawberry pie?" Monty asked the waitress, then turned to Georgina. "And whatever sounds good to you. My treat."

"We've got strawberry rhubarb, if that'll do. Best in town, folks say. Even in December. The diner imports those fresh sweet winter-harvest strawberries from Florida," the waitress chimed in.

*So does the B and B...*

"Then I guess we'd better try it," Georgina said.

"Sold!" Monty said.

"Two pieces, or just two forks and a slice cut in half? The servings are very generous," the waitress said.

Monty leaned in to Georgina. "If it didn't have rhubarb, I'd say let's get three pieces and take a piece back for Dylan. Strawberry pie would make his day. But rhubarb's too tart for him."

"I was thinking if we get two, I'll need to take half of my piece home anyway. That way Dylan could give rhubarb a second chance," Georgina said.

"To tell you the truth, I don't need a whole piece either. I have to be able to fit into those tailored trousers."

"One slice, two forks," Georgina said to the waitress, who promptly jotted the order down, then walked behind the counter again.

Monty looked up to the ceiling. "'One slice, two forks.' Sounds like a good title for a country song."

She had to laugh. "It does! Maybe that should be your next one, if you decide to come out of retirement."

Monty shook his head. "Well, the thought occurred to me, but that would take me away from Rose, I'm afraid. I'm already pushing my luck with a reunion tour with my old band, Proud River. I'm going to insist that Rose comes with us and hope she finds the prospect intriguing."

Georgina raised her brows. "How could she not? The glamorous life of a musician sounds like so much fun."

"Sometimes it is—I won't lie. But I sure wish I could get that time back and spend it with Dylan instead. Might have made his life a little easier to have a dad around more often."

She wanted to say that he could make it easier for him now, but Dylan didn't want the help. And she sort of understood. But she hadn't really thought about how it might have affected him as a child. Any kind of job that required a lot of traveling would be tough on the whole family. She, for one, wouldn't want to live like that.

"Well, you've made my life easier by being such a cooperative groom-to-be," she said.

"I don't think Dylan would agree. Thinks I'm being stubborn by not giving him any direction. But Rose and I made a promise to put it all in someone else's hands so that we wouldn't have any arguments about it. Little does she know, I was planning to let her have any kind of ceremony she wanted. Ha! But we're so grateful that you and Dylan were able to take time out of your busy schedules to do this for us."

The waitress placed the coffee and a split slice of pie on one plate between them.

"Dylan and I will talk about it more tonight. We're getting together to share notes about you two lovebirds," she said, taking a bite of the pie.

"What do you think?" Monty asked.

Georgina finished chewing and swallowed. "Best strawberry rhubarb pie I've ever tasted. This is certainly a treat."

"To be honest, it's also a bribe," Monty countered.

She felt her eyebrows raise. "Interesting. You *do* know that if you have a special request for the wedding, you can just tell me. No bribe required."

"It's not for the wedding. A friend and his wife want to renew their vows in a couple of days, and they had their heart set on it taking place in a barn in Destiny Springs. They both grew up here and were even grade-school sweethearts."

"How precious!"

At least the *grade-school sweethearts* part. The barn idea, not so much, even though she'd put together an amazing one for her sister Hailey, if she did say so herself. It was pretty obvious what Monty was about to ask.

"Maybe you should be bribing my sister instead of me," she said.

"Possibly. But even though it's a family-only deal, so my friend says, they've already made a mess of the whole thing, and I'm afraid the stress is ruining it for them. Was hoping you might be able to help coordinate a bouquet for her and find an officiant. And, most importantly, see if Hailey wouldn't mind letting them have it at Sunrise Stables."

Georgina wanted to say that she was the one who should be buying him a cup of coffee and slice of pie. Sure, it was a small-scale plan, but she had a favor to ask of him as well.

Besides, contrary to how Dylan might've felt, it was good to have connections. In this case, she was the one being sought out for hers.

"I'd be happy to help. I can make a few phone calls when I get back, and I can also help the couple with last-minute invitations and any decorations they may want for the space." Georgina took another bite of the pie, and it melted in her mouth.

Monty finished chewing and swallowing, then wiped his mouth and looked at her. "Thank you. This will mean the world to them. Back at Kavanaugh's, you said you wanted to talk with me about something."

"You mentioned inviting Ethan. Do you and Rose have a preference on wedding size? Without spoiling the surprise, I can find accommodations for at least sixty folks, assuming the majority are couples, which would cut my room search in half. Or we can go higher," she said, even though she hadn't exactly confirmed it. A cursory search for area hotels and motels and their availability afforded her the confidence, however. That and assuming some folks wouldn't mind staying on the outskirts of Destiny Springs. She'd had to find accommodations for much larger groups at the last minute when she'd been wedding planning full-time.

Monty stared straight ahead and took a sip of his coffee, seemingly lost in thought.

"I can honestly say I don't have a preference. Though, just between you and me, I'd love to brag and show her off to the whole world." Monty didn't seem to even try to hide his smile. He then chased it with a bite of strawberry rhubarb, closed his eyes and shook his head as if it were too delicious to be true.

"What's your favorite kind of pie?" she asked.

"Now, that's an easy question. Chess pie."

"How would you feel about a groom's pie rather than a groom's cake? No promises, because you want to be surprised."

He looked at her. "I would be. Pleasantly."

"I'm still in the planning stages, but do you know what Rose's favorite flavor of cake is? Or would she prefer a pie as well? Now, that would really be a surprise," Georgina offered, although she had no plans of veering that far off course.

"Strange, but I don't recall her having a sweet tooth at all. Always orders coffee at the end of a meal but no dessert. As far as the wedding goes, when I asked her if she had any special requests, she said no," he continued. "All I really want is for it to be extra special and one of a kind. Like Rose herself."

Georgina's hopes, exactly.

"That said, Dylan has access to all my contacts," Monty continued.

Unfortunately, he didn't really answer the question she needed. Equally unfortunate, he answered the one she was about to ask, which was if he could give her a list of his contacts. At least she could use Monty's desire to show off his new wife to the world as a reason for a larger wedding.

Except Dylan had the list. And something already told her he wasn't likely to simply hand it over to her.

*Unless he can be persuaded...*

"So, is strawberry pie, without any rhubarb, Dylan's favorite dessert?"

Monty laughed and shook his head. "That's a tough one. If it's not his favorite, then it comes in a close second."

Georgina smiled and nodded. With her baking skills, it would be easy to "make Dylan's day" with strawberry pie, as Monty had put it.

And if things went accordingly, it would make her day as well.

# CHAPTER EIGHT

"BEST SEAT IN the house, Mr. Legend."

Dylan tried to not roll his eyes, but he had only himself to blame. This was the second time in his life that he'd used his given name.

And it would be the last.

But tonight he needed every advantage he could get, because the whole guest-list topic was about to bubble over if they didn't come to an agreement, and fast. He needed to make a quick two-day trip to Fort Worth to record the promos, and that would mean leaving his co-planner unsupervised.

The host had led him to the back table for two, nearest the fireplace and as far away as possible from a raucous table of forty.

"Special evening?" the host asked as he handed Dylan one of the menus.

"Yes. The other party should arrive shortly," he said, although he stopped short of saying *date*. "Blond hair, brown eyes, warm smile. Georgina Goodwin."

The host simply nodded.

Dylan was going to suggest that he and Georgina ride together, but that really would sound like a date, even though there was no reason for it to feel that way. They were wedding co-planners. That was all.

He'd arrived at Ribeye Roy's well ahead of her, hoping to get his choice of tables, because even the thought of being here with her was enough to scare off the words. And he needed to speak tonight—get his point across and resolve this whole issue once and for all. It was messing with his concentration.

But then Georgina walked in and messed with it some more.

Dylan stood and pulled out her chair before the host had a chance. But not before the man graciously took her long wool coat, revealing a stunning pale pink dress. He expected no less, but the woman in front of him was so much more.

*Stay focused.*

He opened his mouth to tell her she looked pretty, but nothing came out, so he referred back to the menu.

"The food looks amazing," he said as he eyed the photo of the twelve-ounce T-bone steak and the accompanying loaded baked potato. "Have you eaten here before?"

"Just once. Since this is where your dad and

Rose first met, I thought it was appropriate that we meet here to talk about them."

He looked at her just as a waiter set down two tall glasses of ice water. "May I start you off with any appetizers, or do you need more time to look at the menu?"

"We need a few more minutes," Georgina said.

After the waiter nodded and turned away, she took a deep breath and smiled.

There was something about her that both eased his fears and terrified him, because he had a way of turning beautiful smiles into looks of concern—even pity——once he started stuttering.

"How was the f-f-fitting?" he managed to say without tripping up too badly.

"It was amazing. Monty is such a sweetheart. So cooperative."

He couldn't argue with that. His dad was great. Maybe a little too great at times.

"Rose couldn't have been nicer. We all agreed on the same dress," he said while watching the dessert cart pass by their table.

"The long silk one with the plunging cowl in the back?" Georgina asked.

At that, he looked at her. "You've seen the sketches?"

"Actually, yes. In fact, I suggested that kind of design to Jess as an option. Didn't want to put my thumb on the scale, though. It's what I envisioned for Rose. These things just come to me sometimes when I'm planning a wedding."

The way she lit up sent a shiver down Dylan's spine. Although he wasn't a fan of weddings, especially big ones, she radiated more warmth over the subject than the roaring fireplace nearby.

Not to mention that was quite a talent. He was no expert, but she sure nailed it on that dress, which made him momentarily second-guess his thoughts on the wedding size.

Very momentarily.

The waiter returned. "Have we made any decisions?"

"How about we both pick out an appetizer and share them?" Georgina suggested to Dylan.

"The portions are quite large," the waiter pointed out.

"I like that suggestion. We can share those, then go from there. You first," Dylan said to Georgina. Not that he wasn't craving a full-on steak. Maybe they could share one of those as well.

"Hmm. Let's try the baked brie," she said.

"Excellent choice. And for you, Mr. Legend?" the waiter asked.

Dylan winced. He looked at Georgina. Her eyes narrowed to a suspicious squint. He referred back to the menu. "The jumbo lump crab cakes, please."

The waiter nodded once more and left.

"Excellent choice as well, Mr. Legend," Georgina said. The squint dissolved and the smile had widened.

"We didn't have a reservation," he said.

"The restaurant isn't even full," she pointed out.

"Maybe I just wanted to impress you and get the best table." No *maybe* about it.

"Well, it worked," she said.

At that, he looked at her again, unsure how to interpret it since she'd already suggested he use the power of his last name anyway. Was she impressed on a personal level or a professional one? Or maybe even both?

But when the full waitstaff came out and started singing "Happy Birthday" to some lucky soul at the table of forty behind them, Georgina's beautiful smile deflated.

"Apparently, the Legend name didn't get us the best seat in the house after all," he said. Not that there was anywhere to get away from it.

He'd expected her to laugh, but he got a semi-chuckle instead.

Perhaps she realized, as he did, that they'd been avoiding the topic they were supposed to be here to discuss and making small talk about the menu selections instead.

"Rose mentioned she has a small family. About ten people in total," he said, diving right in.

"Yes, I know. But that only seems to be a big deal in church weddings. Besides, Monty said he'd love to 'show off' his new bride to the world. He told me you have the list of his contacts," she said.

Once again, his voice failed when she smiled and batted those gorgeous brown eyes of hers. Like chocolate kisses, but with a hint of gold dust in the center. Made him wonder why he thought he ever stood a chance on getting his way when meeting face-to-face.

But he wasn't ready to give up.

The waiter positioned the two appetizers equally between them. Dylan insisted Georgina go first, and she didn't disappoint. She took nearly half of both appetizers. Nothing better than good food, in his opinion.

He loaded his plate as well, leaving a decent amount behind in case she wanted more. The waiter had underplayed the size of the portions. He, for one, probably wouldn't have room for even a split entrée.

Just as he got up the nerve to resume making his case for a small wedding, someone at the large birthday table clinked his knife against the side of his glass, then proceeded to shower his "special lady," as he put it, with birthday praises.

Georgina set her fork down, turning from seeming ravenous to being fed up.

"Hopefully, they'll be done soon." The words came out surprisingly smooth, even though he was looking directly at her. Maybe because she was staring down at her plate. He, too, was a bit annoyed, along with other tables of couples who had stopped trying to talk over the party.

Finally, the celebration quieted as a birthday cake was cut into squares and distributed at the table.

Dylan placed his fork across his plate, signaling he was done with the appetizers. "Should we order some entrées?"

Georgina hadn't resumed eating, so perhaps it had nothing to do with the noise and more to do with saving her appetite for the main course.

She finally looked up and shook her head. "Not for me, but please order something for yourself."

"Is everything okay?" he asked. Maybe she simply didn't feel well.

At that, she sat up a little straighter. "Just lost my appetite for a moment. And maybe I'm being a little childish." She picked up her fork and took another bite of the brie.

That wasn't even remotely what he was thinking. Sounded like this went pretty deep, but he wasn't sure what to say. If it had to do with birthdays in general, they kind of made him lose his appetite too.

"Bad birthday experience?" he asked. "I've had a few of those."

She looked up. "Really? I would've thought you'd have had the best birthdays, considering..."

"Considering my dad was a star? I guess that's a fair assumption." In that moment, he felt a little ungrateful for everything his parents had tried to do. Their intentions had been good, but over-protecting him never did sit well.

Georgina nodded. "I was born on Christmas Day. Never had a party on my actual birthday. Not even on Christmas Eve, which I would have gladly embraced. If I got one at all, it was after the new year. And my Sweet Sixteen was barely acknowledged."

"I'm sorry to hear that."

"But something good did come out of it, because that's why I got into wedding planning. No one can overlook a bride. She gets one special day where all eyes are on her," she said. "I know that must sound pretty silly. I should be over it by now anyway, right?"

Dylan gulped. Silly? No. But it definitely explained a few things.

She started toying with her food again. Of all the things he'd planned to say, what was about to come out of his mouth wasn't one of them. But it was direct and honest.

"Georgina, look at me," he said.

She raised her chin, and he felt the words sticking to the back of his throat. But he had to try, and she had to see his eyes while he did.

"You're special *b-because* of your birthday."

GEORGINA TRIED TO SPEAK, but nothing came out.

Not only because he'd said something no one else ever had, but because he looked into her eyes while doing it. Without hesitation.

Without looking away. Until now, when he finally seemed to realize what he was doing.

Although she was convinced of his sincerity, she wasn't convinced of the logic. She picked up her fork and played with the remaining piece of brie on her plate, even though she couldn't take another bite. Too full.

"Thank you, Dylan. But I still bet you had some amazing birthday parties growing up. Then again, any party would have been amazing to me."

He leaned back in his chair and gently nodded while fixing his eyes on the lit candle between them. "You're right. I did. More famous country singers and producers and promoters in one room than you could count. A few rock stars too."

Georgina sat up straighter. Talk about a fairy-tale childhood.

Dylan finally smiled. Maybe now that he was remembering it was special after all, he'd see her point of view about the guest list. Hope swelled within her heart for the first time since Becca asked her to help with this whole thing.

"Tell me more," she said.

"Not much more to tell, really. They were there for my famous father, not for the little boy who didn't have any friends to invite."

Georgina's breath caught in her throat. Not the way she thought this story would go.

"I don't believe that," she said. He had to be teasing. Even though he was a grown man and not a little boy, she could tell he must have been adorable and likeable.

"It's true," he said. "I had trouble...talking."

Her first thought was *He still does*. He'd gifted her his full attention for all of five seconds and had barely looked at her again.

"And I was teased for it," he added.

"Shy kids seem to have a tough time of it growing up. Children can be cruel for no reason," she offered, even though she was still stuck on the fact that he got huge birthday parties. She'd take a room full of famous adults and no kids over a forgotten birthday any day of the week.

He looked at her again, straight in the eyes. "Adults can be w-w-worse."

That was when she knew what he was really trying to say, and the sudden ache in her heart for that little boy couldn't go any deeper. She'd had a friend who'd stuttered and remembered how awful it was for her. He didn't need to explain any further.

Georgina resisted the temptation to reach across the table and squeeze his hand. Instead, she simply said, "Not this adult."

He let out a nervous laugh and looked away, once again. This time it didn't sting. It wasn't anything personal against her, yet it was as personal as it could get for him.

"Well, I feel better now that my deep, dark secret is out in the open," he said.

"I'm pretty sure I ran off lots of friends because I talked too much. I was the kid whose teacher would write that on the report card. One even wrote, 'Georgina has such a wonderful, bubbly personality, but it tends to bubble over sometimes.'"

Dylan looked at her again, the earlier distress having drained from his face. "I can't imagine anyone being bothered by anything you say."

"I'm pretty sure people tune out after a while. Too many bubbles, not enough substance."

"Not this person," he said.

Georgina gulped. Again, no hesitation on his part. And no looking away.

"Well, I know, from my experience with you, that when you speak, your words are always meaningful and precise. No pointless bubbles," she said.

He held her gaze. In it, she could tell he was wrestling with whether she was telling the truth.

"Problem was I pretty much chose not to speak. Too risky. Until I discovered that I could talk about the rodeo. I'd hold events in the bedroom with my stuffed animals and talk the night away. That's what led me to announcing professionally. No one pays attention to those guys when they're in the booth. I finally felt heard for the first time in my life. And if someone does decide to look at me, Sundance steals their attention."

"*I* hear you," she said, taking the opportunity to riff on his own words. She didn't say the part about how if she were at a rodeo where he was announcing, she would barely notice that sweet golden retriever. Although she'd thought he was a handsome cowboy when they first met—even when he seemed to be ignoring her—he was even more handsome now.

"I've heard that works with singing," she continued.

"My dad wanted me to follow in his footsteps.

And I'm not half bad when no one is looking at me."

"Yeah, me too. I'm a regular Dakota Rush when I'm alone in the shower."

Georgina had to laugh at her own joke. She could never sound like the popular country singer, but she tried. Except Dylan barely cracked a smile. He even shook his head, almost imperceptibly. What was that all about?

And just when she'd thought they'd had a breakthrough.

"I'm curious," she said. "You never answered my question about why you barely look at me when you talk. Yet you seem to speak fine to other people. Do I make you nervous?"

That had been Becca's take on it, and it got a smile out of him.

He shifted in his seat. "Maybe a little. Which doesn't exactly help the words flow."

"Well, I've been told that I'm a lot to deal with sometimes, so I can't say that I blame you."

"Okay, then. Maybe a lot. But in a good way," he added.

"That's a relief, because you know we still have lots of things to check off our wedding-planning list. But something tells me the guest list isn't one of them. Do you still want a small wedding for your dad and Rose? Because I put on an excellent large wedding. Just ask my teddy bears.

While yours were playing rodeo, mine were getting married or attending lavish ceremonies."

"Oh, I have no doubt about it," he said with a grin.

"How about this. We send a Save the Date to immediate family and closest friends and add two more rungs of potential guests for the actual invitation, which needs to go out by the end of next week, latest. Either we'll reach an agreement by then or Max will decide for us. But at least we'll be prepared. And I won't make the wedding cake until the last minute anyway. I know you have Monty's list, and I won't even ask to see it. You decide who else is worthy of being invited."

By the way he exhaled a long breath, she could tell he wasn't fully on board. But his slow nod indicated there was a still a chance.

The waiter came back around. "May I take these plates away? Would you like to order an entrée?"

They shook their heads in unison.

"You were right about the portion size. I'm full," she said.

At that, the waiter produced some smaller dessert menus. "In case you have a little room left or would like to take a dessert to go. Marie is on her way with the dessert cart, if you'd like to take a look at the selection."

"You're pure evil," she teased the waiter.

Dylan was obviously and immediately under a spell as soon as the cart arrived, and she suddenly felt like the evil one. Although the desserts in front of them looked phenomenal, none of them were strawberry pie.

But there was something else. She'd gotten a taste of his full attention, and she wanted more. And she was pretty sure she knew how to get it.

"Everything looks so good, but I don't have any room left," he said.

Georgina concurred, and the waiter bowed and left.

"That was the right call," she said.

He looked so wistfully in the direction of the dessert cart, it was all she could do not to laugh.

"I hope so, but I'm already having doubts."

"It was. You need to start saving your appetite because tomorrow I'm baking wedding cake and groom's pie options. And you're taste testing all of them."

*Prepare to be spellbound.*

# CHAPTER NINE

BY THE TIME Georgina heard the stampede, it was too late.

She took a broad sidestep, but Max and Penny brushed her leg anyway, which caused her to teeter—and then for the beautiful fresh strawberry pie to fall to the floor. The one she'd stayed up late last night to make.

The only saving grace was that she'd put it on a decorative plastic plate rather than glass.

She'd carried it out to the parlor area to find the best morning light for a quick photo. Which reminded her: She and Dylan still needed to discuss hiring a photographer. A videographer as well. Camera phones had come a long way, but a celebrity wedding deserved the best, regardless of the size. If she ended up losing the guest list battle with him, she intended on winning the social media war.

Another thing of beauty this morning: watching little Max's face light up when he saw that Santa had left another package beneath the tree.

Georgina's heart quickened a few notches when she glanced up at the nanny cam and saw that nothing was obstructing its view this time. Santa was sure to have been caught.

She resisted the urge to stop what she was doing, rush down the hall and wake up Becca. Cody was around somewhere, so that might be her best bet for getting the scoop.

Dylan, by contrast, had yet to come downstairs. Unless he'd taken Sundance out while she was in the kitchen. Entirely possible. This morning, she'd been extra busy making a small batch of bride's cake samples for their tasting today. Classic vanilla, coconut-cream and lemon-zest cupcakes, which could also double as all-you-can-eat afternoon treats for the few B and B guests.

The groom's pie would be easy, now that she knew Monty's favorite. Of course, she could always make a variety of mini pies with different fillings, with the full chess pie at the center of the culinary universe.

So many possibilities. Made her giddy just thinking about it.

Becca finally wandered down the hall, just as Georgina was cleaning up the last bits of pie crust, looking sleepier than ever. She was holding her back as though it might otherwise snap in two.

Oddly enough, Georgina couldn't have been

more envious. The more she was around Max and his friends in Destiny Springs, the more she was envisioning one or more children of her own.

She closed the space between herself and Becca and put an arm around her waist, if only to help relieve a little of the pain as they made their way toward the parlor.

Becca tilted her head and looked as though she might cry.

"Oh, no! What's wrong?"

Becca shook her head. "Nothing. Just ready to give Max a baby brother or sister."

"I can imagine!" Personally, Georgina would be yearning to know in advance whether she'd be having a son or daughter. But at least Becca and Cody already had a name picked out either way: Alexander if it was a boy, Alexandra if a girl. And Max had already decided that, either way, his new sibling needed to have a purple nursery.

"Thankfully, my wonderful husband can't wait to take on all the middle-of-the-night crying sessions and daily changing of the diapers since he missed out on it with Max," Becca said, stopping short of the archway but within view of her precious little boy who was now shaking the newest package.

"Cody volunteered for all that?"

Becca nodded. "He thinks it's going to be easy and fun. Should we tell him?"

They looked at each other for a long moment, then both burst out laughing. Still, Georgina had a feeling Cody would find a way to make it fun. The man got a kick out of being thrown off bulls for a living, for goodness' sake!

Becca was one lucky wife to have such enthusiastic support from a man who gave up a national bull-riding championship career, complete with travel and awards and admiration, to be a full-time daddy.

"Do you have your phone with you, by chance?" Georgina drew a large imaginary circle around the Christmas scene in front of them, then discretely pointed up to the nanny cam.

"I do. I figured you would be asking to see it. Let's go to the kitchen."

Georgina steered Becca around the sticky part of the floor, and her boss didn't even ask what had happened.

She wished that Becca could move just a little bit faster. The Secret Santa suspense was unbearable.

Becca sat on one of the wobbly bar stools, pulled her phone out of a robe pocket and handed it to Georgina, who typed in the password that her boss had entrusted her with.

She didn't even have to squint to see who it was.

"Just to be clear, you said not to tell you who it is unless it's Santa, right?" Georgina asked.

"That's correct," Becca said.

Georgina bit her lip and contemplated her next move. The person in the video was dressed like Santa, except it looked to be a woman. It clearly was not Vern. This Santa was too graceful and slender. She also must have tucked her hair beneath the red hat. And she kept her face down. So much for repositioning the camera.

"Does that include Mrs. Santa?" Georgina asked.

"Why? Is that who you see?" Becca asked, sitting up straighter this time.

"Do you really want to know?" She was hoping so, because it would be fun to have someone beside her on this journey of discovery.

"I do now because I was so sure it was Vern." Becca eased the phone from Georgina's hand, studied the footage and nodded.

"I'd be sure that Vern put Sylvie up to it, but she's out of town visiting relatives. Won't be back until next week," Becca continued.

That had occurred to Georgina as well. Vern's fiancée would've been a likely bet. But if she wasn't even in town, that ruled her out.

There were a couple of other local women who could fit into a size-small Santa suit.

"Are you going to show Max? At least he'd have his imagination confirmed."

"Or shattered." Becca shook her head. "The 'real' Santa will be in the square, starting tomorrow, for photos with the children. And they usually hire someone in a traditional size range."

They wandered back into the parlor in time to catch Dylan and Cody vying for Max's attention. In that moment, an unwelcomed thought crossed Georgina's mind. How would Dylan be as a father?

She'd already seen evidence that he'd make an amazing daddy. The scene that was playing out right before her eyes further confirmed it. Except with his career, he'd be gone quite a bit. So much for her imagination. Just as well—she had work to do today.

Becca, Max and Cody finally left the parlor area, and it was once again down to her and Dylan.

"I didn't see you this morning," she said.

"I had some business I had to take care of."

Of course. Rodeo announcing probably did involve more than simply showing up and talking. Made her realize how little she knew about him.

"Everything is okay, I hope," she said.

Dylan nodded. "Me too. I needed to cancel a quick trip to Fort Worth to record some promos. I'll have to go back for the photoshoots, but it saves me from having to make two trips."

"If you canceled because of the wedding planning, I'd be happy to take up any slack. Both times."

More than happy, actually. The more she thought about that contact list he had tucked away somewhere, the more she dared to dream how exposure and meeting people of influence could help put her back on the map.

"That's part of it. I also agreed to announce at a ranch rodeo in a couple of days for Nash Buchanan. So I made arrangements to record at Indigo Studios in Keaton. Can't be guaranteed of the quality, and I won't get to meet some of the folks I'd wanted to meet. But…"

That was a nearly two-hour drive. Which, of course, would take much less time than a two- or three-day trip for him.

"The ranch rodeo is for a good cause—Toys for Little Wranglers," he continued.

Georgina blinked. She could have melted as easily as a scoop of ice cream on a hot pecan pie, straight out of the oven. Not only because what he was doing was exceptionally selfless, but because he looked at her the whole time without looking away.

"Bad decision?" he asked.

She shook her head. "No! It's a great one. It's just that…"

"What?"

"You keep proving that you're a nicer guy than I first thought you to be," Georgina said.

"Excuse me?" he said in a tone that sounded like it was one cup offended and a half cup amused.

Now she was the one who had to look away.

"Because of what we talked about. How you wouldn't look at me when you spoke."

"You made me nervous. I promise that's it. Still do, to be honest."

She wanted to say that she didn't start out being nervous around him, but she was starting to now.

"I'm used to keeping people either entertained by my enthusiasm or irritated by it. *Nervous* is a new one for me."

He smiled and dropped his chin as if he'd said too much.

In a way, he had. Georgina gulped as the rest of the world seemed to stand still. Although it could be interpreted multiple ways, her heart kept steering her mind back to one way in particular.

"Well, nothing to be nervous about around me. Unless you're afraid I've slipped some kind of secret potion into the cake samples or cast a spell, because I have been known to do that," she said, if only to add some levity to the situation and steer them back to the task at hand.

His brow raised. If he wasn't nervous before, he should be now. And definitely after she made another strawberry pie. In the meantime, the cakes were bound to weaken his resistance at least a little. Except she wasn't only thinking of it in terms of planning the wedding.

"Follow me." She pivoted on her heels and

headed to the kitchen. Might be a good idea to strike while the cake was hot, so to speak.

And before she revealed anything else about how she was really beginning to feel.

WHETHER SHE'D INTENDED to or not, Georgina reminded him of a bride, with the way her hair was done up all fancy. To top it off, she'd removed her bulky pink hoodie. Underneath, she wore a white top with a wide neck that barely clung to her shoulders. And she was wearing a single strand of pearls.

He'd been exaggerating a little when he'd said she still made him nervous. Getting his stuttering out in the open had seemed to relieve it. Until now. Only this was making him nervous for a very different reason.

A cookbook was open to a page that revealed a photograph of a statuesque wedding cake. Looked exactly like the one at his reception, although they all pretty much looked the same, in his opinion.

But the beauty of it couldn't compete with the ugliness of those memories.

Georgina pulled a cupcake tin from the oven and stuck a toothpick into the center of each. A mixture of delicious scents—vanilla, coconut, lemon—wafted in his direction.

"Perfect! The guests are going to love these,"

she said, setting the baking tin on the counter then walking back over to the bar area where he'd settled.

"You mean those aren't for us to sample?" He didn't even try to hide his disappointment.

"No, but those are," she said, pointing to some cupcakes sitting on a rack of some sort. "I made an earlier batch so that they'd have enough time to cool. The timing should be perfect."

That was enough to make him sit up straighter.

"Can I help with anything? Besides the taste testing?"

"As a matter of fact, you can. You can pick out your favorite style of cake." She started turning the pages slowly in front of him.

Pure torture, but also surprisingly...interesting. They each looked a little different after all. And each one could feed an entire rodeo.

"We'll have to hold the reception in the barn. That's the only place around here with a high enough ceiling," he joked. "We're really only gonna need that top layer, you realize."

Georgina gave him a sly grin and shook her head as if she knew what he was implying.

"Better to have leftovers than to run out. Besides, the bride and groom keep the top tier and freeze it. Then, on their first anniversary, they thaw it out and eat some," she countered.

Funny, he didn't remember his ex-wife, Dakota, keeping any in the freezer. All he remembered was the way his bride had seemed to want to get the whole cake-cutting part over with, saying it was taking away from her mixing and mingling.

It also brought to mind how Georgina had mentioned singing and sounding like "a regular Dakota Rush" at dinner last night. Not that she could have known. He'd tried not to let the gut-punch show. In that moment, he didn't feel comfortable explaining anything. At least hearing her name again hadn't hurt as much as he thought it would. Didn't hurt at all, to be honest. What had was when Dakota changed her mind about taking his last name, at least on paper. Instead, she kept *Rush*, even though he was completely supportive of her using her stage name anyway. That didn't keep her from taking full advantage of the Legend name, and of his father, to make professional connections, however.

But that was the past, and his immediate future looked mighty sweet.

"Not that we're going need a tiebreaker, but have you seen Max this morning?" he asked.

"Becca and Cody took him to the square to see Santa. Becca didn't think Max should be part of the taste testing, if we could avoid it. Way too much sugar. But I'm going to make him a special cupcake out of the flavor we choose. And until they get back, I'm on call for any guests. Fortunately, we don't have many today. This coming weekend, however, we're pretty booked."

She selected three cupcakes from the cooling rack and placed them on a platter, then proceeded to cut them into bite-sized bits while she talked. "Okay. Try these three while I ice the others. I'm leaning toward royal icing over fondant, if that's okay with you. And I'd love to cover it with white sugar roses and greenery, like in one of those pictures. But I've also whipped up a Swiss meringue buttercream."

He wasn't sure what language she was speaking, but he was all ears as he took a bite of the first sample.

Lemony. Mouthwatering. He usually wasn't a big fan of tartness, but this was enough to make him change his mind.

She rushed over with a glass of sparkling water. "Almost forgot. A little something to cleanse your palate between samples."

The second flavor was coconut. The third, and his favorite, vanilla.

She turned around in time to catch him reaching for seconds of the latter.

"Slow down, cowboy. We have a lot more taste testing to do, including the groom's pie."

*Pie?* Now that was something he'd never seen, and he'd attended enough "mandatory" weddings for an adequate sample because, in his opinion, that was the only reason worth going.

She placed another batch of three cut-up cupcakes in front of him, except these had icing. "I'm guessing your favorite was classic vanilla, but try the others with these icings. It changes the flavors a bit."

"You mentioned something about pie. That isn't traditional, is it?" he asked, then popped one of the samples into his mouth. She was right. The tart lemon cake turned into a sweeter bite that melted in his mouth.

"Actually, they were tradition in the sixteenth and seventeenth centuries, in England, I believe. In this case, your dad expressed a preference for pies, so I thought we'd go with that. Start a new Legend family tradition. I'm guessing you had a groom's cake at your wedding?"

"I don't even remember." It was the truth. He'd lost his appetite after the disastrous reciting of the vows and how he'd disappointed his bride in more than one way that night. The thought of creating a Legend family tradition assumed he'd ever want to be a groom in a wedding again. Getting through his dad's without stutter-rendering reminders was going to be difficult enough.

And now he'd disappointed Georgina, it would seem. Her cheery demeanor cooled several degrees as she busied herself again without speaking. She was jumping through a million hoops to get everything just right.

"What other traditions are there when it comes to the wedding cake or pie?" he asked.

His interest perked her up a bit. And her enthusiasm was more powerful than a sugar rush.

"Let's see…there's the bride and groom feeding each other the first bite. Symbolizes their commitment to providing for each other."

Yet another part of tradition that was broken at his own wedding.

"Of course, some couples grind the cake into the other person's face, which can be funny. But only if the other partner is on board with the idea. I planned one wedding where the groom did that to his new bride. I thought she was going to start crying. Definitely got that marriage off to a bad start, in my opinion."

"That does sound awful."

"But then another couple had planned in advance to do it, and it was fun to watch. The guests couldn't stop laughing. And the photographs were priceless."

"Laughter is pretty important," Dylan said without even giving it much thought. Wasn't much laughter in his first marriage. Not much sweetness either.

"So, which type of feeding would you prefer?" he asked.

"Oh, I've always envisioned the romantic kind. But I don't know…might depend on the man. If we have a particularly playful relationship, the latter could be fun. Of course, he'd get cake rubbed into his face too, so he'd better put a lot of thought into it."

"I didn't get either. We cut the cake together, then she walked away. Is that any tradition you've heard of?" he asked.

As soon as he said it, he realized how bitter he sounded.

Georgina's jaw visibly dropped. She then recomposed and shook her head. "Not that I've ever heard. Maybe she just felt awkward about doing that in front of people. Some folks don't want others to watch them eat."

That definitely wasn't it. Dakota always wanted to be watched. Admired. Dylan nodded as if it were a possibility, however.

"Maybe at your next wedding," she said.

"Not so sure I'd want to take a chance on missing out on that first bite of cake again."

Georgina cast him a look he couldn't quite read. Was that sympathy etched on her face or disbelief? Whatever it was, it caught him by surprise. He didn't mean to be so negative about something that was so important to her. But he couldn't have feigned any more enthusiasm if he'd wanted to.

Once again, she straightened her shoulders and pulled herself together. She had an amazing ability to do that.

"In that case, Mr. Dylan James Legend, you should have the opportunity to experience it in a less-traditional setting." She walked around the bar and selected the largest cupcake sample that remained on the plate, then looked him right in the eye.

"How would you prefer your cake? Gentle and romantic, or playful and smashed into your face?" she asked.

"Smash me," he said, closing his eyes and bracing for it.

She didn't disappoint, although it wasn't anything like a smash. More like a loving smear across his closed mouth and chin.

He opened his eyes to find her straining to contain a laugh.

"I can't believe you actually did that," he said, licking his lips, then letting out a laugh of his own, which made her totally burst.

"You asked for it. In more ways than one," she said.

He swiped a finger across his chin just in time to catch some crumbs and icing before it dripped onto the counter or floor.

"The good news is you get to smash the cake on my face in return," she said.

He picked up a piece. She closed her eyes and pressed her lips together lightly.

Instead of smashing, he said, "Open your eyes." She did, then noticed that he was holding it up for her to eat.

"That wasn't the agreement," she said.

"I know."

Georgina took the bite and turned a pale shade of pink.

He dared to lean in just enough to see if she'd lean back the same amount. When she didn't, he leaned in farther. Then a little more.

She closed the distance between them, just enough for their lips to brush, then pulled away and looked him in the eyes.

Had she felt it too? That soft jolt suggested this was going to be more than an ordinary kiss, followed by the urgent pull to find out for sure.

This time, the distance-closing was mutual.

It was, quite literally, the sweetest kiss he'd ever experienced.

A moment later, it wasn't wedding bells he heard but rather the shuffling of feet leaving the kitchen. Their kiss was cut way too short for his taste.

"Vern?" Georgina called.

The man stopped and turned. "I didn't see anything." Vern then added a wink and a smile and shuffled right on out the door, toward the parlor.

"Oops," Dylan said.

Georgina's pale pink blush turned a deeper shade.

He couldn't deny that he'd changed his mind, just a little, about one wedding tradition in particular.

The way she'd responded to his confession about the stutter yesterday? No one had ever expressed such a sensitive interpretation. And the way she was treating him no differently now, as if it hadn't changed her impression of him? That was a first. People often acted as though he was suddenly fragile and might break if they said one wrong thing.

Not this woman, who had actually smashed cake onto his face. And these feelings weren't because she could bake like no one he'd ever met.

Dylan could look at her now while speaking, for short periods, without nervousness triggering his stutter. Yet she was wrong when she said there was no need for him to be nervous.

He was starting to get sweet on this red flag of a woman.

# CHAPTER TEN

DYLAN WOKE UP to sunlight peeking through the denim curtains and Sundance licking his face.

He'd let the pup out much earlier, before sunrise and before Georgina had even begun preparing breakfast in the kitchen. Not his lucky morning, because he'd been hoping to sneak another kiss and chase it with a cup of that delicious coffee she'd introduced him to.

Still, a day off from planning the wedding was exactly what he needed. Perfect timing. For both of them, perhaps, because he, for one, didn't expect for the cake tasting to turn out the way it had. Yet she'd managed to replace his bad memory with something playful. And romantic.

But today he didn't need any distractions. The rodeo committee had gone to great lengths to set up the promo recording in Keaton. Which also meant the takes had to be perfect. With the studio time being paid for by the half hour, he didn't want to run up the bill. Even though his nervousness had lessened in one way around Georgina, it was heightened in another.

No, this day apart was the best thing to happen.

Dylan sat up in bed, and Sundance practically crawled into his lap to lick his face some more. That was when he realized why. He'd washed the smashed wedding cake off his face after it happened, and again last night before going to bed. Yet, he had still managed to miss a spot underneath his chin both times.

"You inherited my sweet tooth, I see."

He stood, much to Sundance's chagrin, and took a shower while the pup sat patiently at the threshold. Fortunately, he'd also picked up some disposable razors in the square while he was getting gifts for Sundance, Max and Georgina. A package of inexpensive but festive red-and-green ones, in fact. Destiny Springs didn't overlook anything when it came to celebrating Christmas.

Not that he needed to shave for what he had planned this afternoon. Rather, in case something happened that he hadn't planned. After all, such a thing had happened yesterday with Georgina.

Dylan shook his head and laughed at the thought as he tapped the extra water off the blade, then returned to the task of ridding his face of all stubble.

By the time he and Sundance got downstairs to take their proper walk, the entire B and B had awakened. After taking care of his baby and getting him situated in the room once again, Dylan headed down to the barn. Although he would've liked to have taken Sundance, they'd be spending plenty of quality one-on-one time together today.

For now, he needed sustenance. A full breakfast was being served, despite the small crowd. And there was Georgina, flitting around from guest to guest, while Max filled their glasses with orange juice from an oversized glass pitcher. Cody was also helping by serving up something from one of the warming trays.

Dylan grabbed a plate and made his way down the buffet table. Georgina glanced up in time to catch him getting an extra serving of fresh strawberries with the tongs. When they locked eyes, he was pretty sure she blushed that pale shade of pink again. Or maybe that was mere projection, because his face all of a sudden felt warmer than usual.

She walked over and leaned in. He thought, for a moment, she was going to kiss him on the cheek. Instead, she whispered into his ear.

"You have to try the migas, if you haven't already."

Georgina returned to whatever she was doing over at the coffee station. He made his way to Cody, who plopped a large portion of the egg concoction onto his plate.

"How's everything working out with the wedding planning?" Cody asked, adding a sly smile. Unless Vern had told everyone that he'd witnessed their kiss, there was no way for Cody to know. Then again, this *was* Destiny Springs. He'd been warned that nothing stayed a secret for long.

"It's working," Dylan said.

Cody leaned in. "Just between you and me, Becca's a little worried about Georgina this morning. She seems distracted."

Dylan bit back the urge to smile. He was pretty sure he knew why. He felt a little distracted as well.

"Georgina seems like an expert multitasker. She just has a lot on her plate," he said. He, for one, couldn't do what she did, but he admired her for it.

"I'd ordinarily agree with you, but Georgina made a whole pot of coffee this morning, only without the coffee. That's not easy to mess up."

"Maybe she didn't get enough sleep. We both sampled cakes yesterday. Added up to a lot of sugar."

"Could be. By the way, I'm taking Becca for a checkup after I finish up here. She has a few concerns. I personally think her aches and pains are because she's about to burst. I'd rather Max not be there, in case there is some problem we have to deal with."

Dylan's lungs constricted. Felt like a bull just

plopped right down on his chest. Becca already felt like a sister, and Max was so excited about maybe having one of his own. But Dylan didn't want to show his concern, even though Cody wasn't doing the best job of hiding his.

"Sounds like a wise plan. Better safe than sorry," Dylan said.

He hadn't been around many pregnant women in his life, but he always appreciated what a delicate miracle was happening. That was another thing he worried about—having a child and him being on the road if something happened. If his bookings kept up the momentum he gained last year, he could be away more than he was home.

"Do you need me to watch Max for a while?" Dylan offered.

Sure, he really needed the morning to go over some of the promo spots and fine-tune his inflection points before his recording session. Perhaps Sundance and Max's own pup, Penny, could keep the little boy company while Dylan supervised.

Even that would be inconvenient, but nothing compared to what Cody and Becca might be dealing with.

"That's a nice offer, but Georgina's going to take Max with her to pick out some wedding decorations. Said it was a two-person job, but I suspect she was doing what she always does, which is more than a normal person can handle.

Becca isn't entirely comfortable with it. But she's uncomfortable in general, so…"

"I'm beginning to see that," Dylan said, about both Georgina and Becca. He nodded at Cody and took a seat at the far end of the community table.

Max immediately seized upon the opportunity. "Would you like some orange juice, Mr. Dylan?"

"Why, yes, I would. Thank you, Max."

The little boy somehow managed to set the pitcher down without it toppling and ran to a separate table that had the clean glasses and coffee mugs and such.

He started to run back, but Dylan called out, "Take it slow, cowboy."

Max overcompensated and walked very slowly to the table. Once there, Dylan held the glass for him while the little boy poured, filling it to the brim.

"Perfect!" he said.

"I'll be back," Max said, then wandered down the table to the other guests.

Georgina was going around the long community table and picking up the used dishes. She then tried to balance a few coffee cups on top and attempted to walk with the precarious stack. Doing exactly what Cody had mentioned: too much for one person.

Fortunately, her timing was impeccable. As she

approached, Dylan rose and swooped in as her balancing act threatened to topple. From there, he helped her carry the dishes to a portable sink.

"Thanks," she said. "I would have made it, though. I do that to amuse the guests. And if I ever drop a plate, it's on purpose."

"I have no doubts," he said, playing along.

She unsuccessfully tried to hide a smile. Another thing he noticed about her: She had trouble asking for help.

And he suspected she would need it this morning. Dylan knew from his brief time there that the square was going to be a zoo. Becca was probably correct to be uncomfortable with the idea in this case. Max could be more than a handful. Even watching him with that giant pitcher of orange juice, going around the table and filling everyone's glass to the brim whether they needed a refill or not, was making him a little dizzy.

"Cody tells me that you and Max are picking out decorations behind my back today."

Her eyes flew open. "Oh, nothing like that! I just wanted to pick up some small things, like ribbons for Rose's bouquet. And for the flower arrangements, depending on how many white roses they can find for us. Off-white ribbons, for a whisper of contrast. Perhaps in velvet, to add some warmth. I didn't think you'd mind. Plus I was going to let Max pick them out. Within reason, of course."

Dylan tried to put on his most serious expression. "I was actually looking forward to that part," he said.

Her brows furrowed as she studied his face as if trying to figure out if he was serious. All of a sudden, his throat tightened again and he couldn't speak. And just when he thought he'd had a breakthrough in talking to her.

But there was one thing he couldn't help but do: break character and laugh.

Georgina playfully slapped his arm. "You had me going there." She shook her head and turned to resume her tasks.

"Wait. How about if Sundance and I go along to help? Then y'all can come to the studio with me afterward and watch the session. Might be fun for Max."

The first part was a calculated decision; the last part he'd offered on impulse. But it might be the only option. Shopping in the square could take a while, considering the holiday crowds. And he couldn't afford to be late to the recording. The rodeo committee was already doing more than enough to accommodate him.

Plus what Cody had said stuck in his mind. About how if there were any problems with the pregnancy, they would have to deal with it.

Dylan's offer would at least solve the issue of everyone having to worry about Max's care.

*Who am I kidding?* He didn't want to go a full day without seeing her again, no matter what he tried to tell himself earlier. Nor did he want Georgina to have to juggle even more.

Sure, that could ease a potential problem for her, and even for Cody and Becca.

But in turn, he'd just created a huge one for himself.

GEORGINA RUSHED DOWN the hall to the master suite, knocked lightly on the door and opened it before Becca had a chance to answer.

There was the mother-to-be. Sitting on the edge of the bed, in tears.

Georgina rushed to her side.

"Cody said you wanted to talk to me. What's wrong?" Georgina asked. She had been in the middle of cleaning up from breakfast when Cody eased a plate and dishrag from her hand and said that Becca was having a 911 moment and requested her.

Although it was pretty obvious. The poor woman looked miserable—but glowing. Georgina reached for a tissue from the box on a side table and handed it to Becca.

"I don't have anything to wear to the doctor's office. Even my maternity clothes are too tight."

"What you have on looks beautiful. Besides, they don't care what you're wearing."

Becca sniffled and looked down at her hands as she toyed with a tissue. Meanwhile, Dylan and Max and Sundance were waiting in the parlor. Georgina really hadn't intended for Dylan to come along, much less for her and Max to go to his recording session. But it did sound exciting, in a way. And her sister Hailey offered to come over and serve afternoon coffee and sweets in the barn in case Becca and Cody weren't back in time. After all, her little sis did the same job as Georgina before starting her trail ride business.

However, Georgina wasn't going anywhere until Becca felt better.

"What about the wedding? What am I going to wear to that?" Becca asked.

Georgina had been thinking about that as well. But it was one detail lost in a haystack of a million. She got up and walked over to Becca's closet. The woman was right. She didn't have a thing to wear that would fit and be appropriate.

"I'll do some personal shopping for you tomorrow," she said. "Kavanaugh's has a pretty good selection of blouses and skirts."

The look on Becca's face was priceless. Yeah, even Georgina didn't believe what she'd just said. The place was perfect for western wear, and they'd even managed to put together a decent groom's outfit for Monty. But the women's section was much smaller. Still, not many other options nearby.

Becca's look of disbelief melted into a full-blown tear fest. Her boss was usually so together, but her world was about to change.

There was one other possibility.

Georgina pulled out her cell phone and searched for maternity stores between Destiny Springs and Keaton. Thankfully, there was one—Expecting the Best. It was about ten miles out of the way, but a quick glance at their website offered adequate assurance that the detour wouldn't be in vain.

Probably wasn't something Dylan would be interested in helping with, however. She wouldn't blame him for that. He probably couldn't even pretend to be interested, as he had with the ribbon. But perhaps he could drop her off and Max could go with him and watch his session. The little boy would like that better than shopping for maternity clothes.

Yet she didn't want to get Becca's hopes up. She retrieved a pair of tall boots from the closet and helped Becca squeeze into them with those swollen feet, then gave her a hand up and led her over to the mirror. She went back into the closet and grabbed a long, colorful scarf and draped it around Becca's neck.

"There. You look very chic. And don't you worry about a thing, because I'm going to find the perfect wedding outfit for you. Okay?"

Becca nodded but still looked like she was on the verge of tears again. Hopefully happy ones this time.

"I just want Mom's day to be super special. I don't want to ruin it by looking like I'm about to go to a yoga class. And I know it sounds funny, but I want to look good for Monty's former band-mates if y'all decide to invite them and they can come. Not many people get to hang out with platinum-selling artists. I mean, Monty already feels like a dad. But getting the Proud River guys together again reminds me that he really *is* a legend."

*Wait...* "What?" Georgina asked.

"Dylan didn't mention it?"

"No. I'm pretty sure I'd remember something like that."

Very sure, in fact. Monty had mentioned a re-union tour when they were at the diner, but that was where the discussion ended. It hadn't even occurred to her to include them for the wedding. Georgina felt a mix of excitement and frustra-tion. True, she and Dylan hadn't really talked about the guest list any further. Under the influ-ence of the kiss, she'd probably agreed to less than she was ultimately willing to settle for in that area. But her knees had gone weak, along with her resolve.

"Well, it was a busy morning, picking out Mom's wedding dress. In fact, I was going to ask Jess to make an outfit for me, but Mom wanted a version of the jumpsuit as well, for her and Monty's dinner with the bandmates."

"Do they live nearby?"

"They're spread out. But they'll all be in Jackson Hole over Christmas and into the new year to start planning their reunion tour. That's what sparked the idea of inviting them to the wedding in the first place. Rose was thinking the surprise would be a nice gift for Monty, so don't mention anything to him. We really didn't decide on anything, so please don't be mad at Dylan."

"Of course I'm not," she said.

Georgina stood up straighter now. Dylan might very well regret asking to tag along today. He'd be a captive audience, and this subject *would* come up.

Then again, Becca could be right that perhaps the whole conversation didn't register with Dylan, or he was still mulling over the concept. Or perhaps their kiss had clouded his thinking as much as it had clouded hers.

She gave Becca a hug, and they proceeded downstairs together, with Georgina taking the lead. Not that she could necessarily break Becca's fall, but...*precious cargo.*

Cody rushed to the bottom of the stairs to assist his wife with the last few steps.

"Would it be selfish of me to ask you to stay pregnant another month? Because you're absolutely beautiful this way," he said, giving Becca a tender but extended kiss.

"Yes, it would be. Don't even *think* about asking the doctor if it can be done. Now, let's get this visit over with," Becca said.

"Everything is going to be fine," Georgina assured her.

Cody escorted his wife out the door and across the threshold, where they disappeared into a fog that had set in at some point.

Dylan and Max were watching and waiting, holding hands, just inside the parlor. Sundance was by the little boy's side and was being unusually obedient. They looked like a picture-perfect family.

Georgina couldn't help but be envious of her boss's too-pregnant-to-fit-into-anything predicament because in less than a month, she'd be welcoming a new member to her family. It got Georgina thinking about a certain lifestyle that she wanted someday but otherwise hadn't felt any urgency or longing about.

Until now.

# CHAPTER ELEVEN

*BABY ONESIE.*

Dylan blinked and reread the garment tag. He'd seen such outfits before on babies, but he never realized they had a name. Or that they even came in such a small size. And in such soft material.

Were all newborns that tiny? If so, he'd be afraid to hold one. Even imagining it made him nervous. A tidal wave of protectiveness washed over him at the thought of it. Over a silly onesie that no baby was even wearing.

That was the last feeling he needed to sort through. He was dealing with enough just trying to figure out this thing with Georgina. She had been awfully quiet on the ride over to Keaton. He'd already figured out that she was only quiet when she had something she really wanted to say. And it usually wasn't something good.

At least Sundance was behaving beautifully on leash. Dylan didn't want to leave his best friend in the cold truck, unattended, and could've stayed outside with the pup and cranked up the heater if needed, but the store owner was nice enough to allow them inside since there was no one else in the store.

If he'd known they were going to come here instead of the square, he would've left his own little baby at the B and B. Yet he really needed support today, perhaps more than ever. His anxiety was inching up at the fact that he wasn't the least bit prepared for the promos.

Max, by contrast, was having all sorts of fun picking up baby toys and blankets, then setting them down in odd places. Dylan took inventory of his every move and went in behind him occasionally to return the items to their proper place. That way, the saleswoman who was currently assisting Georgina with finding an outfit for Becca wouldn't have a huge mess to clean up in their wake.

"Mr. Dylan. Are you gonna buy that for Sundance, 'cause I think you need a bigger one 'cause he's big." Max pointed to the onesie that Dylan was still holding.

How had Max snuck up on him so easily? Which led to another thought about how parents must keep track of their child at every point of the day. Not to mention if they had more than one.

"Actually, I was thinking of buying it for you. Do you like it?" He held it up to Max's chest as if pretending to see how it might look on.

The little boy jerked and giggled. "I'm not a *baby*, and it's too small, and it's pink, so it's for a girl."

"I'll see if they have one in purple, in your size," Dylan said, struggling to keep a straight face.

"Nooo!" Max giggled even harder and shook his head, then ran back over to Georgina's side as if seeking protection from this hopeless teaser.

Fortunately, she seemed to be wrapping up her shopping and was purchasing a couple of items. Just in time. They needed to head over to the studio soon.

He walked to the register with the onesie still in hand. It was like he couldn't let go of it. Hopefully, Becca and Cody would like it.

"What a cute little boy y'all have," the saleswoman said as he approached.

The assumption caught him off guard in a surprisingly good way. Georgina had a deer-in-the-headlights look but otherwise didn't correct the woman.

"Thank you. I'll take this one." He set the onesie on the counter and pulled out his wallet.

"Oh, a preemie! How adorable!" The woman practically cooed as she took the little garment off the hanger.

Georgina leaned in and whispered, "Is there something you're not telling me, sweetheart? You have been looking quite radiant lately. But if that's for Becca and not you, I'd suggest a regular size."

"Can you help me out here?" he whispered in return.

"Before you ring that up, we're going to need a regular size. Definitely not a preemie. And maybe in yellow or purple or green instead of pink?"

Again, all this sounded like a foreign language to him, but he was glad he was navigating this unfamiliar landscape with someone who was fluent. At the same time, he felt rather silly. Especially after Georgina and the saleswoman shared a knowing look.

The woman took the preemie onesie and returned with a larger size in yellow, then rang him up.

"We have complimentary giftwrapping, if you have a few minutes," she said before placing it in a bag.

"That would be great. Thank you, ma'am," Dylan said.

After the saleswomen stepped to the back to wrap the gift, the atmosphere turned serious again. Just like on the ride over.

"So, I hear Proud River is having a reunion. And that the band members are all going to be in Jackson Hole through the new year," Georgina said, looking him straight in the eye.

He wasn't sure how to comment. Not something he could deny.

It wasn't that he was keeping it from her. Well, maybe a little, until he could figure out what to do. The buzz surrounding the reunion would draw too much attention, including the wrong kind for him. The reunion had yet to be announced to the public, but it was already gaining momentum. Obviously, Becca or her mom had not kept it to themselves.

"And I hear there was some discussion about inviting them to the wedding while y'all were at the fitting," she continued.

Now inviting them to the wedding was on the menu. As if the guest list issue wasn't already becoming a big enough sticking point. Adding the bandmates to the list promised to set it in super glue.

Maybe nondisclosures weren't such a bad idea after all.

Even though she folded her arms, her tone wasn't necessarily accusatory, as he would have expected. And deserved. He should've mentioned it at Ribeye Roy's, and he knew it. But their co-planner date had felt so much like a real one and he hadn't wanted to mess it up.

"I should have t-t-t…" he said.

Georgina waited a few beats, then unfolded her arms.

"Told you," he said, finishing the thought.

"You're right. You should have," she said.

He'd been doing so well, but this whole discussion was beginning to make him nervous. And the setting didn't help. It was bad enough that they'd grown so much closer. That their relationship had evolved from professional to personal. But shopping for maternity wear and baby clothes?

Before he could even attempt to explain it in a way that didn't sound as though he'd considered withholding that piece of information, she pushed her shoulders back.

"It's no big deal," she said, adding a soft smile that wasn't the least bit convincing. "But that doesn't mean I'm letting you off the hook."

He wasn't sure whether she was showing sympathy, which he didn't want, or letting him know who was ultimately in control of the outcome. Either way, he was reluctantly in awe of her composure. He was starting to feel like a total mess.

They stood in relative silence for the next few minutes until the saleswoman returned with his wrapped package. The drive to the studio promised to be awkward. Even worse, his head and heart were no longer in the game as far as recording.

Fortunately, Max spared them the need for discussion. He was chatting up a storm in the back cab with Sundance, whom Dylan could tell was under the little boy's spell. What creature wouldn't be?

Dylan was under someone's spell too, even though it didn't make complete sense. He didn't know her well, but he recognized a perfectionist when he saw one. He also recognized that he was destined to ultimately fall short, should they take this relationship any further.

Georgina looked out the window for the next few miles, then finally spoke. "Sorry to drag you shopping. Becca was panicked before we left. I had to help her."

"I'm glad we made the stop. And you didn't drag me anywhere. I did feel out of my element, though."

"Does the thought of babies make you nervous?"

It was a fair question. "Maybe a little. Haven't been around very many of 'em."

"Me neither, to be honest. But if fatherhood ever happens to you, there's nothing to be too nervous about, because they stay babies for only a few minutes. The next thing you know, they're in school, then graduating, then starting careers and families of their own."

He wasn't so sure that was helping, even though he knew she meant well.

"You're a natural with Max," she added. "I'd never know you were a newbie."

"He makes it easy. Does most of the talkin'. Takes the pressure off me."

That made her laugh, which broke through some of the tension. Hopefully, what he needed to say wouldn't ratchet it back up.

"I wanted a family when I first got married. Or make that I was always told I should want one, and I believed it," he said. "Turns out it was a good thing we didn't have a child. She wouldn't have been home enough to help raise him or her. And once my career got off the ground a little, I was home even less."

"Hmmm. It's important that both parents be present, if possible. Then there's the timing. I wouldn't want a child to have to share a birthday with Christmas or any other holiday. And I'd want either one or two. No middle child."

"You're a planner. No doubt about it."

Georgina shook her head and laughed. "When you're a woman with a biological clock, you're smart to give it at least a little thought without taking the romance completely out of it. How about you? What's your plan?"

Dylan exhaled. "To learn from my first mistake. Don't rush into marriage. I was too young and was pressured into it. Takes time to know whether you're compatible and want the same things in the long haul."

Not to mention the importance of honesty. The

only thing Dakota Rush had loved about him was the professional doors his last name and his father could open for her. But no use saying that. At least with Georgina, she'd been up front about wanting to benefit professionally from the wedding. Part of him even admired her ambition. He just had to be sure he wasn't used as a stepping stone again.

Dylan pulled into the drive of the recording studio, and not a moment too soon. The conversation was getting way too serious for his comfort.

"I hope y'all won't be too bored. Take the keys in case you want to drive around or get a bite to eat."

"No way I'm going to miss this. I can't wait to hear you," she said.

He gulped back the realization that no one had ever said such a thing. Not even his mom or dad, because they were afraid to watch. Afraid that he'd choke up in the middle of an event and everyone in the rodeo world would be watching and listening. Afraid that he'd be crushed if it didn't work out. Or, according to their fears, *when* it didn't work out.

Except his career was working out more beautifully than he could've imagined, if not as fast as it could have, had he'd taken advantage of his dad's offer to "make a few calls" when it was clear their son wasn't going to give up.

If only it could work just as beautifully with Georgina.

GEORGINA WAS BEGINNING to see things more clearly now. How she and Dylan were getting closer, yet there was something separating them.

Physically, it was a thick panel of glass. Dylan was in the soundproof booth with Sundance. The glass and insulation between them further added to the disconnect she'd felt with him in the car.

It was the emotional part that wasn't so easy to define. Was he putting up a wall when it came to family and children? She hoped she'd sounded casual enough about it, because she wasn't talking about the two of them. Just talking in general.

But even that seemed to make him nervous.

The control room of the recording studio felt like the cockpit of a plane. Max was sitting quietly with a thick coffee-table book in the corner. Not that he could read many of the words yet, but it was mostly pictures of rodeos gone by. That would hold his interest for a while.

Two men fiddled with some knobs and ran some sound checks while Dylan's words spilled into the small space.

"Whoa! Now *that's* a voice," one of the men said.

"I'll say," the other one added.

Her thoughts exactly. It not only filled her ears, it filled her heart, adding even more confusion to the issue.

"Hey, Max," she whispered as the two men

seemed to be finalizing whatever they needed to in order to get the recording started.

The little boy looked up.

"Have you come across any pictures of rodeo announcers in that book?"

"I don't think so. I'll look for one."

"Awesome," she said, just as she heard one of the men in the control room announce, "Okay, Dylan. Whenever you're ready."

Dylan gave them the thumbs-up and cleared his throat. One of the technicians pressed a computer key and leaned back.

"Where the West begins is also where the new year begins for rodeo-lovin' cowboys and cowgirls of all ages.

From mutton bustin' to bustin' broncs, there's something for the whole family to enjoy watching. Can you think of a better way to kick off the new year?

I didn't think so. Neither can I, which is why I'll be there for every event.

The Fort Worth Charity New Year's Rodeo, benefitting ovarian cancer research, is doing its part to help with new beginnings...*and* happy endings.

Make a resolution today to attend, and you can help make that happen too.

And tell 'em Dylan James sent ya."

"Sounds good, Mr. James. Let's do a few more takes."

"I'll vary the speed and add longer pauses," Dylan answered.

One of the men let out a hearty laugh. "The editors will appreciate it."

Not only did Dylan give them several options, he captured her interest in the whole process. Who knew so much went into such a short promotion?

Max seemed equally impressed. He'd been turning pages of that big rodeo book, searching for photos of announcers, but it was as though he'd completely lost interest in looking, and only wanted to listen to Dylan.

If she didn't know about Dylan's stutter, she would've never guessed in a million years that he had one.

"That's a wrap," one of the men said after five more reads. "And look at the time."

"My thoughts exactly. I wasn't sure what to expect, but this guy's a pro," the other one said.

Georgina felt herself beaming with pride, even though the compliment wasn't directed at her in any way. It was kind of like she was a fly on the wall. One they'd all but forgotten was there.

"Yeah, I was worried for nothing. Glenn Guillory doesn't like to be kept waiting."

"*The* Glenn Guillory?" Georgina piped in.

She couldn't help herself. The actor had just gotten engaged to his longtime girlfriend, and they'd yet to set a date. Talk about a dream opportunity for a wedding planner...

"One and the same. Maybe you and Dylan and Max could hang around town for a while. We're taking Glen out to dinner at Fancy's down the street."

"I'm not sure we're dressed for it," she said.

The man laughed. "You're probably overdressed. It's good old-fashion home cookin' that's anything but fancy."

Her heart was now beating through her chest as possibilities raced through her head. What could she possibly say to Mr. Guillory that didn't make her sound like a fangirl? Her immediate thought was that they shared the same initials: GG.

*Ugh. How corny.*

Best to let the conversation develop naturally. Talk about how she and Dylan met, and how they were thrust into the task of planning a wedding together because she was a professional wedding planner, and he was the son of the groom, Montgomery Legend.

Or not. She had to keep reminding herself that

he didn't want his real name out there or for people to make the connection. Yet it already was out there in many ways, wasn't it? And the world hadn't ended.

"Is this an announcer?" Max turned the book around and pointed to a figure at the top of the stands. A little blurry, but he appeared to be in a booth, above the crowds.

"I believe it is. Good work!"

One of the men swiveled, rolled over a few steps in his chair and took a closer look.

"Yep. That's Bob Tallman. Talk about a legend. Doesn't get better than that. Although your friend here might be a contender."

The guy then rolled back to his spot and resumed his task.

Georgina looked at the picture again and imagined how it might feel for Dylan. And how far he might be able to go. The gentlemen here knew a good voice when they heard it—that was for sure.

Once the professionals confirmed that they had enough to work with, Dylan removed his headphones and emerged from the booth. One of the men opened the door and exited into the common area, where they shook hands with Dylan. They'd finished early. No sign of Glenn Guillory.

"Can I make a recording?" Max said.

"Absolutely, young man. We have a few minutes." The man led Max to the booth and helped him with the headphones, while the other returned to the control room, leaving her and Dylan alone yet completely in view.

"How did I do?" he asked. "Could you tell I stumbled in one of the takes?"

"I thought the pause was intentional. You sounded amazing." And she meant it. She didn't know much of anything about what he did or the importance of it. Now that she'd gotten a sample, she was more impressed than ever.

Dylan nodded toward a hallway and started walking. She followed to where they were no longer in anyone's line of vision. In the background, Max could be heard reciting the story he always told when he helped out with Hailey's trail rides at Sunset Stables.

Then there was the man standing in front of her. Looking into her eyes. Looking as though there was something important he wanted to say but couldn't get the words to flow.

Georgina understood why he might have felt too nervous to speak when they first met. She was feeling the same way at the moment, because every brain cell was trying to warn her that whatever *this* was could never work. But every other fiber of her argued that maybe it could, with a little extra time and patience.

Unfortunately, having patience wasn't a strength of hers. But perhaps there was a compromise somewhere in there, because it felt as though there was still a thick glass wall between them.

Instead of speaking, he leaned in and kissed her without hesitation. So different from the first time, which was playful and light. This felt deeply serious for some reason. And seriously right.

"Sorry. I couldn't wait any longer," he said as he pulled away, even though she could have kissed him until Max stopped talking and the coast was no longer clear.

"Lucky me," she said.

Their gazes locked, and she was about to initiate another kiss when one of the men called out, "It's a take!" Followed by the scrambling of Max out of the booth.

They emerged from the hallway. Georgina hoped her face didn't look as pink as it felt. Being the only blond, super-fair-skinned sister in her family, the blushing gave her away every time.

Max ran over and practically screamed, "I made a recording like you, Mr. Dylan!"

"I heard! You sounded terrific. I'm very proud of you, cowboy," Dylan said.

"I'll send you away with some zip drives. Mr. Legend, we've already sent digital copies to Fort Worth. I don't expect they'll want any retakes."

"Th-thank you." Dylan then turned to her, but his eyes had turned…darker. "I guess we're done here. Y'all about ready to head back?"

It took her a moment to realize they addressed him by his real last name. They'd called him Mr. James earlier.

"Actually, we were telling Georgina that y'all are welcome to join us for a bite to eat after our next client is done. He came all the way from California to do some voiceover work for a documentary we're helping produce on the state of Wyoming. Least we can do is feed him."

"Glenn Guillory," she added. "How fun would that be?"

Dylan looked down at his boots and tapped at the tile below, although there was nothing there. "Th-that's a kind offer, and very impressive, but I have to get up early to help Nash with the ranch rodeo tomorrow. I need to learn the lineup in advance as well. But if you want to stay, Georgina, I could take Max home and either Cody or I could drive back and pick you up afterward."

Not the response she'd hoped for. Georgina struggled with the logic. His offer to come back for her was a nice one, though. But that would mean he'd spend nearly six more hours on the road today, with Keaton being nearly two hours from Destiny Springs. Considering Becca's emotional state—and depending on what she found out from the doctor—Georgina couldn't ask Cody to make the trip. Not to mention, it would make more sense for Dylan to just go to the restaurant and save an extra round trip. He *had* to have known that. This was about something else.

"Actually, I have to do some preparing for tomorrow as well, but for a vow-renewal ceremony. And I'm behind in my duties at the B and B. But thanks for the invitation."

She hoped the disappointment didn't come through in her voice. Not only because she'd be missing out on an incredible networking opportunity, but because she knew this went a lot deeper for Dylan than merely having to get up early the next morning.

If nothing else, it did give her a glimpse into what a future for them, as a couple, might look like: Specifically, her doing social things alone and always being asked why her partner wasn't by her side. Even the thought of it made her sad. Her hopes that whatever they had going could turn into something serious and possibly permanent threatened to sink as surely as the *Titanic*.

Fortunately, she was good at treading water. For a while.

# CHAPTER TWELVE

ORDINARILY, GEORGINA LOVED baby goats.

Not so much at the moment.

She also loved her baby sister. Hailey was letting Georgina hold the vow-renewal ceremony in her barn at Sunrise Stables. Except the goats kept *baaa*-ing at her, making it difficult to focus.

"*Bahhhhh* humbug," she called back.

She didn't actually blame them for her mood. Rather, she blamed the whole incident yesterday at the studio. She kept replaying the missed opportunity to meet a celebrity who might very well have been in need of a wedding planner. In retrospect, even if it had been a much shorter round-trip drive for Dylan or even Cody, the dinner wouldn't have been the same without him there to enjoy it with. Not after that amazing kiss in the hallway.

But all was not lost. The couple today were friends with Monty, so no telling what other celebrities they might lead her to. *If* she did a good job for them, that was. Although her heart and head weren't in sync this morning, she intended to make her first vow-renewal ceremony the best ever.

Fortunately, the meeting with the couple today was for planning purposes only. Georgina had secured an officiant. She also made sure the local florist had enough roses and calla lilies and white anemones available for a proper bouquet, unless the woman had something specific in mind. At which time, she could offer her expertise in elevating the idea to something extraordinary. Aside from that, they might just have to take whatever they could get for any additional arrangements or embellishments. Hailey offered an old turntable and some albums, which could be used in place of an organist or soloist.

The inside of the barn itself had been recently renovated. It even had an antique chandelier hanging from the rafters. Hailey kept it super tidy ever since she'd started her goat yoga classes, petting zoo and pony rides for the folks of Destiny Springs, so there would be little to no cleanup required.

The yoga equipment was tucked away in shelves against the wall, so that was fine to leave as is. They would have to work around the carousel in the middle, however. There wasn't time to deconstruct the thing, never mind the effort it would take to reconstruct it afterward. The ponies could probably remain in their stalls, if it was okay with the couple, unless they wanted the reception to be in the barn as well. The ponies added a certain charm and authenticity to the whole setting.

The goats, however, would have to be temporarily relocated before the ceremony, even if she had to move them herself. They had to make room for chairs for the guests and a pathway for the bride to make her walk from the house, where she could get dressed, to the barn.

Visualizing the possibilities within the actual space was breathing life back into Georgina. Unfortunately, her imagination was bigger than the barn.

"There you are!" someone called out.

Georgina whipped around to find Hailey walking through the open barn door, with an older couple trailing closely behind her.

"Oh! I didn't hear you drive up," Georgina said as she closed the space between them and extended her hand to each. "You must be Frank and Helen. So nice to meet you."

"Likewise," Frank said.

"I'll leave y'all alone to talk business. Come on inside when you're done here, if you'd like. I'll put on a pot of coffee." Hailey turned on her heels and walked away.

Helen walked deeper into the barn. "This is perfect. What do you think, Frank?"

He followed suit, looking up at the rafters. "I agree. Good job, Ms. Goodwin."

Meanwhile, the *baaa*-ing resumed as if concurring with his statement.

"I'm so glad! The goats, of course, will be relocated," she said.

Helen walked over to the pen, which made the goats *baaa* even louder. "You don't need to go to all that trouble. Their talking doesn't bother me."

"It wouldn't be any trouble," Georgina insisted. "This is a very special day. The focus should be on you and Frank. Plus the guests might not be able to hear you renew your vows over the noise."

A pretty good argument, if she did say so herself.

"It's just going to be the two of us and another couple as witnesses. And the officiant, of course. And you're certainly invited," Frank said. "After all, you're doing all this for us at the last minute."

She was about to say she hadn't done a thing. But she quickly picked up on the fact that this nice couple didn't want to be of any bother. Except planning a wedding was never a bother. It was a joy. In fact, more ideas of how to make it extra special came flooding in.

"I'm not trying to change your mind, if that's what you really want. But believe me, people adore weddings, and most really don't mind last-minute invitations. Even if they can't come, you're proudly announcing your love for, and rededication to, each other. And this world needs much more of that."

Another reasonable argument, although one she wasn't used to making. She often had to work hard to reel the bride and groom in on the guest list because of venue or budget limitations.

Again, they looked at each other and smiled, with Frank pulling her even closer.

"We don't have all that many friends or relatives. We're just not that social. Maybe we enjoy each other's exclusive company a little *too* much," he said.

Okay. His argument was better. But she was curious about one thing.

"So, how do y'all know Monty?"

"He played at our daughter's wedding. She's been in a wheelchair most of her life, and it was her dream. She contacted him, and he actually responded, if you can believe it. A huge celebrity like him," Frank said.

"Sounds like something he would do," Georgina offered.

"I followed up to thank him and explain that we might not have the budget but we'd be glad to pay him to FaceTime her and send his best wishes. He offered to drive in and perform at the reception instead, for free. He's stayed in touch with all of us ever since." Helen's eyes suddenly filled with tears.

"That is a beautiful story," Georgina said as she battled to hold in a few tears of her own.

Monty was a sweetheart. Hadn't taken long to figure that out. She simply hadn't realized how much. Now she really wanted to make his and Rose's wedding special.

Georgina straightened her shoulders, opened her notepad to a clean page and jotted down their comments, even though there was no way she'd forget them. It never paid to get too emotionally attached to her clients, but these folks were making it nearly impossible.

"I'll make sure there are some folding chairs on hand in case you change your mind and want to invite others at the last minute," she offered. "I want to make this as stress free as possible for you."

As the wedding planner, it was her job to absorb all of it.

They put their arms around each other's waists and smiled. "We want it to be stress free for you too."

The sentiment caught her off guard. No one had ever indicated that her feelings mattered. She was used to bridezillas, in fact, but she still took great pride and joy in pleasing them.

"Seriously, doing this is more fun than stress for me. Especially since you love the barn and you've set the date. So, let's talk about flowers.

I checked with the local florist and have a few ideas based on their inventory."

Monty was insisting on picking up the tab. Not that they were aware of that fact, but she didn't want to take advantage of his generosity by suggesting something too extravagant.

"Oh, you didn't have to go to all that trouble," Helen said.

Who were these people? Of course she did!

"Believe me, it's no trouble. And I can already tell you deserve a beautiful, lush bouquet." *Even if no one will be there to see it.*

Frank smiled as his wife. "She sure does."

*Yes!* A possible ally.

"We talked about this, sweetheart," Helen said to him, then looked at Georgina. "Just a single rose."

Georgina practically felt her hope and enthusiasm deflate right in front of them. She wasn't about to give up, but there were a few other things they needed to discuss.

"Music. My sister has a turntable and a collection of records," she said. That was when she realized her planning skills were slipping. She hadn't even seen what Hailey could offer, much less narrowed it down to a particular song or two. Thankfully, Vern had an extensive collection to choose from as well. No doubt he'd insist on letting her borrow an album for a day.

"Or I can hire a quartet. Maybe a harpist," Georgina continued. Not that she'd checked on those possibilities either, so she probably shouldn't have mentioned it. They were in Destiny Springs, after all. Not some cultural metropolis.

"I like the idea of the turntable. We have an album that has the song we used in our wedding. If that's okay, we can bring that," Helen said.

Frank nodded in agreement. Something told Georgina that his wife could've requested nails on a blackboard and he would have wanted it for her. Grooms usually left such details up to the bride, in her experience, but this man seemed fully engaged. And enthusiastically agreeable.

Not only did that make Helen happy, Georgina felt suddenly relaxed and even happy about it herself. Was there anything they needed for her to help with?

"Of course that's okay! It's your special day. Now, about the flowers…" Georgina said.

"Whatever Helen wants," Frank said, all but sealing the deal.

"I want what you brought to me when you first proposed," Helen answered.

He shook his head. "Those were the lean days. We can do better than that."

"No, we can't. It was perfect." She gave him a solid kiss on the cheek, which made the man blush. Georgina could almost envision him laboring over which flower to bring her to get her to say yes to his proposal. As if the woman would've said anything else.

"I could have the florist add some pine or sage along with some twine or a ribbon to tie it all together," Georgina said. There wasn't much left in her bag of tricks.

"Just the rose. A light pink one," Helen said.

Georgina's breath caught in her throat. She still had the single pale pink rose on her bedside table. The rose that Dylan had given her. It was already wilting—having been damaged and older in the first place—but she couldn't bring herself to throw it out like she'd had to do with the arrangement in the foyer. A poinsettia now sat proudly in its place, much to her chagrin.

Her original argument about the bouquet would've been to suggest at least a dozen pale pink roses in a spiral design and with twine to bind them together to give it a chic but rustic look. Much more appropriate than traditional ribbon for a barn wedding, now that she thought about it. It was all in the details, which had always been Georgina's favorite part.

Yet ultimately, she had no further argument, because she *got* it. Got why Helen would want something so simple and meaningful. At the same time, she appreciated the challenge, because the perfect single pale pink rose wasn't so easy to find in a pinch. Not during Christmas. If anyone could locate one, however, it was her.

Helen's husband got it right, and not only the first time around. A man that thoughtful was equally rare to find.

But maybe—just maybe—she'd found one of those too.

"HERE GOES NOTHING."

Dylan climbed out of his truck first, then opened the back door of the extended cab and unleashed the beast. Sundance always seemed to know when they were going to work a rodeo and would barely sit still the entire ride. Today was no exception. Once that door opened, the pup was like a bull leaving the chute.

While Sundance was taking care of his own business, Dylan retrieved his laptop, tucked it securely beneath his arm and took the deepest breath possible. The cold, crisp morning air filled his lungs and calmed his nerves.

The closed arena up ahead was an impressive structure for a county fairground. Small enough to get in and out quickly, but large enough for him to remain somewhat anonymous.

Even though he hadn't pulled an all-nighter in a long time, he'd come close last night. Had plenty of homework to do since the contestants were area ranch hands rather than rodeo names.

Thankfully, there were only three events scheduled, because he'd never announced stray gathering, goat roping and trailer loading before. Not that he wasn't familiar with those ranch tasks. And it certainly wasn't his first rodeo. It was simply his first *ranch* rodeo.

Still, this was for a good cause. The adrenaline it was giving him felt better than a solid night's sleep or two cups of Georgina's morning coffee.

Sundance dutifully returned to Dylan's side and was calm and focused, as the pup knew he needed to be.

"Let's go have some fun," he said, taking hold of the leash but letting Sundance lead the way.

The grounds were bustling. Dylan smiled and nodded at the cowboys and cowgirls, wondering if some were the competitors he'd be talking about as if he'd known them personally and for a very long time. He wasn't able to find photos or social media on a lot of them.

If he had time to spare after he got set up in the booth or box and tested their sound system, he'd pitch in where he could. Not that he'd need to. This event seemed to be running like a well-oiled machine.

Just inside the door sat two large metal cages that were already starting to fill with unwrapped toys—the price of admission for attendees. All the entry fees were going to Toys for Little Wranglers, and he was gladly donating his time and expertise.

Sundance stopped and sniffed with great interest.

"Sorry, but those aren't for you." If Dylan had planned a little better, he would've brought one to contribute, along with a special treat for his copilot.

Seeing all those toys lassoed his thoughts and yanked him back to the maternity shop yesterday, to the good thoughts first. He hadn't spent a lot of time with children in his life, but being around Max made him wish he could.

Then to the bad thoughts. Georgina didn't say a word on the ride home, and he suspected it had nothing to do with the fact that Max and Sundance were sound asleep in the back-seat cab—and that neither he nor she would have wanted to wake up the "children." Rather, it likely had everything to do with the opportunity he'd spoiled for her.

Glenn Guillory was a big deal, but between the possibility of being outed even further and the likely anxiety-induced stuttering, Dylan knew he couldn't have gotten through that dinner. He just couldn't. His offer to make another round trip back to Keaton was one he wished she'd taken. It would have greatly cut into his preparation time, but knowing how happy it would have made her would have been worth it.

He shook his head to dislodge the memory. What was done was done, and he needed to focus. The competitors and audience deserved his best performance. Not that it was work for him.

He grabbed a program flyer from a stack sitting at the entrance. It took only a cursory glance to stop him in his tracks. In big, bold letters, it read:

Ranch Rodeo Cowboy Christmas Challenge
Benefitting Toys for Little Wranglers
Special guest announcer: Dylan Legend

"Oh, no." Dylan closed his eyes and reopened them, hoping they were playing tricks on him. The long, sleepless night of research and preparation exited his brain in that second, and he felt a familiar lump in his throat. One that the words may have trouble getting around.

Even though it still happened outside of his professional commitments, it had never once happened while calling a rodeo. Largely because he was *Dylan James* during those hours.

There was nothing he could do about it now, and he couldn't blame the well-meaning volunteer who designed and produced the flyer. Even though he usually enjoyed talking rodeo with the workers and guests, that couldn't be the case today. He'd entertain and inform, then head back to the B and B and hope folks wouldn't think twice about it.

Even though he was tempted to wad up the flyer and throw it in the trash, he held on to it to compare the lineup in case there were any inconsistencies with the schedule that Nash had emailed him yesterday, which Dylan had practically memorized overnight.

He passed a few more cowboys and cowgirls and could pretty much pick out the flag man and pickup man. Dylan recognized the chute boss from Nash's description.

"Benny McDonald, right?" he said as he approached and extended his hand.

"In the flesh. And you're, let me guess… Dylan Legend. Our announcer."

"Th-th…"

*It's happening.*

Dylan took a deep breath and looked down at Sundance, who was staring back with those warm brown eyes. The pup always seemed to sense what was happening and offered a look that made Dylan not feel like a little boy struggling for words on the school playground in those moments.

Benny had to have noticed, but his expression didn't register any discomfort. Dylan had gotten good at detecting such subtleties from people who either weren't quite sure what was going on or knew exactly what was happening with the stutter.

But once again, shifting his attention to his best furry friend and biggest supporter always saved him.

"The one and only," Dylan said, this time without a hitch, as he gave his lifesaver's neck some serious scratching. "And this is my partner, Sundance."

Benny reached down and gave the pup an equally brisk petting. "I know you, but you don't know me. Nice to officially meet you." He turned his attention back to Dylan. "We're so glad you're here. Both of you. It's not a rodeo without you callers. I heard you announce somewhere in Colorado last year, and your voice blew me away. And dude, you were funny! You were the star of the day, but don't tell the others I said that."

"Riverstone Roundup." Hard to forget. It was quite a feather in his cap to be able to fill in at the eleventh hour.

"That's the one. Say, do you mind giving me a hand with this gate? It's a little sticky, and I can't figure out why," Benny said. "Just need you to open and close it a few times so I can get a close-up of the hinges."

"Of course." Dylan set down his laptop.

Benny pinpointed the culprit, then sprayed something on it and instructed Dylan to open and close it a few more times.

"Thank you. Appreciate it," he said.

Dylan wanted to say that he appreciated being treated like a normal person—one without a stutter and a famous father. One who could be looked to for help fixing a gate rather than receiving the white-glove treatment.

"Hey, Beau! Dylan and Sundance are here. Want to show them to the booth and let 'em get situated?"

A young man ran over. "Sure thing. I'm Beau, but I guess Benny just said that. Follow me. How many events do you do a year?"

"Last year, sixty-two performances. Fifteen venues," Dylan said as they walked.

"Any in Fort Worth, by chance? That's where I grew up. Lots of family still there."

"A couple. I'm doing one on New Year's Day, in fact. If you don't have any plans, I recommend the event. Benefits ovarian cancer research."

"Talk about a small world. I already bought a ticket for me and my girlfriend, but I didn't realize you were announcing. That's the icing on the cake, now that I've had a chance to meet the legendary Dylan James. If I had a voice like yours, I'd give rodeo announcing a try."

*James.* Not Legend. He felt his heart practically swell in his chest.

Dylan almost said he wasn't exactly a legend. Not even close, really. But why draw attention to it? If the guy had made the connection, it seemed to be no big deal. Yet another reaction he wasn't used to.

But Beau's words did trigger a fond memory about...*icing.*

Specifically, the icing on the wedding cake samples and the kiss with Georgina that followed. The longer kiss in the hallway yesterday. He didn't get a kiss good-night last night, but he wasn't giving up on the possibility of another.

Talk about something that could totally wreck his focus today.

They made their way up the steps of the bleachers. The booth was small but mercifully at the top. Always a good thing. He was forced to announce on the ground once, with a wireless mic and a spotlight bearing down on him. With Sundance at his side, he made it through. Otherwise he could barely stand to imagine how brutal his stutter could have been.

"So, what do you think?" Beau asked.

"I'm impressed."

"After you get set up, head on over to that room behind the bleachers and grab yourself something to eat. And if there's anything in there that Sundance can safely eat, he's welcome to it too." Beau pointed to the far corner.

"We just might take you up on that offer."

This time, however, Dylan was lying. The fact that he'd been outed in print raised his anxiety level, even though the two folks he'd talked with so far had seemed unimpressed by it.

"Hope so. I'd love to hear about your journey into announcing."

Dylan fully intended to tell the world about his journey. Someday. After he was fully established. How he still dealt with an occasional stutter but had learned how to conquer it at its worst. It would do kids who dealt with the same disability a world of good.

But the timing would have to be right, and it was much too soon.

"You have a great voice. Maybe you should give it a try," he said.

Beau seemed to light up. "You think so?"

"I do. And I'll help however I can," Dylan said.

"Wow, that's too kind," Beau said. As he walked away, he kept saying "Wow" and shaking his head.

The young man's reaction seemed a little over the top. *Too kind.* It wasn't like he was world famous or anything. But he'd take it. It felt good to be in a position to help someone else.

That was when Dylan realized what he'd done: offered to help someone get a foot up in a career that wasn't easy to break into. And how he'd done the exact opposite by refusing his father's help. Had he denied his father that same feeling Dylan felt now?

*Nah.* The man was already charitable beyond

belief with so many others. He likely enjoyed that kind of feeling all the time.

Dylan realized something else: As many strangers as he'd talked to at rodeos, he'd never made a personal connection with someone as he had with Beau. And even though most folks were as nice as pie, it wasn't easy for him to keep the words flowing sometimes.

But conversations here had been easy so far— dare he say *fun*.

Just like his conversations with Georgina had become, although those had moved on to a whole different level. For both of them, judging by the kisses.

After seeing her disappointment yesterday at his refusal to have dinner with Glenn Guillory, he wasn't so sure they could stay at the same level. He'd never want to hold her back. But hobnobbing with the stars simply wasn't what he wanted. He'd already lived more of a glitz-and-glamour life than most, and it wasn't everything that people seemed to think.

Then again, maybe it would be everything for her.

Even the thought of it hurt. Fortunately, he'd had a lot of practice in handling such feelings.

And even more practice at not giving up on something he really wanted.

# *CHAPTER THIRTEEN*

"READY...SET..."

Georgina lifted the strawberry pie from the top shelf of the refrigerator and placed it on the counter, taking no unnecessary chances this time. Whatever pictures she could capture with this lighting would have to do.

She examined the pie from all angles as she rotated it with the utmost patience and care. It looked even more delicious than the first one. Before it met its fate on the parlor floor, of course.

"Perfect!" Just like her timing.

Two hours had passed since she added the strawberry and glaze filling to the pre-baked pie crust, which should be the exact amount of time needed. The only thing missing? Her personal taste tester—the one she had to impress most.

She'd called out to Dylan when he returned from his ranch rodeo ten minutes ago, requesting that they talk. He said he needed to feed Sundance and put him in the room and would be back down in a sec.

He didn't ask what she wanted to talk with him about, but he likely didn't have to. Everything was now hinging on that single thorn that remained in the otherwise beautiful sacrament of making a marriage official.

Becca promised to keep Max around the B and B in case they needed a final tiebreaker. In fact, she was being agreeable to just about everything since getting a good report from the doctor. Georgina wanted to think that the outfit she'd picked out for her at Expecting the Best had something to do with her emotional shift as well.

But pulling Max in for his vote was a wild card she didn't want played if they didn't have to. She did go ahead and bake a fresh batch of chocolate-kiss cookies, just in case. At this point, she needed to score every point she could.

The strawberry pie would hopefully earn her points with Dylan too. Aside from her obvious intention of wanting to soften him to the idea of a big wedding for Rose and Monty, she really wanted to hear all about the ranch rodeo and tell him about her meeting with the vow-renewal couple.

Maybe even ask for a makeup kiss.

Even *she* realized she might have acted a little childish and pouty about the whole dinner issue with the studio crew and Glenn Guillory. Not that she wasn't sad about it. She would've accepted the invitation in a heartbeat if he'd been at least half interested in going with her.

The bigger question now was: Was his reluctance because he wasn't comfortable with the types of activities she enjoyed most in life, or was he simply disinterested? By that, she meant activities that involved other people, and sometimes lots of them. Because what would be the point in being together if they couldn't do things together?

Not that she was even sure they were headed down that road. But after that second kiss, it was safe to assume they were pointed in that direction.

She carefully slid the pie back into the refrigerator, then sprinted upstairs to her room to freshen up a bit. Instead of trying to consolidate her talking points, the only thing she could think about was what to wear. All of her lucky pink clothes were in the laundry bin, so she retrieved a long, dark gray cashmere maxi sweater dress. Very… *cozy.*

By the time she added some black boots and returned to the kitchen, Dylan had taken a seat at the bar. He'd obviously done some freshening up too. She could smell the B-and-B brand of soap from where she stood. His hair wasn't quite dry either. And his flannel shirt still had fold marks but otherwise looked even softer and cozier than she felt.

Now who was the one trying to tip the scales?

"You changed," he said, standing briefly and leaning in for a quick kiss.

On the cheek.

She felt like being playful by saying that he must be mistaken because she would never change for anyone. Take her or leave her.

But the man had a serious sweet tooth. No use adding anything that might come across as the least bit bitter if taken the wrong way.

"I felt like putting on something a little warmer. I see you changed too."

"I smelled like livestock after being in a closed arena all day. Didn't think you'd appreciate it," he said.

"I probably wouldn't have even noticed, but I do appreciate the consideration."

They looked at each other for the longest time, and she couldn't begin to guess what he was thinking. Felt like he was taking a step back from her after pulling her in yesterday.

"So this is it, huh?" he finally said.

Georgina gulped. "For us?"

His eyes widened. "What? I hope not. I meant the discussion we keep kicking down the road. We're finally having it."

*How embarrassing.*

"Oh, that? I'd forgotten all about it," she said in her most playful voice.

"Me too," he said, adding a wink and a smile.

Funny how any words he spoke, which sometimes didn't flow so easily for him, had the power to soothe.

"Maybe that's one reason I called you down here. But I realized I never let you sample the groom's pie, for your approval."

That got his attention. His posture straightened.

After pouring a glass of sparkling water for each of them and placing the glasses on the bar, she opened the refrigerator door, but not wide enough for him to get a peek inside. Instead of retrieving her most recent work of art, she pulled out the chess pie she'd made earlier and placed it on the counter in front of him.

When she sliced into it, the filling didn't disappoint. It was the perfect consistency. She retrieved one plate and two forks, then cut a small slice for the two of them to share. Didn't want him to fill up before she played her full hand, along with what she hoped would be a winning card.

"It's your dad's favorite," she said as he took a generous bite.

"It was never mine, but this could be a game changer," he said after savoring and swallowing.

She tried a bite. Not bad, but not perfect either. Monty deserved her best effort.

"I'll sift some powdered sugar on the top as well. Make it extra sweet and pretty."

That earned her a smile but nothing more. The heaviness and inevitability of what they needed to discuss was clearly setting in.

"If you otherwise approve, I'll just need to know how many to make," she said.

*And off we go...*

Dylan set down his fork and reached for the sparkling water.

"I know you do. And I also know my father and what he would like. Trust me, he'll show off his new bride every chance he gets. But in the moments that mean the most, he doesn't care about the outside world. He shares special moments with only the most special people."

"And I love that about him. At the same time, I would bet he wants something special for Rose. The couple I met with yesterday for the vow renewals convinced me of that, with the way the husband wanted her to have only the best. If his wife hadn't been so modest, I would've been able to make it something really special. This is a huge deal for the bride. It's the most important day of her life."

Dylan audibly exhaled as if she'd said way too much. Unfortunately, she was just getting started.

It was already beginning to feel like that strawberry pie wasn't going to be nearly good enough.

"Oh, I know how important it is for the bride. I ruined my ex-wife's wedding," he said.

Georgina cocked her head. "I sincerely doubt that."

Dylan looked straight ahead now at some undetermined point. Not at her.

"It's true. It's all on video. Longest reciting of vows in history because I couldn't get them out. I single-handedly turned Dakota's dream wedding into her worst nightmare."

"Dakota? You don't mean Dakota…as in *Rush*." No, it couldn't be. Although it would explain his odd response when Georgina had tossed out her name during dinner the other day.

He looked at her now as if trying to read her face. "Before she was famous."

Georgina blinked and shook her head, wishing she could somehow unhear it. It made sense, considering the circles his family traveled in. Still, the fewer details spilled about past relationships, the better.

"I couldn't handle the pressure," he continued. "Weddings are too stressful on grooms anyway. If I ever get married again, I'd take Max's suggestion and 'lope.'"

Yet another thing she wished she could unhear. "But that's what we're here for and trying to do.

Take the pressure off Rose and Monty. Unfortunately, *loping* isn't an option."

He looked at her now, but he otherwise didn't budge.

As a professional, she found his statement concerning. Even though yes, weddings were stressful. For everyone. She'd encountered her share of cold feet on both sides.

But as a woman who had her heart set on an extra-special day for herself someday and had already developed feelings for the man in front of her, it was disheartening.

It wasn't just about that one day. She needed someone who appreciated the special moments she created for couples. Someone who wanted such moments not only for her but for himself. Dylan didn't seem interested in either.

And all the strawberry pie in the world wasn't likely to change that.

FOR MUCH OF Dylan's life, he'd been at a loss for words. Quite literally.

Today it seemed as though he'd spoken too many. Not only that, but he'd spoken the wrong ones. By now, he knew Georgina well enough to know when something affected her...without her having to utter a word.

At the same time, he wouldn't be doing either of them a favor by pretending he was looking forward to a wedding of his own or thought that a lavish one was something his dad would want. Or any groom that he'd never known, for that matter.

That said, did the process now intrigue him?

Yes. More than it ever used to, thanks to Georgina.

True to form, she turned her frown upside down in record time. It was only then that he realized she was probably masking a hurt that ran painfully deep.

*Takes one to know one.*

Even though he'd revealed more than he ever intended to, there was something else he couldn't articulate. Something that also ran deep. She was listening to him, but...

*Does she hear me?*

"Well, then! I think it's time to call in the tie-breaker. Do you agree?" she asked.

Before he could answer, she whipped out of the kitchen and disappeared.

He downed the rest of the sparkling water, then took his glass to the sink. She was right. Letting Max decide was the only solution. Except the little boy wasn't experienced enough in life to understand the complexity of this decision, or the ramifications.

But an agreement was an agreement. He'd

abide by whatever Max decided and deal with the consequences later.

He eyed the chocolate-kiss cookies on the counter and realized he didn't have an equivalent bribe to offer Max. At least, not a fresh one.

Dylan stepped out of the kitchen and looked down the long hallway, toward what he now knew to be where Cody and Becca's suite was located. Max's room was supposedly across the hall. But all seemed perfectly quiet.

He returned to the kitchen, covered the chess pie in cellophane and slipped it back into the refrigerator. Not that he knew all that much about pies, but he for one didn't have the appetite for another piece. That was when he spotted his favorite type of pie, along with a handwritten note placed on top.

Becca—Do *not* touch this! Or let anyone else. I made this pie for someone special.
Love, Georgina
P.S. Not that you aren't special. I'll explain later.

FINALLY, FOOTSTEPS DREW NEAR, including the now-familiar sound of tiny, eager ones. Max entered the kitchen first. He was wearing the decision hat Dylan had bought.

*Yessss!*

"Don't you look nice! Love the hat," he said.

Max touched his head as if he'd all but forgotten he had it on.

"You gave it to me! Miss Georgina told me I should wear it 'cause you need me to make a decision."

"She's right. We do. Where is she?"

"Talking to Mommy and Daddy."

Dylan stood, then walked over to the plate of chocolate-kiss cookies. "While we're waiting, how about we steal one of these? Georgina must've made them for you."

Max looked up at him, his mouth agape.

"Go ahead! I'll take the blame," Dylan said.

"Are you gonna have one too?" the boy asked.

"I'm saving my appetite for some strawberry pie."

Thankfully, no more questions were asked. Max was getting animated, even though the sugar hadn't had time to enter his system.

Soon enough, Georgina joined them in the kitchen.

"There you are!" she said to Max. "I see you found the cookies."

"Mr. Dylan said you made them for me and that I could have one. I told him he could have one too, but he said he would rather have strawberry pie."

Georgina looked as though she froze in place.

Dylan simply smiled and shrugged.

Max situated himself on the barstool next to Dylan while Georgina poured the little boy a glass of milk.

"Anything for you?" she asked Dylan.

"Maybe later," he said. If that pie tasted as good as it looked, it might weaken his defenses. Yet, he didn't need them anymore. Seemed the fate of the list was now in Max's chocolate-and-crumb-covered hands.

Rather than offering him a piece of that strawberry pie, she simply nodded. Maybe she hadn't made it for him after all, because how could she know it was his favorite?

"So… Max. We have a dilemma we need for you to help us solve," she said. "It's about who we should invite to the wedding."

Max finished chewing and swallowing a rather large bite, then washed it down with a huge sip of milk, resulting in a white mustache on his upper lip.

"I think we should have family and only the closest of friends. Ten to fifteen people. And, of course, Penny and Sundance, and all of your stuffed animals. Which would mean there would be more cake and pie left for all of us at the end of it," Dylan said.

Georgina cast him the side-eye, followed by a sly grin.

"And I think we should include lots of friends

and family. I'm thinking a hundred or more after we include all of your stuffed-animal friends, because no one wants to feel left out. I can always make more cake and pie, but a wedding only happens once," Georgina countered.

Max took his time mulling it over. Then he said, "I need another cookie so I can make a decision."

Dylan laughed, and Georgina practically snorted. And they probably each thought they were the best negotiator in the house. Max proved them wrong.

Georgina lifted the Saran Wrap and retrieved another cookie. Max intercepted it and took a bite before she so much as set it down on the napkin in front of him.

The longer they waited, however, the less cute all of this became. Had the biggest decision of the wedding really come down to this? A six-year-old boy? Either way, one of them would be disappointed. The fact that they couldn't reach a decision on something so unimportant in the grand scheme of things made him wonder if they'd be able to compromise on other issues, were their relationship to move forward.

And he wanted it to move forward.

Sure, Dylan had professional reasons for wanting to keep the ceremony small and private. Similarly, she had professional reasons for wanting a high-profile event. The more publicity, the more connections.

"I've made my decision." Max wiped his heads on his napkin but failed to wipe the chocolate from the corners of his mouth or the milk from his upper lip. It should have seemed adorable. But in this moment, it was unsettling.

He and Georgina both seemed to be holding a collective breath.

"We should invite everyone in the world so no one's feelings are hurt, including Santa because he keeps coming by the house anyway. And all his reindeer and helpers. And Mrs. Claus too," Max explained.

So much for that. Georgina should be happy, however. Max's decision was more in line with her preference. Except he could tell she wasn't entirely satisfied.

"Thank you, Max. We appreciate your thoughtful input," Georgina said. "Now, go brush your teeth and wash your face, please."

Max hopped off the barstool and pattered back down the hallway, leaving a bigger mess than ever in his wake.

"I guess the authorities have spoken. Not sure how we're gonna pull this off, though. Where are we going to put all the people and animals in the world?" Dylan said.

It was as much of a concession of defeat as he could muster.

"Actually, part of me was secretly hoping he'd pick your option, if only because it would be so much easier," she said.

Not sure whether she meant it, but the thought was appreciated.

Georgina turned, opened the refrigerator and pulled out the strawberry pie he'd caught a glimpse of. His mouth began to water.

"This calls for a celebration. We're one step closer to not having a clear decision."

She grabbed a plate, cut a slice and pushed it in front of him.

He sank the fork into the piece. "I'm not going to be a sore loser. His decision is closer to your vision."

"You do know I want what's best for Monty and Rose, right? A glamorous wedding with big names just comes with an extra benefit for me."

"I know that."

"I tell you what—if that isn't the best strawberry pie you've ever tasted, then we'll go with your guest list idea."

He tilted his head and studied her offer. "Sounds like a trap."

"That's because it is. I'm pretty confident in that pie. I'm also confident in my ability to plan this wedding. And I would do all the additional work required. But it doesn't mean anything if you don't share that sentiment and if I don't have your full support and confidence."

What could he say? There was no doubt it would be a beautiful wedding, and she could pull it off. And that pie…

"You could plan a beautiful wedding with your hands tied, which is what they've been anyway in having to plan with me. But are you sure? Because I intend to be completely honest about the pie," he said.

He wasn't just saying that. This pie was made to influence him, and he refused to allow it. But he sure wasn't going to refuse to eat it.

"I expect no less," she said.

"You're willing to hinge the whole thing on this one bite?" he said, scooping it on his fork and holding it up between them, giving her one last chance to back out. A coin flip would make more sense. And it would certainly be less pressure on him.

"Why not? We've exhausted every other avenue to reaching a decision."

"Okay, then." *Here goes nothing.*

He took the bite and chewed it slowly. The crust was impeccable. The strawberries and filling were nothing short of perfection. Was it the best strawberry pie he'd ever had?

*Absolutely.*

Not entirely true. If he were to be honest, it would probably tie with his own mom's. But that had been so long ago, and she'd set an impossible bar for anyone, so...

Of course, he could lie and get his way. She wouldn't be able to prove otherwise. But that wasn't the deal he agreed to. Besides, it was better to let her take the reins and confirm her true priorities, with her being fully informed of his own preferences and reasoning, before he fell any deeper for her.

In fact, it might be the only way to know if she'd listened at all.

He had said his piece. More than once. He needed to leave for Fort Worth to do the photoshoot promos for the rodeo in a couple of days. He'd put off the PR folks as long as he could. Even though he'd be gone only a few days, it was yet another reason to leave it in one person's hands. They had officially run out of time to negotiate any further. Someone had to step aside.

And that someone was him.

# *CHAPTER FOURTEEN*

GEORGINA HUMMED A familiar tune as she adjusted the new package that appeared beneath the tree overnight.

Surprisingly, she was kind of loving the Christmas songs, even though she was struggling to recall the lyrics of this one. Ordinarily, she would have put on some country music. But she was feeling unusually festive this morning. Must have had something to do with the fact that they had finally made some progress on the wedding plans yesterday.

"I don't believe it. Are you really humming 'Rudolph the Red-Nosed Reindeer?'" someone said behind her back.

Georgina spun around.

"Becca! Yes, I am. And you're just who I'm looking for. Santa was here again last night. I want to see the footage!"

"Okay. But first things first—coffee. Or whatever you drank this morning, because you're way too happy. I'm not sure what to make of it, but I'm a bit jealous."

Georgina turned her attention back to the tree and adjusted some of the ornaments that weren't evenly spaced. Funny, she hadn't even noticed that about them before. Besides, this was actually fun. Maybe she'd volunteer to decorate the B and B tree next year, just so it would look as perfect and balanced as possible the first time.

"I didn't drink anything this morning. I just didn't get any sleep," Georgina said.

"Oh! Well that explains everything."

"It kind of does, because I was up all night putting together the evites for the wedding."

"Y'all reached an agreement? Max said he helped."

"More than you know. He recommended we invite everyone in the world. I narrowed it down to a good chunk of Monty's contact list, which Dylan handed over. Along with the list you gave me for Rose's friends and your side of the family. And a special invite to his Proud River bandmates, who I thought could stay here at the B and B, along with some other VIPs. I managed to book enough additional rooms in scattered hotels. Only problem will be if people don't RSVP but show up anyway, because I'll have to cancel whatever rooms we can't get a commitment for ahead of time or else have to pay for a night."

"Very thorough of you, Georgina."

"And I have a call in to the florist. And I've figured out how big the cakes—and Monty's pie—will need to be and when I'll need to get started to be done on time without them being made too far in advance and getting stale, and—"

"I need to sit down," Becca said.

Georgina swept in to hold her up and help her to the sofa. A couple of guests came downstairs and offered a concerned look.

"Hi, folks!" Becca called out and waved, which seemed to ease their concern. However, it did nothing to ease Georgina's.

"Are you okay?" she asked.

"Yes. And I say this with a heart full of love, but all your talking is wearing. Me. Out!"

"Really? That's all? I'm sorry. I'll keep quiet... after I see Santa. Is your phone in your room? I can go get it." Georgina assumed the sprinting position.

"Slow down, Prancer. I have my phone right here. Somewhere," Becca said as she dug into the deep pocket of her oversized sweater. "I haven't looked, although I have to admit that you've awakened my curiosity. Most of all, I'm enjoying the fact that you're *finally* getting into the Christmas spirit."

Becca handed her the phone.

Georgina played it a few times, zooming in as

close as possible. "Good news! It's Santa again. Looks like the real one this time."

She showed the footage to Becca, even though she didn't ask.

"Looks like a man, for sure."

Georgina played through it again. "It still could be the same woman, couldn't it? Just a bulkier suit? Or she could have padded it to throw us off. Of course, that would mean she's aware of the nanny cam."

"May not even be someone who lives here. Could be someone from the outskirts."

She sat back down and deadpanned, "Like the North Pole."

Becca squinted. "Please tell me you don't believe that."

Georgina stood again. "After yesterday, I believe in just about everything."

That included the fact that she was enjoying the holiday for the first time ever, thanks to the gift of getting to finish planning this wedding and making it extra special. But she was especially having fun with the whole mystery surrounding Santa, although she was determined to find out who it was.

It was helping her to *not* think about Dylan. Or overthink it. True, the wedding wasn't going to be what he envisioned, but it wouldn't be nearly as large as she'd like either.

Speaking of her co-planner…

"Have you seen Dylan this morning?" Georgina asked.

"I'm pretty sure he went to the county fairgrounds."

"Are they having another rodeo?" Surely he would have mentioned it.

Becca shook her head. "No. Cody said there's nothing going on today. Probably completely empty, in fact."

"Maybe he wanted to take Sundance there for some exercise."

"That would've been my guess, but Cody said Dylan asked him to look after that sweetheart for a while. I was still half asleep, but I'm pretty sure Cody also mentioned something about sunrise snowball fights. They're probably all out back."

Georgina had heard some shrieks and barks, but she assumed it was Cody and Max and Penny.

Becca tried to get up from the plush sofa but wasn't having any success. Georgina swooped in to give her a hand.

"I'm gonna lie back down for a while. But first, I'm making a glass of warm milk. Forget the coffee," Becca said.

"I'll get it for you."

Becca shook her head and squeezed Georgina's hand. "No, ma'am. I need to get in some steps. Otherwise, I won't be able to fit into that pretty dress you picked out for me. And if that happens, I'll have to corner our Secret Santa and borrow his suit."

"At least we'd finally find out who it is," Georgina offered.

Becca's brows pinched. "So you agree? That I may have to wear a Santa suit to Mom's wedding?"

"What? No!"

Her serious expression cracked, and a sweet laugh followed. Georgina was grateful to hear it. Her friend and boss hadn't done nearly enough laughing lately.

"Just giving you a hard time. Besides, you have a big wedding to finish planning," Becca said.

A big one was right. Even though Georgina didn't want to have to resort to a wedding in the B and B's barn, where breakfast was always served, Dylan had wanted a barn wedding, so it was actually a good thing. Besides, it was the only space on the property that could possibly fit more than one hundred people. Assuming everyone whom she'd slated to invite actually came. In reality, she was guessing there would be closer to eighty or ninety guests, tops, considering the short notice and the holiday.

Still, it was Montgomery Legend they were talking about.

This was what she'd wanted all along, right?

To plan a lavish wedding that would put her back on the map? To be in control? Except something wasn't sitting right with her, and she couldn't quite pinpoint it.

No doubt Dylan was disappointed, although he seemed to take the whole decision much better than she would have. But perhaps he was feeling left out of the planning now. If the boot was on the other foot, she would feel that way. But that gave her an idea.

She wanted to show him her final plan before she pressed Send on the invite email anyway. Wanted to show him how it was going to all come together. How she'd scaled back the social media presence so as to not draw too much attention to the former band members, which seemed to be an issue of concern for him. At least, not until the reunion tour was formally announced, even though it could work so beautifully to have people see the band back together in one place and for such a romantic event.

Then there were the cakes. Dylan had been a huge help with those. Classic vanilla it would be. Leave it to a serious sweet tooth to make a solid decision. Also the groom's chess pie, which had his approval. She'd like to offer up some single-serving pies as well and would like his opinion on flavors.

At the thought of it, she could practically taste

their first kiss. In doing so, she realized it wasn't his opinion she really wanted or needed.

It was more times like the ones they'd already shared.

DYLAN STOOD IN the middle of the empty county fairgrounds arena and breathed it all in.

Nothing like it to calm the nerves, clear his mind and put his priorities in perspective. Funny, but it was going to be tough to say goodbye to this town. For some reason, it already held a special place in his heart.

It did for many other reasons, actually. He loved the people here. The way they assured him he was "no big deal" despite his true identity. Treated him like they most certainly did anyone else in Destiny Springs. With respect and kindness.

He settled onto one of the benches, then leaned back, closed his eyes and played the past two weeks over again in his mind, wondering what he could or should have done differently.

Couldn't say he was happy about handing over the reins to Georgina. But whatever she came up with would ultimately be fine. She was the professional wedding planner out of the two of them, after all. He trusted her to make it beautiful. Besides, it was officially out of his hands.

But this wasn't about him anymore or the risk

it could pose to his own image. At the end of the day, he'd still have a career. Potentially an even better and easier one, once the right influential people found out he was Monty's son—something he had somehow managed to avoid by being extra careful.

Who knew? Once the cat was out of the bag, he might even be able to pick his jobs rather than hoping to be picked by them.

That knowledge alone—that his future was secure either way—gave him some comfort, if not the level he'd tried to accomplish.

This wasn't about his dad and Rose either. They wanted to be surprised, and if they didn't end up liking what she planned, they allowed it to happen by not speaking up. Yet he'd always been quite sure his dad would strongly prefer an intimate ceremony. With the exception of his birthday parties, every event of importance that Dylan remembered while growing up had included family only. On the stage, Montgomery Legend belonged to the world. Off the stage, he belonged to those he cherished most.

No, everything was now about Dylan's future with Georgina.

*Or without her.*

Dylan closed his eyes and took another deep breath. Maybe he should have brought his best friend along after all, but he really needed to be truly alone for a short while. It was the only way he'd ever found to clear his head and soothe any frayed nerves. Always had been, always would be.

But the sound of footsteps in the distance threatened to cut it short. Maybe if he sat very still and kept his eyes closed, whomever it was would keep walking. He sure didn't want to have to make small talk at the moment. Such talk was never fun. Except in very special circumstances, like at the ranch rodeo.

The footsteps continued to draw near, so he opened his eyes. Maybe a nod and wave would keep them moving.

Instead, he gulped at the sight. Georgina was headed toward him, a vision in pale pink and black, carrying a folder and paper bag.

"There you are," she said, settling in beside him.

She set down the folder, then opened the bag and pulled out a paper plate with a piece of that strawberry pie covered in cellophane and a plastic fork on the side.

"You found me," he said.

"I didn't realize you were lost. Plus I didn't want to have to report my co-planner as missing in action."

He forced a laugh. "I thought we pretty much agreed my role in that was done. Besides, I'll be gone for a few days. You'll be completely unsupervised."

Georgina looked genuinely distressed. "What? Where are you going?"

"Fort Worth. Remember? I have to do the photoshoot promos with the rest of the group."

"Oh! Of course. Becca had mentioned it way back. I thought we had a few more days. But you're returning afterward, right?"

"Definitely. I'm not leaving that strawberry pie behind for long."

"Wise decision. I had no intention of dragging you into helping turn my vision into reality. But I did want you to look over what I put together, so I guess my timing was optimal," she said.

"You don't need my approval, Georgina. Not anymore."

"I know. You said you trusted me with this, and I appreciate it. I simply want to show you that your trust wasn't misplaced and hopefully reassure you that you made the right decision to lie about my strawberry pie being the best you'd ever tasted. I tried a piece. I can do better."

If only that meant what he hoped it meant: that she'd reconsidered the guest list based on his input and opinion. If it had ended up with him getting to make the final decision, he would have invited at least a handful of select acquaintances to include to make her somewhat happy. Except for his dad's former bandmates. They'd all been out of touch for too many years to be considered close anymore. Besides, they'd have plenty of time to catch up during their reunion tour.

"I didn't lie about the pie. And you don't need to bribe me with another piece. I think we've moved beyond that by now," he said.

Besides, his stomach was feeling a bit too anxious to enjoy so much as a single bite.

"I think so too." She opened the folder, pulled out some loose papers and handed them over. "I was going to bring my laptop, but I decided to go full-on old school so that you could have your own copy."

Dylan accepted the pages from her and flipped through them. First was a photo of the cake, which looked like the one from that book she'd shown to him. Probably was. This cake had five tiers, but she'd added a notation to make it with only four. Either number of tiers could serve up to two hundred guests, if he remembered correctly. Not the kind of number one would forget.

The sketch she'd done for the ceremony mapped out the logistics for a huge, enclosed space—the breakfast barn at the B and B. She'd noted where the chairs would be placed as well as the location of a makeshift aisle. At least she had conceded to his preference for a barn wedding—he had to give her that. Then again, it was really the only practical choice. Although his math skills weren't the best, a brief glance told him that she'd figured on accommodating at least one hundred people.

The more pages he flipped through, the more anxious he felt. Especially when he reached the guest list. Two pages, two columns, single-spaced.

But the most revealing part wasn't on any of the sheets. She'd come all the way to the county fairgrounds just to prove that she *wasn't* going to meet him halfway. If anything, this list seemed longer than he'd imagined it could be.

Yet she'd asked for his opinion. Time for a heaping helping of honesty.

"It looks like it will be real nice, Georgina. Real nice. Except…"

"Except what? Oh, let me guess, it's still too many people? That wasn't even your dad's full list. I did cull it down."

There definitely was that. But the formality of it—at least from her descriptions—sounded more appropriate for something else.

"It's worthy of a royal wedding. But is it right for Monty and Rose?"

She straightened her back and looked forward at some undetermined point in the distance. No doubt that he'd put her on the defensive. In all fairness, she'd given him clues all along. But something about seeing it on paper put it in perspective.

"Rose and your dad are royalty, in my book. Besides, they wanted to be surprised."

"Oh, they'll be surprised," he said.

Someone looking on would have thought he'd thrown ice water on her. Figuratively, he supposed he had. He was aiming for seriousness in jest. But the jest must have been undetectable.

"I'm sorry, Georgina. I don't mean it in a bad way. Everything here is…beyond beautiful sounding. The bouquet, for instance. White roses will look great with her dress."

Not that the guests would be able to even *see* the dress.

"Uh-huh. I bet I know what you're thinking and, okay, it's a lot of roses. I'll give you that. How about we cut the greenery in half? That would make it more compact and proportionate," she said.

She wasn't wrong. That had stood out.

"How about a single rose instead?" he countered.

At that, she turned perfectly quiet. He wasn't sure whether she was thinking about the single rose he'd picked up for her, but he for one hadn't forgotten, because the beautiful expression on her face when he pulled it out of that paper bag was something he'd never forget. There was nothing dishonest about her response. And then again, when she'd tried to hide the fact that she was holding it when he came downstairs that morning.

"I suppose we could do just one. I mean, that's what my vow-renewal clients ended up wanting as well. At least, that's what she said she wanted. *He* wanted her to have a big bouquet, which I thought was sweet of him."

Yet even Dylan knew that one rose wasn't meeting her halfway, which was what he hoped she would do. Maybe his role here wasn't completely over with after all.

"Actually, a half dozen might be perfect," he said.

She looked at him for the longest time. "But is it perfect for this client?"

That he couldn't answer. Then again, neither could she with any certainty.

They sat in silence for the longest time. Both trained on some undefined point in the distance.

"Are we back to square one?" she finally asked.

He inhaled, held it for an extended moment, then released it in a slow and steady stream.

"No. If we were, I'd still be insisting on a Christmas wedding. But I reached the conclusion that my original plan had flaws. You convinced me of that. Monty and Rose shouldn't share their special day with it. You shouldn't have to share a birthday with Christmas either. I'm sorry you've had to live with that."

He looked at her now. And she was looking at him.

"And I'm glad you were honest about the conflict with New Year's Day. I was wrong to push it so hard to begin with, because even though it's a new start for the bride and groom, a lot of folks might prefer to start their year focusing on their own lives rather than other people."

"Excellent point," he said, placing the loose sheets back into the folder and setting it on the bench. It wouldn't do either of them any good to hash over any more details.

Once again, they sat in silence for what felt like the longest time.

"Are *we* back to square one?" he asked.

At that, he looked at her. The way she gulped back what appeared to be tears forming in her eyes suggested she knew exactly what he meant. And that they shared the same doubts.

This wasn't about their differences in the final wedding plan. It went much deeper than that, and they both knew it.

"You're a beautiful butterfly, Georgina. You deserve to soar in your career, and this wedding will help. I'm not judging at all. In fact, you're probably a lot smarter than I am about making connections and getting ahead. And I've seen how happy it makes you to be around people. And how they respond to you. It's a gift I wish I had."

"I don't want to soar alone, though. I want to soar with you."

"I can't soar. I already tried. I need the comfort of a cocoon. I'd rather stay at home and eat popcorn in bed and watch a movie than make small talk with anyone…except for a pretty woman who loves pink and who makes the best strawberry pie I've ever had. The only person I'd want to share that cocoon with is you."

She turned her face away from his, but not before he caught a glint of a tear. It was all he could do to swallow back his own.

"It wouldn't be fair to either of us to live separate lives or for one to give up what makes them happy and comfortable," he said.

She retrieved a tissue from her handbag. "I know."

Funny, but that wasn't what he hoped she say. But it was honest.

"I think we should call in Max. He could give us a solution to this," he said.

That made her laugh just a little. He reached out and tucked a windswept strand of hair behind her ear. "So, where do we go from here?"

"I've thought about that. Over the course of planning your dad's wedding to Rose, it got me thinking that that's what I want too. Sooner rather than later. And hanging out with Max? Motherhood wasn't something I was even considering so soon. But hey, weddings and wedding planning tends to do that to people. You'd be amazed at how many folks get caught up in the romance of it all and make rash decisions."

It was the perfect summation.

"And there's nothing wrong with feeling that way. I'm just not—"

"The impulsive type. You want to be very sure. Not rush into things," she said, finishing his thought. "And there's nothing wrong with that. Neither of us is wrong. About the wedding or how to enjoy life."

The brutal honesty of the statement felt like the most painful blow. One he all but knew was coming, but one that he wasn't prepared for.

She looked to him with eyes full of hope, as if she wanted him to disagree. But he simply couldn't. The bottom line was this whole thing wasn't about them. Or even about his dad and Rose. It was about their own futures. If this relationship were to move forward, would her painstakingly cultivated network of famous clients and friends come first? And would he be the sidekick who would inevitably embarrass her?

Unfortunately, he had his answer.

Once again, the silence enveloped them for

what felt like the longest time. Until the pain thankfully turned to numbness and acceptance.

"You know what?" she finally said. "I wish I'd known about this place a long time ago. I can totally visualize a wedding here. One of any size."

His heart could have stopped. Although he'd had trouble visualizing so much of what she'd laid out, *this* he could see.

"What do you know? We found something we can agree on," he said.

If only they could agree upon even more important things. But the fact remained that neither was wrong.

They were simply wrong for each other.

# CHAPTER FIFTEEN

GEORGINA PRESSED THE COLD, wet washrag against her eyes and held it there in hopes of reducing the puffiness.

After a good long minute, she removed the compress, looked in the mirror and gasped.

Her own reflection was bad enough, but Becca had come up behind her and was standing there, looking equally horrified.

Washrag still in hand, Georgina put her hands over her heart. "Don't sneak up on me like that. You scared me."

"*You're* scaring *me*. What happened?" Becca asked.

*My whole world is falling apart.*

"Nothing. I'm fine. Are you okay?" she asked.

"I'm doing better than you, clearly."

"I look that bad, huh? Don't answer that." Georgina dabbed at her eyes with a dry towel, then reached for her liner and mascara, although the effort would be futile. She'd end up crying it all off anyway.

Meanwhile, Becca looked on as if she were watching a horror flick.

"If you're okay, what are you doing in my room? Not that you aren't welcome to hang out here," Georgina said.

It was true—she pretty much had an open-door policy for Becca, especially in her condition. No need to go through the formality of knocking in case her boss needed something and Cody wasn't there to help. Lately, Becca had been popping in for nonemergency reasons as well.

"You mean what are *we* doing in here," Becca said as she rubbed her swollen belly.

"You're right. My apologies. I keep forgetting you're carrying a little person around in there," Georgina said, laughing at her own joke as she struggled with drawing a straight line with the eyeliner pencil. And failing miserably.

"At least you haven't lost your sense of humor. But I wasn't talking about my soon-to-be little one," Becca said.

Georgina's heart sank. Of all the moments for a surprise guest. "Then who?"

"Come out and see!"

She followed Becca out of the bathroom, and there stood Rose in her wedding dress. Seeing her was like an immediate salve had been applied to her heart.

"Oh, Rose, you look so lovely!" Georgina said.

"Jess has a few more details and plenty of finishing to do, but I went for the fitting today. I told her I had to come here and show you."

Rose did a couple of slow three-sixties. The dress looked amazing from all angles. But the best part of all was the happiness that practically radiated from the bride-to-be.

It also made Georgina realize how wrong Dylan had been when he'd indicated they couldn't agree on anything. They'd agreed on the dress, hadn't they? And on the classic vanilla cake as well, come to think of it.

While she had Rose here, she was tempted to show her the wedding plans. See if she was as off-base as Dylan seemed to imply. But that would not only spoil this joyous moment with too much seriousness, it would definitely spoil the surprise.

"I'd better change out of this dress before I get something on it, and then return it to Jess so she can finish. Becca, you stay here." Rose added a sympathetic smile and tilt of the head, just for Georgina.

Although Rose didn't say it, Georgina knew why. Her eyes looked like they'd been stung by bees. Yet she'd momentarily forgotten all about her own problems in favor of seeing the dress executed so beautifully.

After Rose left, Becca closed the door, walked

back over to her and gripped her shoulders. "Talk to me."

"There's nothing to worry about—I promise."

"If you're saying that just because I'm about to burst, don't. You've been there for me and heard me out too many times to count."

That wasn't entirely untrue. But Georgina had been there because she wanted to be.

"I'm not leaving until you do, and I won't let you leave either," Becca continued. "We both know I can successfully block the door without even trying. So spill. Let's get comfy."

This time, Becca was the one doing the helping. She took Georgina's hand, led her to the edge of the bed and pointed. "Sit."

Georgina did as she was told, then took a deep breath. "Dylan doesn't like the plan I came up with for the wedding. Especially the length of the guest list."

It wasn't the entire truth as to what had really caused the puffy eyes. But their disagreement had initiated more truths coming out and the ending of a relationship that had barely begun.

That was probably a good thing overall. They would've found out sooner or later that they weren't compatible. One thing she didn't want to do was go to parties and socialize without the man she loved by her side. And staying at home wasn't her thing, even though she'd enjoy nothing more in the moment. With him. Their brief time in that empty stadium, just the two of them and before everything fell apart, was admittedly… magical.

Then again, she'd been under Cupid's spell. Christmas's too. Not anymore.

"Why does he even care about the wedding size?" Becca asked. "Dylan isn't the one getting married now, is he? Nor is he a professional planner. Don't tell him this, but I was kind of relieved that Max broke the tie in your favor."

"Really?" The waterworks threatened to start again, but for a good reason this time. Someone was actually on her side.

"Oh, yes! I was a bit worried about what Mom and Monty would end up with, leaving Max in charge. But I was sure you wouldn't let anything bad happen. And you pretty much had Dylan eating cake out of the palm of your hand. At least, that's what Vern says." She gave her a sly smirk.

Georgina had all but forgotten that he'd walked in on their kiss.

"Vern told you about that?"

"I don't think he meant to, which is why I didn't ask you about it sooner. Not that I needed to. It's obvious you two like each other, even though you couldn't agree on very many things."

"Which is part of the reason why I look so scary. We figured out we probably never would."

"I figured that was the real reason for the eye bags, because a guest list dispute certainly wouldn't be worth it, looking like you do. No offense. Although I think all the tears may be a bit premature. I've seen the way he's looked at you since day one. And the way you look at him. My guess is he's sporting some eye bags himself about now."

Georgina wasn't sure whether that theory helped. But it sure didn't hurt.

Becca stood, with a little help from Georgina.

"I'm going to find Cody and Max and tell them the good news about the dress. They won't be particularly interested, but they've both been super attentive during this pregnancy. I might as well take advantage of it because once baby gets here, I won't get any attention."

"Don't worry. I'll make sure you have plenty," Georgina said.

Once Becca was gone, she was faced with something scarier than her reflection, and that was trying to spot any loose ends in her plan through bleary eyes.

At least she'd held herself together long enough to say goodbye to Dylan before he left for Fort Worth. Becca and Cody offered their bon voyages at the same time. It was a blessing that it hadn't been a private goodbye. Besides, he'd be back in time for the reception dinner on Christmas Eve, which was now less than a week away.

In the meantime, she had to move forward. The invites should have gone out already, but her and Dylan's final chat made her doubt pretty much everything about her plan. Especially the most pointed question.

*Is it right for Monty and Rose?*

Her ex-business associate had posed a similar question to her about a wedding she was planning for another couple right before he severed the partnership. Creating beautiful weddings for any couple was always her goal. The one her associate had questioned in the end didn't fall short in any area.

Neither did the one in front of her. Even though it wasn't Dylan's vision, why did he question hers after entrusting her with it?

Georgina tried to shake it off as she focused on her laptop screen.

But she had to blink to clear her vision. Not because it was blurry, but because she wasn't even looking at the right plan.

Was she?

Georgina blinked again and scrolled through the file. Even double-checked the document name.

No, it was the right file. She was just tired and distracted. Except something became very clear. How had she not noticed before? Her plan for Monty and Rose was almost identical to the Martin-Rodriguez wedding plan. Or was it the Sinclair-Thompson wedding?

No. *Both.*

Georgina put her elbows on the desk and covered her face with her hands, as if she could hide from the truth of the matter. She now understood what Dylan was trying to tell her.

And she had chosen not to hear it.

But there was something else she realized. Her wedding plans, past and present, were variations of *her* dream wedding. Not necessarily her clients'. Dylan had voiced so many preferences on behalf of his father, not for himself. But she couldn't see it at the time. The worst part of it was she hadn't listened to the person who needed listening to the most.

Perhaps she'd messed up her chance with him, but there was still time to get one thing right.

She picked up the phone and called a person she'd never have imagined would be in her contacts list. Maybe Dylan didn't believe in accepting his dad's help with anything, but she did.

Furthermore, she wasn't afraid to take advantage of it.

Is THAT HIM?

Dylan sat in his truck, trying to collect his

words while watching people pass by the silver-haired man who was sitting on the patio outside of the restaurant without realizing who it was.

If Dylan were a stranger, he might not recognize Montgomery Legend either.

From his vantage point inside the truck, his dad looked so much older than the image Dylan carried around in his mind, even though it hadn't been all that many months since he'd last seen him. Yet his father would always be that tall, dark-haired country crooner to the little boy who looked up to him.

Monty had come all the way from Jackson Hole, Wyoming, to Fort Worth to spend some quality time with his son before the big wedding, when they could have easily talked on the phone. Part of that was to attend the photoshoot and filming that Dylan had just completed.

Dylan, however, successfully dissuaded him from coming, suggesting instead that they meet for a bite to eat afterward. The folks there would ask too many questions and likely make the connection between the two. His dad had seemed to take it in stride.

Unfortunately, Dylan wasn't in much of a mood to talk. He'd long been looking forward to doing the promotion work for this rodeo, but the flight from Destiny Springs had been a blur. The photoshoots that followed, and even the promo video in which he'd made a cameo appearance, were equally hazy.

That last afternoon alone with Georgina, however, was still clear as day. And the hurtin' remained fresh.

Yet somehow, he delivered his lines today without a stumble or hitch in spite of it, thanks to his best four-legged friend by his side.

Dylan got out of the truck with Sundance and headed to the outside patio. Perfect weather for it. A sunny, mild day in Fort Worth. Soon enough, he and his father would both be back in Wyoming, where winter earned its name and outdoor dining was more of an extreme sport than a leisurely meal.

Monty spotted him as he approached and stood to give Dylan a big bear hug and Sundance a brisk petting.

He then stepped back. "You look good, son."

"Maybe a little tired around the edges."

"Aren't we all? Have a seat. I had 'em bring us a couple of sweetened peach teas," Monty said, pointing to the glasses. "I hope that's okay. I know you used to love it, but you can order something else if you'd like."

An older couple passed by and stared a little too long, as if Monty did indeed look familiar. But they must not have been able to place him. Otherwise, they would've likely stopped and asked for the man's autograph or picture. Dylan remembered the days when a meal out wasn't complete without his father's fans.

His dad retired a few years back and had since worn his signature longish hair in a slicked-back ponytail. Add to that the sunglasses he sported today and he could be mistaken for any number of trendy seniors.

Then there was a table full of young people looking their way. Probably at Sundance, however. Who could blame them?

"I'm sorry I couldn't have you sit in today," Dylan said. "But I did bring you this. It's a zip drive with the voiceover I recorded in Keaton and the promo video and photos they took today."

Monty looked at and handled it as if he'd been gifted a bar of gold. "I'll watch this as soon as I get back to my hotel room," he said.

"Where are you staying?" Dylan asked.

"The Drover."

"Stockyards, huh? Nice."

Monty nodded. "How about you?"

"Well, I don't want to brag, but there's a motel down the road that has a swimming pool, right out front, with a slide. I splurged and requested a king, but they upgraded me to two queens and a larger room."

His dad let out a deep, hearty laugh.

Dylan couldn't help but smile. Obviously, his

dad hadn't forgotten all the two-queen-bed rooms they had stayed in when he was little and had taken family road trips across the country. No set plans, no itinerary, no reservations.

"Whew! That brings back some memories. We'd always have to drive around and check out two or three different motels to find one with a swimming pool and a slide you liked."

"I know. I can't believe y'all went to all that trouble."

"Trouble? Are you kidding? Those were some of the best times of my life, watching you swim. Even joining in sometimes."

"The Drover is a definite step up."

Monty shrugged. "Not without the people you love to share it with. Say, I have a suite. You should join me tonight. We could stay up late and watch television."

Now that was something he hadn't anticipated.

"I'll give it some thought. The motel does have a nice swimming pool, so…" Although even saying that in a teasing way felt like he was rejecting his father again. The way the man dropped his chin and nodded seemed to confirm it.

The waitress came around and set some chili con queso, guacamole and chips on the table.

"I took the liberty of ordering this, but we can get entrées," Monty said.

Dylan loaded a chip down with a big scoop of queso. "Actually, this will probably fill me up."

Monty dug in as well. "Same here. They just make it better in Texas, don't they?"

"Sure do. Are you excited about the big day?" Dylan asked. Seemed like a good time to finally get some feedback because he'd suffered nothing but doubts ever since questioning Georgina's plan.

That question visibly perked Monty right up again.

"I am! Especially after Georgina called to tell me what y'all had planned for us. I begged her not to, but she insisted. She promised that Rose would still be surprised. But before she finalized everything, she wanted to make sure I'd be happy and get my blessing. The young woman doesn't give up."

"That's the truth. How do you feel about it?"

His dad didn't have to utter a word. The smile on his face said it all.

"From the way she described it, I couldn't imagine anything finer," Monty said.

Not the answer Dylan was expecting, but it was exactly what he needed to hear. He was suddenly humbled but also genuinely happy for her. Georgina had been so right all along about what would make this couple happy.

And he'd been so wrong.

Not only about the wedding, but about letting the relationship end. He was so afraid of rushing in that he'd rushed out way too quickly. She'd been kind to him in ways other women hadn't been. Besides, the opportunity had presented itself to her, not the other way around. She'd been smart to take it and make the most of it.

Now she'd have a beautiful portfolio piece for her wedding business. And his dad and Rose would be the beneficiaries of her talent.

"Is there anything you *don't* like about the plans?" Dylan asked.

Monty cocked his head seemed to think about it. "Maybe the guest list."

So he hadn't been wrong after all.

Dylan nodded. "Yeah. We went back and forth on that."

As much as this could be considered a small victory, it didn't feel like one. He wasn't about to throw Georgina under the bus and let her take the blame. No, he'd share that.

Monty loaded a chip with guacamole this time, taking his time while chewing and seemingly mulling over everything.

"What would you have changed about the list?" Dylan asked. He grabbed a chip of his own and got a generous scoop of guacamole. He hadn't had much of an appetite since leaving Destiny Springs, but it was starting to come back.

"I was kinda hoping to have more folks there, so that I could show off my new bride," Monty said.

*What?* Dylan almost choked on the bite. That was what Monty had told Georgina, and Dylan assumed the list had reflected that. He'd even seen the list.

"I do love the idea of family only, though," Monty continued. "Other folks probably couldn't have come on Christmas Day anyway."

Now Dylan was sure he couldn't speak. Not with his head spinning. But he had to try.

"The wedding is now on Christmas Day?"

A look of confusion crossed Monty's face. "Of course! She said that was your suggestion. She said y'all went back and forth about it, and that she was rooting for New Year's Day, which would have been perfect. New year, new beginnings and all. But then *you* wouldn't have been able to be there, and I couldn't have that."

What Monty was describing went against nearly everything she'd presented to Dylan. They'd agreed on a New Year's Eve wedding. He didn't even know where to start with the questions.

Then he realized that a very important question *was* answered. She *had* listened to him after all. A little too well, it seemed. Between the guest list and the wedding date that his dad now indicated he would have preferred, that made two decisions she would've been correct about from the beginning. But this situation wasn't too late to fix.

"Dad, I'm going to need your help with something."

Monty sat up straighter. "Of course."

"The PR firm you're using to promote your reunion tour with Proud River? Would they be able to help me put together some social media posts?" he asked.

"I'll ask. You know I'll do anything to help you, son."

Except it wouldn't be for his own personal benefit. There was a way for his dad to show off his new bride to the masses. It would also show off Georgina's skills as a wedding planner. Maybe she'd cut the list down from one hundred plus to around twenty or thirty, but the whole world should know about her skills in planning a celebrity wedding—one that was perfect for *this* couple.

"I'll need a copy of the final plan that Georgina sent you as well. I may add a little surprise in there for you, after all."

If it wasn't too late. And if the Proud River band members could attend.

He also thought of a surprise for Georgina, albeit a good one, if he could manage to pull it off.

It could backfire royally, but he had nothing left to lose. Because he'd already lost her.

And if it worked, he just might be able to win her back.

The table of young people were still staring at them from across the patio, except three of them had stood and were headed over. And they didn't seem to be looking at Sundance.

Dylan figured it was a matter of time before someone recognized his father.

"Excuse me," one of the young women said to him. "Are you Dylan James?"

Had he heard that correctly?

A simple yes threatened to logjam in the back of his throat at the twist of being recognized. He looked down to best friend's big brown eyes and goofy grin for support. And Sundance delivered.

Dylan took a deep breath and looked up again. "Yes, I am."

"Can I have your autograph?"

Dylan tried to remain calm and cool as she placed a napkin and pen in front of him, and he obliged.

"There you go," he said, handing the napkin and pen back to her.

"Thanks so much. Is that Sundance?"

"Sure is. And that gentleman over there is my dad."

Monty offered a single nod but otherwise didn't say a word.

Two of the young women reached down to pet the pup.

Once they'd walked away, he looked at his dad, who was now beaming. Hopefully, with pride.

"My son. The famous rodeo announcer," Monty said.

"Not quite, but I'm working on it."

Monty shook his head. "No, sir. Once someone recognizes you in public, you've arrived. And you earned it all by yourself. I couldn't be prouder. Your mother would be too."

Unexpected tears threatened to fill his eyes. He needed to hear that, more than his father would ever realize.

"You know, I was thinking. I'd like to do something extra special for you and Georgina, to pay you back for all the hard work you did on the wedding," Monty said.

"You don't have to do anything for us. We were both happy to help."

"Oh, you know me better than that."

He certainly did. No favor went unreciprocated. But that gave Dylan an idea.

"Actually…there is something you could do. It would be for both of us. Help me plan a birthday party for Georgina. She's never had one," Dylan said.

The look of confusion on his dad's face was priceless.

"She looks young, but maybe not *that* young. I was thinking late twenties or early thirties," Monty said, then let out a snort.

Dylan had to laugh. "She was born on Christmas Day, and her birthday was never made special."

"Well, we can't have that! We'll come up with something extra nice for her. Go fetch your suitcase and stay with me at the Drover tonight. We'll talk about it."

That, of course, would be the logical thing to do. However…

"I have a more special place in mind. One with a slide," Dylan said.

It took Monty a minute, but he finally understood. What better place for them to hang out but in the type where his family had made the best memories?

"I love that idea, Dylan James," Monty said. "Let's go buy us some swimsuits."

# CHAPTER SIXTEEN

HOT COFFEE IN HAND, Georgina stepped out on the patio in her fuzzy slippers and flannel nightgown and bathrobe and looked out across the white blanket of snow. The Christmas lights strung along the roof cast interesting shadows as some of them flickered and danced before the sun began to erase them.

She'd awakened before dawn, and without the help of her alarm, even though she could have slept in. The B and B was empty, for the moment. No big breakfast to cook for guests. Becca, Cody, Max and Rose were all still asleep.

Christmas Eve mornings had never felt this calm and peaceful.

Maybe it was because today—and tomorrow—wouldn't be about what she was missing personally. She'd gotten her hopes up that something special and "just for her" would happen every Christmas growing up. Even if it could have been nothing more than a few hours she didn't have to share with the holiday.

This year, something even better was happening. Rose and Monty's rehearsal dinner tonight was already perfect, since she'd arranged it to be in the place the two had met. That was the part of her plan Monty seemed to like the best.

Usually, she'd be under a little stress to make sure everything was in place for that. But there wasn't even any need for a rehearsal, it being such a small, informal gathering. The dinner tonight was more of a formality and tradition, although she was having some decorations delivered for it anyway. But the waitstaff at the restaurant would be setting those up.

Georgina did have something to be very nervous about, however. She had yet to talk to Dylan since he'd left for Fort Worth. He'd be there tonight and probably wasn't going to be happy that he wasn't consulted over the change of date and venue. In fact, she thought it was a little odd that he was staying so quiet about it.

She'd sent out the invitations, including one for him. She'd also given Monty a copy of the wedding specifics, in case there was anything he wanted to change. But apparently there hadn't been.

It was getting too late to make changes anyway, even for a professional juggler like herself. She'd felt a little guilty about ruining the surprise for Monty. That was her only regret.

Georgina wandered back inside and stoked

the wood in the fireplace. Hopefully, the parlor would be nice and warm for the Sayers by the time they awoke. Once they did, she'd be there to cook their respective favorite breakfasts and pamper all of them. And make a special breakfast for herself, while she was at it.

Then, she'd simply enjoy the day and finally relax by watching Max shake the new packages that had mysteriously appeared overnight and seeing Becca absolutely glow in her final days of pregnancy.

"Might as well get this over with." Georgina set her coffee down and powered up her laptop, which she'd brought downstairs. But when she opened her email, a sudden sweat covered her face and neck.

"Nooo!"

In her inbox was an email from Dylan with RSVP in the subject line. But it clearly wasn't in response to the invitation she'd sent out. At least there weren't any similar RSVPs from anyone else.

*Don't panic. Probably a weird email glitch.* With such a small list, she could always call everyone and straighten it out.

She opened the email to find a marked-up copy of the invitation she'd sent out, with a proposed new date of New Year's Day rather than Christmas Day.

In his text, he wrote:

Georgina—I checked with Robbie and Tom and Billy, and they already have plans for tomorrow. But they're free on New Year's Day to attend the wedding. And even play.

"Who?" But then she remembered the names of the Proud River band members. Guitar, bass and drums, respectively. She'd intentionally left them off the guest list since they weren't family. Monty knew they weren't invited, so what was going on?

Below, there were a few links. She was almost scared to look.

She clicked on the first one. It was the band's website. It mentioned Montgomery Legend's up-coming nuptials and instructed visitors to check back for more details and photos, along with up-coming reunion-tour specifics.

This was huge. But why?

She clicked on the second link, which was Monty's personal social media page, asking his fans to check back on New Year's Day for some exciting news, along with photos and video of his and Rose's upcoming wedding.

But it was the last line that caused her breath to hitch:

Special thanks to Georgina Goodwin and my son, rodeo announcer Dylan James. If you want to know more about him, check out his page.

Her hands trembled as the pointer hovered over the hyperlink, then clicked on it.

Dylan's headshot filled the page. She'd only thought she missed him for the past few days since he'd left. Seeing his face, his smile, those Nikko Blue Hydrangea–colored eyes looking directly into hers from the screen, took her back to their first introduction.

And to the last goodbye.

But it was what he'd written that made her feel as though he was holding her heart in his hands at the moment.

Plans are still being finalized for my father's marriage to the lovely Rose Haring, in a private ceremony that is scheduled for New Year's Day.

You'll want to check back for details, along with photos and video of this very special and heartfelt event.

And if anyone is looking for a wedding planner, Georgina Goodwin is your gal. My dad would second that. Message me with inquiries.

Georgina wasn't sure what exactly he was trying to accomplish with all this, but one thing was for certain: She wasn't going to let him out himself any more than he already had. Nor was she going to let him miss the rodeo in Fort Worth or his dad's wedding. Those things were too important.

She ran upstairs and retrieved her cell phone, then called Dylan. This couldn't wait until tonight to discuss. But it went straight to voicemail.

"Call me. ASAP," she said.

*What a mess!*

Anxiety began to course through her entire being as she thought of so many loose threads. Did the family members they'd invited know about this possible change? His email to her looked as though he was seeking her permission, but who knew? And what about the flowers that were supposed to be delivered late today—not only the bouquet but those she'd ordered to decorate Hailey's barn for the wedding that was supposed to take place tomorrow? Had those been canceled or rescheduled for delivery? The florist really needed to know. The guests needed to know.

She needed to know. And if nothing had been officially changed, she needed to make sure it didn't happen.

It also begged the question: Had Hailey been consulted about this? Her barn was the site of the wedding, after all. And if so, why was Georgina left out of it?

*Grrrrr.* The anxiety was being replaced by full-on stress.

Next call, her sister. But she got the same thing. Voicemail.

At least her sister's house was nearby. If Hailey wasn't answering the phone, she'd have to answer the door. And if she didn't do that, Georgina would use the key she'd been given in case of an emergency. This certainly qualified as one.

Without so much as changing into regular clothes, Georgina slipped on her cold-weather boots, bundled up and headed to Sunrise Stables.

The sun had indeed risen, at least partially, within the several minutes it took to warm up the truck and drive over there. It was light enough for Georgina to see her brother-in-law, Parker, going in and out of the barn.

She climbed out of the truck and walked over to him.

"I hope you're getting the barn ready for the wedding tomorrow," she said, looking for some confirmation that the actual ceremony had not been canceled.

Parker gave her a hug, which calmed her a little.

"Hailey asked me to bring out a few extra chairs. Can't say why," he said.

Dylan's email did indicate the bandmates would be at the wedding. *The one on New Year's Day.* That would explain the chairs, except they weren't needed this soon. It was also a good idea to have extras on hand, in case someone brought a guest who wasn't invited.

"So Hailey didn't give you any indication as to why? Not even a hint?" Georgina asked.

"Oh, she told me everything. She also told me that I can't say why. At least not to you." He laughed a little at his own joke.

"This isn't funny." Georgina huffed, turned away and headed to the house. Fortunately, Hailey and Parker had yet to get any blinds on their side-door window, and she could see her little sister in the kitchen. Probably burning something for breakfast.

Georgina didn't even bother knocking. She let herself in and fast-walked toward her little sis.

Hailey's eyes widened.

"Don't even try to run away. I'm pumped up on adrenaline right now, and even though you're faster and younger and skinnier, you will *not* get away until you tell me what's going on."

"Sounds like someone needs some hot chocolate," Hailey said.

"Someone needs some answers. And I'm not leaving until I get them." Georgina walked over to the sofa and plopped down.

Hailey simply smiled and poured some warmed-up milk into a couple of mugs, then stirred in some chocolate powder and topped them off with a mountain of marshmallows.

She brought them over, and Georgina reluctantly accepted one.

"Please tell me you made this for your husband instead, and now he won't get any. Parker laughed and wouldn't tell me anything."

Hailey took a seat in the nearby recliner. "And you think I will?"

Georgina shook her head and took a long sip while collecting her thoughts. No doubt Dylan put her up to this.

Hailey's kitchen skills had obviously improved since she got married, because the hot chocolate wasn't half bad. She was practicing in anticipation of an adopted child, and this small home—their grandparents' old house, which Hailey inherited—was perfect for raising a little boy or girl. Cozy.

"I suppose you won't, but do you mind giving me a hint? This is ruining what was promising to be a joyous Christmas Eve."

Hailey furrowed her brows. "Who are you, and what have you done with my sister who hates Christmas and everything that goes with it?"

"Consider this a blip. I'm already turning back into Ebenezer Scrooge."

"Okay. I'll give you a hint. You won't go back to being Scrooge. I promise. Even though you're dressed like him. Pretty sure he had a flannel nightgown too."

"Very funny. But what about the—"

"Dylan has taken care of everything. You'll see him tonight. It will all work out."

Relinquishing all control, with no access to details, was torture for a planner.

"I'll give it a good-faith effort," she said, then released a long exhale that negated it.

"That's all we can ask."

"But what Dylan doesn't understand is how much juggling needs to be done. How one change will unthread the whole plan," Georgina said.

"Would that be the end of the world?"

"No. But he's already put my name out there on his and Monty's social media as the wedding planner. It might not be the end of the world, but it could end my career. For good, this time."

"Try to calm down. You're worrying over nothing. I have a feeling it will all work out. In more ways than one."

"I suppose you're right. It's not like everyone will have a copy of what I'd intended the wedding to be. Good photography and strategic angles can mask a lot of flaws."

"You're right about that too. But I wasn't talking about the wedding."

"If you're talking about it working out between Dylan and myself, I can assure you that our future has been discussed and settled."

"Yeah. Just like the wedding plans have been

settled," Hailey said, trying to mask a smile behind a long sip of hot chocolate.

Which, of course, they clearly hadn't been.

All of a sudden, the wedding issue seemed small. Her sister had talked her down from that particular ledge. Everything would be fine, one way or another.

Yet Hailey had suggested an even higher ledge directly in front of her.

"RAISE THE LEFT CORNER, just a pinch," Rose said, pointing to Dylan's side of the *Happy Birthday* banner.

In his humble opinion, the right side—which Monty was holding in position until his wife-to-be gave her approval—needed to come down a little instead. They were getting awfully close to the ceiling.

Dylan wasn't about to argue. Rose and Monty were doing him a huge favor by sacrificing their rehearsal dinner tonight to help him do something very special for a super special woman.

One whom he hoped would forgive him for changing the wedding to her originally preferred date of January 1 and expanding the guest list, albeit not as much as she might want.

"Better?" Dylan asked.

"Perfect," Rose said.

Good, because the clock was ticking. He wanted

all the guests to be hiding and for their private party room at the back of Ribeye Roy's to be dark when Georgina arrived. Not that she wasn't going to be surprised anyway. But he wanted to pull out as many stops as possible to make this a birthday to remember.

Dylan finished tacking the banner to his side of the wall. He stepped down from the chair and surveyed the sign, which was framed by ethereal pink-and-silver balloons. Below the banner, gifts were stacked on a folding table.

A local florist had managed to round up enough pale pink roses for a nice centerpiece. The long table should be just the right size for a total group of fourteen. He would've invited the whole world if he could have.

Maybe next year, if everything went as planned. And on her actual birthday.

He silently counted eleven folks so far, which meant everyone was there except Vern and Sylvie. And, of course, Georgina. But Vern had warned Dylan that they might be late because his back was acting up and he was "moving slow."

Vern wasn't the only one. Cody had to get Becca to the restaurant extra early and seated in a comfortable chair. The poor thing looked miserable.

Worst case, if Vern and Sylvie missed the party, he'd take over some of the birthday cupcakes to the ranch. Hailey had baked and decorated three dozen for Georgina in lieu of a cake, with the help of their oldest sister, Faye, and their mother. The latter two had driven all the way from Missoula, Montana, and were staying at Hailey and Parker's for a couple of nights.

Those guests, he suspected, would be the sweetest surprise of all for Georgina. The way she'd made her family dynamic sound, he was rather surprised when they'd agreed to drive seven-plus hours to attend a party. That in and of itself was a gift.

When he'd played Georgina's short voice message from this morning, she'd sounded none too happy. Yes, he'd pretty much hijacked the whole event, but for good reason.

He never did return her call but did text to let her know he looked forward to seeing her tonight. And to let her know that the revised invitations had been sent, on which she'd been CC'd anyway, and the appropriate vendors had been notified. No doubt he overlooked some details and there might be a mess or two to clean up.

As of now, there had been no response.

Hailey rushed to his side, a look of panicked excitement on her face. "Georgina just texted. She's almost here. She was supposed to let me know when she was leaving the house."

"Hey, everyone! Take a seat now," Dylan called out.

The guests all scrambled for a chair at the table.

Once everyone was in place, he turned off the lights and felt around until he found the empty seat.

Lots of hushed chatter and giggles ensued. Without being able to see everyone, he was struck by the thrill of it all because it had the innocent excitement of a child's birthday party. He also realized that he'd missed out on the very same thing in his youth. Only in a different way than Georgina.

The doorknob finally twisted, and the room turned deathly quiet.

Georgina cracked the door open and talked to herself. "Huh. This is weird. Did I book the wrong room?"

Someone tried to mask a snort. Becca, perhaps? That made Georgina's silhouette freeze against the hallway backdrop. Max giggled. Up until that moment, he'd blended into the child-like atmosphere.

"What is going *on*?" Georgina said a little louder herself as she felt around the inside of the door frame for the light switch and finally located it.

"Surprise!" everyone called out in unison as brightness flooded the room.

Whatever Georgina had been holding fell to the floor, along with her jaw.

The first to rush in to greet her were her mother

and sister Faye, which only seemed to confuse Georgina even more. In a good way, judging by the smile that followed.

They ushered her fully inside, but she stopped cold in front of the banner and balloons and stared. Dylan swooped around behind her and picked up what she'd dropped—a wrapped package that must've been for Rose and Monty.

From that point, he remained in the background and watched her mix and mingle. All attention was lavished on her. *As it should be.* But her eyes kept finding his as if searching for an explanation.

There was plenty to explain.

Hopefully, this surprise birthday party would make up for some of the grief he'd caused her. And she needn't worry about the wedding decorations that she'd ordered for the rehearsal dinner. The staff at Ribeye Roy's had been poised to get everything in place. But after being let in on Dylan's plan, they kindly agreed to store the items in a utility room for a while.

Convenient, because his own revised wedding plan included returning to the restaurant on New Year's Eve for a proper rehearsal dinner anyway, followed by the wedding on New Year's Day at Hailey's.

He'd sent the Fort Worth Rodeo a generous donation and recommended another up-and-coming announcer to fill his spot. As important as it was, he realized that gigs like those would come around again.

A chance at love with Georgina, however, might not.

After the birthday girl finished her socializing, she made her way over to him.

"Monty tells me you planned this whole thing," she said.

"Not true. He and I planned it together, and it's a gift from both of us, and from Rose. They wanted this to be about you and not about them as much as I did. But Monty turned the reins over to me for final decisions. Not sure I made all the right ones, but I made a very wrong decision before I left. And I'm trying to offer whatever bribe I can to make it right."

Georgina smiled at the joke, then visibly gulped. "This is certainly an interesting way to go about it. A beautiful one. If you ever get tired of rodeo announcing, you should consider birthday-party planning."

He was pretty sure that wasn't going to happen, although there had already been a priority shift within him.

As if sensing that, she quickly inhaled and grabbed his arm. "You changed their wedding to New Year's Day. You're going to miss the whole thing. I see you sent out the revised invitations before I could stop you. And I would have. But it's not too late to change it back to tomorrow. The guests are already here, and we can probably still get the flowers but—"

"I'm not going to miss anything. The wedding plans are final," he interrupted.

She pushed her shoulders back. "No, sir. You can't miss the rodeo. Monty and Rose would not want that. Neither would I."

"Better to miss the rodeo than to miss being with you New Year's Day. And I don't want to miss the wedding either," he said.

"But what about your mom? The charity?"

"She'd want whatever Dad wants. And he wants to have it on New Year's Day. Christmas had been our family's special day. He wants another holiday to be his and Rose's. He didn't say anything before, because he didn't want me to miss the rodeo either."

Spending time with his dad in that roadside motel with the slide made Dylan realize that being at the rodeo wasn't the same as having her back. Now was the time for him to be present for his dad and with his dad. Before such opportunities were gone forever.

Same went for a future with Georgina.

"And he probably wants to spend Christmas with you," she said.

"He wants whatever I want. We had a long talk

in Fort Worth. And I told him that I want to spend tomorrow with the woman I love. To see if we can find a way to have a future together, because I'd rather be in a crowded room full of people with you than be alone. Maybe there is even something in between."

She stared at him as if she didn't quite understand.

He had to admit it was a lot to wrap a mind around. He'd gone over the logistics in his head a dozen times to map out a workable plan and to make sure they were together on Christmas and New Year's.

"Wait. Did you say you love me?" she asked.

"I was hoping you already knew. But I didn't want there to be any confusion."

The unrelated chatter and excitement in the room faded into the background, and it felt as though the two of them were in their own cozy little cocoon but with him now wondering if she'd choose to stay a while. Or would she fly away?

He couldn't read her expression. When Georgina opened her mouth to speak, nothing came out.

In its place, however, was something else. A shriek. "My water broke!"

Dylan had hoped that nothing would upstage everything he had planned for tonight. But it had. Time to cut the party short.

And get Becca to the hospital.

# CHAPTER SEVENTEEN

"IS IT REALLY YOU?" Georgina asked.

Because if she was only dreaming that Santa was right there in front of her, placing gifts beneath the Christmas tree at the B and B, then her birthday party at Ribeye Roy's wasn't real either. And she wanted it to be.

More than anything.

Santa obviously hadn't heard her come in. At first, he froze when she spoke, then slowly turned around to face her.

"No way," Georgina said. "Becca was sure it was you, and I finally convinced her it couldn't be."

Vern shrugged. "Guess you caught me, but you weren't supposed to. There's something very special happening at Ribeye Roy's as we speak."

"*Was* happening."

"Well, that was quick. Sylvie is headed over there now. She was gonna tell 'em I'd took a pain pill for my back and needed to lie down. But I was gonna show up a little later, actin' all achy and stiff, after I finished up here. Didn't want to miss the party entirely."

Georgina closed the gap between them, still suspicious that somehow her eyes were deceiving her. She poked his belly. Yep. He was real.

"Hey! That smarts," Vern said, placing both hands on his stomach.

"Oh, I'm sorry!"

Vern let out a cackle. "I'm messin' with ya. You didn't hurt me. I added some padding to make me look more Santa-like, get into character. More fun that way."

"Good. I had to make sure. You'll need to call Sylvie, because there was an unexpected development."

"Something good, I hope," Vern said.

A few somethings. Dylan had told her he loved her. Also, he threw her a surprise birthday party, which proved that he did. For someone who wasn't impulsive, he was sure coming up with doozies.

Then there was the main event.

"Becca's water broke. Everyone is headed to the hospital."

Vern's expression lit up brighter than the lights on the tree behind him. Then his obvious delight morphed into something more quizzical.

"Then why are you here?" he asked.

"I volunteered to swing by and pick up their

go bags. Cody and Max need to be by her side right now."

"Where's Dylan?"

"He stayed behind at the restaurant to collect the cupcakes and gifts and whatever else, and settle the tab. We'll both catch up with everyone else at the hospital."

And with each other. When they did, she was ready to tell him that she loved him too. Yet had anything beyond that really changed between them?

"Well, then, you'd better get moving! Don't want to miss the best part," Vern said.

He was right about that. Georgina started to turn, but he touched her arm.

"Would you do me a favor, though? Pretend like you didn't see me here."

She cocked her head and squinted. "See who? I don't see anyone."

Vern smiled. "Thank you. I'd like to let Becca keep on wondering—or possibly believing—for a while. It's such a magical time, what with the baby and all."

It was her turn to pat his arm. "Of course. Your secret is safe with me."

"Then again, she's gonna find out anyway." Vern cast his eyes toward the hutch and pointed at the camera.

Georgina looked to the hutch as well. It had

certainly captured not only his face but hers. She reached into her handbag, pulled out a cell phone and held it up.

"In the excitement of everything, I grabbed Becca's phone from the table and put it in my purse. Guess who she entrusted with her password?"

Vern gave her a knowing grin and wagged his finger.

Georgina logged in, located the app and footage, deleted the clip and disabled the camera.

"The problem, as they say, has been solved." She slipped the phone back into her purse for safekeeping.

Even though she was relieved to have solved the mystery, she felt a certain sadness in knowing. This Christmas had ended up being more magical than any she could remember from her childhood. Believing in Santa again, if only in jest, was a big reason for it. As much as she'd originally wanted Becca to share her enthusiasm, there was no way she'd spoil that for her now.

"Oh! You still need an alibi, because they'll notice the packages," she continued. "While I'm collecting Becca and Cody's things, how about you lose the Santa suit. Assuming you're wearing something underneath."

Vern cackled. "Oh, no worries there!"

"Good! We'll go to the hospital together. I'll

tell everyone I dropped by your house to check on you and that you were feeling much better."

"Always the planner," he said.

At that, Georgina wandered down the hall to the primary suite, where she located both go bags and made sure nothing was missing in either, and that a few items for Max's care were included.

While there, she straightened and fluffed the pillows and blankets and folded down the corner of the bedspread, creating an envelope that Becca could just slip right into when she got home.

Cody had set up a crib in the corner of the room since she'd last been in it. He'd brought in a rocking chair at some point and positioned it nearby. A giant teddy bear was currently keeping the seat warm, and a fuzzy folded blanket was draped over the chair's arm. There was a smaller chair next to it. Probably for big-brother Max.

*I want this too.*

Georgina went across the hall to Max's room, where Penny and Sundance were temporarily holed up. She took them outside, one at a time, through a side door, then refilled their water and food bowls.

By the time she returned to the parlor, Vern had changed back into the loveable rancher she knew and was waiting for her in the foyer.

She set the go bags down, then went around

and turned off all the lights in the parlor except for the tree.

It really was beautiful. She remembered something now, how she and Hailey and Faye used to help their dad flock their Christmas tree in the garage. She could even remember the woodsy smell of the Douglas fir and how the white powdery spray-on mixture looked like snow that had settled onto its branches. Thinking back, the tree was at its prettiest before all the ornaments and tinsel and lights were added. And even before Santa put all the gifts around its skirt.

Or, perhaps, Santa's helper. Which reminded her...

"Who else delivered packages here? The nanny cam showed a quite slender woman at one point. We figured it was Mrs. Claus," she said to Vern, who was still waiting rather impatiently by the door.

"I was afraid you might ask that," he said.

"And?"

Vern shifted from one foot to the other while staring at the floor.

"My wife helped me," he said, finally looking back up.

Georgina blinked. She couldn't have heard that correctly. *Wife?* The man was engaged to Sylvie.

"Do you mean...ex-wife? Or future wife?" Georgina asked.

"Nope. I mean my current wife. Sylvie and I got married."

All of a sudden, she felt a little dizzy. This was too confusing, especially when paired with everything else that had happened within a very short period of time. She would not have forgotten something as important as this.

"When did this happen, and why wasn't I invited?" she asked.

"Sylvie and I eloped a couple of months ago. Or, as Max would say, 'loped.' Before the cold weather moved in. We decided to take the old trail ride that starts at Sunrise Stables. Since Sylvie leads some of the rides, she booked just the two of us on an overnight excursion, and Hailey wasn't the least bit suspicious."

That would have been Georgina's next question: Why hadn't her little sister told her?

"We followed one of the trails to the nearest justice of the peace, just like your grandparents had been rumored to do," Vern continued. "We camped overnight afterward, and it was the perfect honeymoon. Just the love of my life, the fresh Wyoming air and the stars above. Sylvie's been living with me, her husband, ever since. We've just kept it quiet."

Georgina was at a loss for words. So romantic yet unexpected. But it had been a night of surprises.

She walked over and gave Vern a big hug. "Congratulations."

"Thank you," he said. "She wanted a Valentine's Day wedding at first, then decided a summer wedding would be better, but I didn't want to wait that long. So we decided we'll do both. I promised to give her the wedding of her dreams. I've been meaning to ask if I could hire you to help plan it, but you've been so busy."

Georgina's heart kicked up a notch. If only he knew what an honor that would be for her. Not to mention fun. Her head was already brimming with ideas, but there were a million questions she needed to have answered first.

"I love that compromise! And I'd love to help. Let's talk about it on the way to the hospital," she said.

Vern started to open the door, but she said, "Hold it right there. Don't move."

He did as told and froze in place.

She retrieved the go bags that she'd set down, then leaned in and gave the B and B's Secret Santa a kiss on the cheek.

"What was that for?" he asked.

Georgina pointed skyward, to the mistletoe he was standing directly beneath. She totally believed in its powers now.

She was beginning to believe in a lot of things.

DYLAN WAS TRYING not to panic. Rose was doing enough of that for everyone.

So much so, Becca herself asked her own mother to sit in the waiting room for a while.

At least Becca was remaining calm and keeping comfortable in a private room with Cody and Max by her side. The doctor had already come out to let everyone know that since her water broke before she had any contractions, it could take up to twenty-four hours for labor to begin. *Pre-labor rupture of membranes* was what he called it. Since she ruptured at term, the risk of complications was reduced.

With that semi-comforting knowledge, the other guests who had joined the caravan to the hospital had extended their best wishes and returned to their own homes.

Georgina still wasn't back from the B and B. He needed her here, but Rose and Monty seemed to need her more. At least, from what he could overhear.

"What do you think we should do? Becca is set on making this happen for us," Rose asked Monty.

"She gets her stubbornness from her mom."

"Montgomery Legend!" Rose said, giving him a playful nudge. "I knew I shouldn't have told her we *had* to be married before the baby was born."

"But it was the truth. Maybe not *had* to be, but

it sure feels like it," Monty said, pulling her in and holding her tight.

"Yes. But that was before this happened."

"Maybe we should let her do this for us, for me, because I'd rather not wait much longer."

Dylan didn't want to pry, but he was feeling completely useless and out of the loop. He got up from his chair and moved to a closer one.

"Is everything okay?" Dylan asked.

Monty nodded. "Oh, yes. I think we're all a little on edge—that's all. Any idea when Georgina will be back? She might be able to reason with Becca."

"We should have eloped," Rose said.

Dylan couldn't say he was exactly following the train of thought, but it obviously had something to do with Rose and Monty's wedding. He did remember "getting married before the baby arrived" as being the only stipulation they had for Georgina and him because Rose and Monty both wanted to focus on the newest addition to the family and on helping Becca instead of their own wedding plans. That was why they had such a small planning window to begin with. It sure wasn't going to happen now.

He pulled out his phone and tried to call Georgina. No answer, so he left a message. If she didn't show up or call soon, he was going to get into his truck and head over there. Make sure nothing was wrong, because they didn't need any more drama tonight.

Cody and Max finally emerged from Becca's room.

"Becca needs to talk to Georgina. ASAP."

*Take a number.*

"She isn't back from the B and B yet. I was thinking of driving over there. See if everything's okay," Dylan said.

Cody shook his head. "Nope. Becca said that if Georgina wasn't here, you would do. And I'm not about to argue with her right now. Whatever she asks of you, just find a way to do it. I don't want anything upsetting her. I'll run over to the B and B if Georgina doesn't show up in the next ten minutes."

Dylan wanted to say it sounded as if Cody was getting the better end of the deal. But when he entered Becca's room, she gave him the sweetest, reassuring smile.

He sat in a chair that had been pulled close to the bed. "How are you feeling?" he asked.

"Surprisingly good, for now. Also excited. Terrified."

He reached over and squeezed her hand. "I've got you, sister."

She squeezed back.

"Good, because there's something we need to do. I was thinking only Georgina could help, but then I realized that you were here. And you have experience."

He gulped. Cody's admonishment was still fresh on his mind about doing whatever Becca said. Except he'd never so much as been near a delivery room or maternity ward. Pretty sure there wasn't anything he could be trusted to do here.

"Don't look so scared!" Becca said, adding a soft laugh. "It's no big deal. I just need for you to plan a wedding. Here, in the hospital, as soon as possible. For Monty and Rose. I promised they'd get their wedding before the baby was born, and I'm going to deliver."

"Yes, you are, which is why you shouldn't even be thinking about this."

Becca rolled her eyes. "You know what I meant. They're already insisting on staying at the B and B to help for however long I need it. I want them there as husband and wife. It would make them both so happy—I just know it."

"Let's reschedule the wedding after we get through this very important moment. They'll be fine with that. *I* just know it." Although he wasn't so sure. Not after overhearing them and seeing them together. Still, their grandbaby would more than make up for having to wait for who knew how long.

"Oh, I'll give them a beautiful ceremony too. Don't worry. A hospital wedding is a temporary fix. Besides, doing this makes me happy and distracts me from the inevitable pain I'll be going through."

Clearly, she wasn't going to budge.

"Becca, I w-wouldn't know where to begin." He got panicky just thinking about it, even though he'd pretty much re-planned the wedding on his own, already. But at least he'd had a roadmap and a little more time.

"Give yourself a little credit. I have faith in you. Just fill me in as you go. I'll try to make sure this little guy or gal doesn't try to crash the ceremony." She patted her tummy. "Get Monty for me, please, but leave Mom in the waiting room. She'll try to talk me out of this again, and I can't deal with her selflessness right now."

He stood up but paused for a little too long apparently.

"Go!" She pointed to the door so forcefully it caused him to wince.

"Yes, ma'am." With that, he walked out as fast as possible, down the hall to the waiting room.

"Monty. Your turn."

Rose started to stand as well.

"I need *you* to stay here with Cody, if you don't mind," he said to her.

Without further explanation or instruction, he headed down an opposite hallway. He needed to find a place where he could be alone to think

for a few minutes because the words were pil-
ing up in the back of his throat now. He was in
way over his head.

Then he saw a sign. Literally. It read *Chapel*.

Of course, most hospitals had one.

He eased the door open. Thankfully, it was
empty and dimly lit. The benches weren't comfortable, but he didn't plan to be here long.

Dylan closed his eyes and went through the
wedding-planning checklist he and Georgina had
roughly followed. The date was settled. *Now*. The
place as well. *County General, Becca's room*.
The theme: *Emergency*. The color theme: *Hospital white*.

Flowers. *Rose will need a bouquet*.

He exited the chapel as quietly as he came in,
then searched for another sign. This time, for the
gift shop. Turned out, it was just around the corner, and it was still open. He selected a vase filled
with a half dozen white roses and some baby's
breath and greenery. He checked out the price tag,
shook his head and whispered under his breath.
"That's what bank loans are for."

Dylan took the vase of flowers to the register.

"Any chance you can help me make a wedding
bouquet out of these?" he asked.

The older woman cocked her head and seemed
to give it some thought, as if the question wasn't

as strange as it had sounded coming out of his mouth.

"I could take 'em out of the vase and dry off the stems, then wrap some ribbon around to hold them together."

"That'll work."

"Is someone getting married?" she asked as she patted the stems dry using a paper towel.

"If I can pull together a wedding in a big hurry," he answered.

"That seems to be the only way it happens around here. This is the second one tonight."

She finished tidying up the bouquet. It didn't look half bad.

"Need anything else? Rings? Folks always need those. I have a collection of toy ones over here. They're even adjustable."

She pointed to a box that was resting on a ledge.

He walked over and rummaged through them. Found a black one for Monty and a pearly-looking one for Rose. Even though the whole thing would horrify a professional like Georgina, he was actually having a little fun with it.

"I'll take these two. Got any officiants in stock?" It had just occurred to him that they would need one. Georgina had handled that aspect completely, so he wasn't even sure where to begin.

"No, but you can go up to the second floor. That's where the other wedding is taking place.

You better hurry, though, because I'd bet they're finishing up."

He paid for the rings and flowers with cash and left a generous tip, then sprinted upstairs, not bothering to wait for the elevator. Once there, he wished he would've left a bigger tip, because luck was on his side tonight. He correctly identified the officiant leaving one of the rooms. And it only took an offer to pay her double to perform one more ceremony before she left.

Okay, perhaps the fact that Montgomery Legend was the groom might have influenced her decision just a little. Even though he vowed not to drop his father's name ever again, this was an emergency.

By the time they got to the maternity-ward waiting room, Georgina had arrived. And she had brought Vern along.

Dylan had never been happier to see anyone. He gave her a huge hug and didn't want to let her go. "I was worried about you. What took so long?"

"I'll have to fill you in later," she said, then pulled away. "Are those for me?"

*The bouquet.* He'd forgotten he was holding it.

"They're for Rose." He reached into his pocket and pulled out the two rings. "She and Dad are getting married as soon as I can pull everything together."

Georgina blinked and shook her head. "What do you mean?"

"Becca asked me to plan a wedding for, well, right now."

She looked at the officiant, then back at him. "And you didn't consult me?" she asked.

"No, ma'am. I wanted to, but you weren't here."

Georgina smiled. "It's a good thing you didn't, because you have great instincts. I'm proud of you for handling this. I know how much it's going to mean to them."

"Hopefully I had the right instincts earlier tonight as well," he said. "I think you were about to say something, but we got interrupted."

Cody tapped Dylan on the shoulder, interrupting them once again. "Any luck?"

"In more ways than you can imagine. The officiant is standing by, over there. Here's the bouquet for Rose, if you don't mind handing it to her on your way back to Becca's room," he said, officially delegating that particular duty to Cody.

"Max," Dylan called out. The little boy looked up from a toy station that the hospital had set up to keep the youngsters busy and ran their way.

"How would you like to be a ring bearer?" Dylan produced the rings and handed them to Max. "These are for Rose and Monty. They're about to get married."

"Here?"

"Yep. In your mommy's hospital room."

"Cool!" Max said as he tried to get two of his little fingers into the larger black ring, while letting the pearly one dangle from his thumb.

"How about you take the officiant to your mommy's room and ask your grandma and Monty and Vern to join you. Georgina and I will be there in a second."

Max did surprisingly well in rounding up the adults and herding them into the room.

"Now, where were we?" he asked Georgina.

"I've been thinking about what you said about loving me."

"Too soon?" he asked. For him, it didn't feel soon enough. But only if she felt the same way.

She shook her head. "Not too soon. But we still have a lot to talk about."

They sure did. But at least there looked to be some solid footing.

"There's something I need to tell you first," she continued.

"Good or bad?"

"Depends on what you do with the information," she said and smiled up at him. She looked deep into his eyes. "I love you too."

Oh, that was definitely good.

No...

*Great.*

# CHAPTER EIGHTEEN

"Merry Christmas," Georgina said.

"Happy Birthday," Dylan countered.

His words could have melted her, right then and there. Sure, he looked so handsome in his jeans and soft red-and-black plaid flannel shirt, with freshly washed hair and clean-shaven skin. But that was the first time in her life that someone had put her birthday above Christmas, even though she'd since come to understand why the holiday was so special.

In fact, on the way back home from the hospital last night after Rose and Monty's nuptials, she took a detour to look at some of the ranch decorations around Destiny Springs. And to give herself time to think, because everything looked so different now.

That was because everything *was* different. Including her. She had simply refused to see it.

It put her quite late getting home. But she'd let Dylan know of her plans in advance and told him not to worry.

"Looks like someone else didn't want to sleep in this morning. Or couldn't," she said as she poured him a cup of fresh coffee.

"I had a little trouble falling asleep. I guess I needed to know you made it back safely, so I waited until I heard the door open and shut."

"How did you know it was me and not Santa?"

"I didn't. But I did notice extra packages under the tree when I got back. So I figured he'd already made his rounds."

"Ah! Good thinking. Have you thought about what you'd like for breakfast? I'll whip something up, or we could head on over to the hospital and eat there. Rose texted. It sounds like Becca probably still has a few hours to go. May happen faster than expected."

He scrunched his nose. She matched the gesture. Together, they gave the idea of hospital cafeteria food two thumbs down.

"How about you have a seat, and I'll make breakfast? It's your birthday, after all. What would you like?" Dylan stood before she had a chance to refuse. He pointed at the barstool he'd abandoned, and she took a seat.

Truth be told, she liked that he'd offered. In fact, she could get used to this.

"Surprise me," she said.

It was just the two of them in the B and B last night and again this morning. Although her favorite part of this job was having a house full of strangers to meet and mingle with, she was rather glad Becca and Cody had closed for Christmas. And this morning, with just the two of them? She wouldn't want it any other way.

Georgina watched as he scoured the kitchen for the ingredients of whatever it was he'd decided to make, then located all the cookware required. Based on what she saw, they would be enjoying pancakes.

By the time she'd returned last night, Dylan was already tucked away in the Denim Room. But he'd stoked the fire so that the house would still be warm, once again spoiling her.

Discovering the real Destiny Springs Secret Santa last night was another lovely surprise in a day full of surprises. But she promised Vern she wouldn't tell a soul. Not even Dylan until after Christmas, although she otherwise planned to keep nothing from him.

She'd curled up in one of the overstuffed chairs upon returning last night and replayed Monty and Rose's impromptu ceremony in her mind. How the couple got married in an undecorated hospital room, with Becca cheering them on.

Becca was the one who had insisted on the ceremony for her mom. No one had the courage to tell the mommy-to-be no. Not that anyone really wanted to. Rose and Monty couldn't have looked happier, and that was what had mattered most. To everyone. And Dylan had stepped up and met the challenge for planning the thing. Quite expertly. In fact, Georgina had never experienced a more touching ceremony, stripped bare of everything she once thought was necessary and replaced by the most important and beautiful thing of all: having the nearest and dearest loved ones there to share the moment.

Made her think of Vern and Sylvie, how they eloped because he couldn't wait but insisted they have a fancy ceremony later. Everyone got their wish.

Maybe these second-marriage folks were onto something. She was pretty sure she'd never look at weddings the same again. Including the one she'd dreamed about all her life.

Dylan was probably two-thirds through with the pancakes when both of their cell phones lit up.

Georgina answered hers first.

"Becca's going into labor," Rose said.

Sounded like Dylan was having an identical exchange with Monty.

They looked at each other and nodded.

Georgina ran upstairs and threw on some regular clothes while Dylan said he'd take care of turning off the burners and putting the remaining batter in the refrigerator.

By the time they reached County General, Becca was in full-on labor.

Rose and Monty were still in their same clothes, having both stayed all night, as was little Max, who had fallen asleep on one of the sofas.

"We should plan a proper honeymoon for them," Georgina whispered. "What a way to spend your first night of marriage. Then again, what an amazing way to start." They seemed as happy as a couple could be. Even more so, if that were possible.

Dylan pulled her in and whispered, "I'll be right back."

When he returned, she didn't ask where he'd been, although he'd been gone for nearly twenty minutes. Perhaps he needed time away as much as she had last night. They were entering a new phase of their relationship, without a clear plan.

But if there was anything she'd learned, plans should always be written in pencil, because life would change them for you.

After at least an hour, Cody emerged from the room. Looked like he'd either done the actual labor or had been bull riding in nationals—and won—considering the sweat on his brow and the pride on his face.

"It's a girl," Cody announced, then leaned over, placing his hands on his knees for support. "Born eleven seventeen a.m. Alexandra

Rose Sayers. Six pounds, two ounces. Eighteen-point-four inches. Ten fingers, ten toes. And the best part? She's a Christmas baby," he managed to announce through the tears.

As much as Georgina wanted to argue that being born on Christmas was a curse rather than a bragging point, she no longer had a defense. Especially after she was allowed into the room to see the newest addition to not only the Sayers family but to the Destiny Springs one as well.

All it took was one look at those chubby little cheeks and inquisitive eyes to realize that Christmas babies were special after all.

She returned to the waiting area to allow Rose and Monty to visit some more. Dylan had been awfully quiet the whole time. Did he feel the same way she did? That now that the excitement of Alexandra's birth and the impromptu marriage of Rose and Monty had passed, they could no longer hide behind other people's lives?

"Looks like I have someone to celebrate my birthday with from now on. In fact, I'm already thinking I could make the smash cake for her first birthday. We'd also need balloons. Pink ones."

"If you need a co-planner, you'll know where to find me," Dylan said.

"Where would I find you? Sounds like something we may need to talk about. Among other things we will eventually face, as two people who love each other," she said.

There. She opened the door. They hadn't talked about how their relationship was going to look from this point on. The original obstacles hadn't been re-opened for discussion. Maybe it wasn't a romantic topic, but it was a practical one that would affect everything moving forward.

But she did know that with the way she was feeling on this miraculous Christmas morning, she'd choose popcorn and a movie in bed with Dylan over hobnobbing with the stars. Not that she wouldn't insist on going out for an occasional elbow-rubbing and to show him off. Maybe he'd been caught up in all the other excitement and mentioned he'd be open to that on a whim.

"I don't plan to go too far," he said.

"You announce at rodeos all over the country."

"I may do a few in the future. But I plan to stick around here for a while, help with some area ranch rodeos, because I want to see how things work out with a certain gal."

"Well, after witnessing the way you planned and executed that impromptu wedding, I have no reason to doubt that any of your plans will work."

"So you liked the bouquet?" he asked.

"It was lovely."

"And the officiant did a good job, even though she had to wing it?"

"I don't think Rose and Monty even noticed any mistakes. But the rings were my favorite part," she said.

He looked at her for the longest time. Did he think she was joking? She wasn't.

"I hoped you would say that. They were mine too," he said.

"Ah! Look at everything we're agreeing on already. A very good sign," she said.

Dylan reached into his pocket for something. "Hold out your hand."

He straightened her left fingers and slipped a pink, sparkly plastic ring on her ring finger and adjusted the tightness.

Georgina had never seen anything so adorable. She held it up as if it were the two-carat marquis diamond of her dreams.

"So that's where you disappeared to," she said. "You went shopping."

He nodded. "Took me a while to find the perfect one in that gift-shop box."

"What's the occasion?" She knew he wasn't one to rush in, so she didn't want to jump to any conclusions. They still had some important things to figure out, having known each other for only a few weeks. Felt like a lifetime, though.

"I propose we always work through our disagreements before we do anything else. We've already proven that we can," he said.

"I accept. But what if there are times when we can't?"

"We'll do what worked for us in the past, even though it wasn't all that easy. But nothing worth having is," he said.

She couldn't deny that yes, everything ultimately did work out. Rather beautifully. And was definitely worth having...*and holding.* Yet getting there seemed to often involve a struggle.

"What exactly did we do?" she asked.

Dylan smiled and winked.

"We let Max decide."

"I GIVE UP. What is it?" Georgina asked while examining the package from all angles.

"It's a book!" Max shouted.

Dylan cast him a *shhhh* look that even a six-year-old could understand.

Instead of being remotely intimidated, the little boy giggled. Of course, Max would be able to make an educated guess. He'd spent plenty of time shaking every package beneath the Christmas tree.

"What's the occasion? Christmas and my birthday were both three days ago. Besides, you've done more than enough for me."

"It's a 'just because' gift."

It had taken him a few days to find the perfect one, what with all the holiday upheaval. Otherwise, he had planned on giving it to her on her birthday. From this point forward, Christmas gifts would be opened on Christmas Eve and birthday gifts would be opened on Christmas Day. It was a surprisingly easy agreement to reach.

Rose and Monty were upstairs in their room and were planning to spend the afternoon with Max. Becca and Cody were still asleep in the master suite down the hall with baby Alexandra. All of them were taking a well-earned, much-needed nap. Meanwhile, Max was overflowing with energy and needed a source of entertainment.

Enter Dylan and Georgina.

Sundance and Penny were of zero help as babysitters. The two canines had settled on the cool marble tile in the foyer, beneath the mistletoe, and fallen asleep, limbs intertwined.

Yet another reason why he could see himself staying in Destiny Springs indefinitely. He wouldn't want to tear his "child" away from the love and happiness he'd obviously found with a labradoodle.

Not that he needed a better reason than Georgina herself for him to stay here.

They still had some planning and negotiating to do before rushing into anything. Hopefully, the gift she was finally opening would help them each step of the way.

Instead of ripping through the paper as he or Max would have done, she unwrapped it delicately, trying not to tear the corners in the process.

"A new year planner. And it's pink!" Georgina scooted across the sofa and gave him a kiss on the cheek. "You know me too well. It's perfect. Thank you!"

He returned this kiss, except on her lips— which was where his belonged, in his opinion.

Max giggled, which caused an immediate divide and retreat to opposite sides of the couch.

"I figured a new start to a new year deserved a new planner," he said.

She flipped through the pages and paused mid-January.

"Oh, no! This book has been used. Someone wrote in it already," she said, casting him an exaggerated frown.

"It was me. I penciled in my announcing gigs." From now on, that was his rule. Personal life in ink, career in pencil.

"This one says *Ranch Rodeo, Cheyenne.*"

"Yep. It'll be a day trip, and I'm hoping you will go with me."

She flipped through some more.

"Here's another one. *Ranch Rodeo, Gillette.*

You were serious about focusing on ranch rodeos."

*And on us.*

"The rodeo that I did at the county fairgrounds worked its way into my heart."

That place also broke it. But only because it was a reminder of one of the biggest mistakes of his life: walking away from the woman he loved. Someday he'd go back there, hold another ranch rodeo or two for charity—maybe even for ovarian cancer research—and finally heal. After all, he ended up getting the girl. He just never wanted to lose her again, and that place was a reminder that it was possible.

She reached over and squeezed his hand as if she felt it also.

"I have two more tentative ones later in the year. All in the Wyoming area." Even talking about it got his adrenaline flowing.

She cocked her head and smiled. "That's wonderful for me that you're staying so close, but what about for you? I still wish you wouldn't have backed out of Fort Worth."

"Had to. There was supposed to be a wedding that day."

"Only because you went behind my back and changed the date without telling me."

"I wanted to surprise you," he said.

"That's an understatement. At least Rose and

Monty don't want another ceremony, so we don't have to disagree on a date all over again," she said, offering up an adorable smile that didn't even hint at the disappointment she must have felt. He'd seemed more upset than she was about having to modify the social media announcements.

"They let Becca get her way, and they decided a wedding couldn't get any better than that," he said. "But we can do much bigger and better. If we get to that place in our relationship. Make that *when* we get there."

"I love your optimism, but are you sure? I know how you feel about weddings. How nervous they make grooms. Yes, I really was listening."

He scooted over, closing the distance between them. "I'm not nervous anymore. It's amazing how that can change when you're with the right person."

"You're right. It can change. I'm the nervous one now," she said.

He leaned back. "Why?"

"I'm just afraid the planning process could tear us apart."

"Don't be. It's already planned, and we both have approved it."

"Okay, you've totally lost me now."

"The first one you put together for Dad and

Rose? The one you showed me? It's too beautiful to go to waste. It would be perfect for us."

Georgina shook her head. "No, sir. We both may want to make some changes."

"Fair enough. But I say let's go ahead and get it over with. Plan in advance and pick a date later. That way if it tears us apart, at least we won't have wasted each other's time."

Georgina's jaw dropped. "That's an awful thing to say."

Dylan smiled and bit his lip. No way was he going to let that happen. In fact, his plan was failproof. He just needed for her to take the bait.

Georgina squinted and shook her head. "You make a very strange point, but it kinda makes sense on a practical level. And if we don't agree on something, Max will be our tiebreaker?"

"It's the best solution." Maybe not *the* best. Finding things they could truly agree on would be much better, but he'd rather disagree with Georgina than agree with anyone else.

"Don't you have the entire spreadsheet on your laptop? I still have the hard copies you printed out, if not. We can knock it out now, before Rose and Monty kidnap Max. Then, we can enjoy the rest of our day knowing we got the worst part over with."

She stood and headed toward the stairway,

shaking her head the entire way, which only made him laugh harder.

Once Georgina was past the landing and out of sight, Dylan summoned Max over.

"Okay, cowboy, how would you like to earn some free stuffed animals?"

"How do I do that?" Max asked.

"When Georgina comes back down and asks you to choose what's on the computer or what she wants, just choose what she wants. But don't say why. Just pretend you like her idea better."

"I can do that. What kind of stuffed animals?" he asked.

"Any kind you want."

"Okey dokey," Max said.

"Now, tell me again, what are you going to do?"

"I'm gonna pick whatever she wants and I'll get a new stuffed animal every time I do, but I'm not supposed to tell her that."

"Perfect." Dylan was about to have Max go through it one more time, just to be sure, but Georgina didn't waste any time retrieving her laptop and was back in a flash.

Instead of sitting next to him, she placed her computer on the coffee table and sat cross-legged on the floor with her back to the fire.

Dylan nodded for Max to sit beside her.

He should've been getting very nervous by

now, because he was about to commit himself to a royal wedding sometime in the future. But when he dared to visualize it, all he could see was Georgina walking toward him, down a long aisle. Everything else faded into the background.

"Okay! I've pulled it up, and off we go." She flashed him a smile like she was now the one who was up to something.

She leaned in closer to the screen. "I see the Elk Lodge. I'm gonna change that to…"

Dylan waited for it, but she didn't say a thing.

"To what? Buckingham Palace?"

Georgina cast a stern look. "Don't tempt me. And just for that, I think I'll let you be surprised."

"You still need Max's approval for any changes, remember?"

"Oh, yeah." She leaned over and whispered something into the little boy's ear.

"I like your idea better," Max said, perhaps a little too loudly and enthusiastically. But Georgina didn't seem to pick up on anything strange about it.

*Good cowboy.* At least, he hoped it was good.

"And yeah, the bouquet is all wrong. Two dozen roses? I don't think so."

She whispered into Max's ear, and the little boy, once again, enthusiastically picked her choice.

After inputting that revision, she scrolled

down, but barely. She was scrutinizing every single item, even though she'd seemed so confident in those choices in the first place.

"A five-tier cake, huh?" She looked to the ceiling and seemed to be doing some calculations in her head. "That size serves only about two hundred…"

*Only? Yikes!*

Meanwhile, he started to do some calculations of his own. How much did stuffed animals cost anyway, and was there going to be enough space in Max's bedroom for all of them?

Once again, she whispered something to Max. And once again, he agreed a little too enthusiastically with her choice. She gave Dylan a cat-who-got-the-cream smile. He simply shrugged as if it simply wasn't his lucky day. Although if this made her happy, it arguably was.

Four more revisions came and went, and only the biggest thing remained—the guest list. The troublemaker. The bane of their existence.

Not this time. There was no way she could have a problem with that. Unless she wanted to include the royal family in addition to all of Monty's contacts and half of Destiny Springs.

But he didn't dare tease about that, because he didn't want to put any ideas in her head. The whole celebrity wedding she wanted didn't happen, and he knew how important that had been to her. This plan, however, would be an even better opportunity for her to network. It was also her concept of a perfect wedding, after all. At least, he'd thought it was.

She seemed to contemplate the list, then whispered something into Max's ear again.

This time, the little boy had a question. "Can Sundance and Penny come too?"

"Of course!" she said, then looked at Dylan. "I think there will be enough room."

*Oh, boy.*

"Thanks so much for the help, Max. Just for that, I'm gonna make whatever cookies you want," Georgina said.

"I want the ones with the powder on the top this time."

"Snowball cookies it is."

"Can you make extra for all the new stuffed animals I'm gonna get?" Max asked.

Dylan held his breath, hoping she wouldn't ask him to elaborate. Max must've realized what he'd done, because he put a hand over his mouth.

But once again, Georgina didn't seem to notice anything strange. Maybe all little kids his age did the unexplainable.

"I sure will. And I'll make some extra for your mommy and daddy too. What do you think?"

Instead of answering, Max gave her a big hug, then ran down the hall. Probably to start rearranging some things to make room for the newest plush friends.

Whatever it ended up costing would be worth it.

She shut down her laptop, then stood and stretched.

"You do know you'll have to tell me the location at least," he said.

Georgina walked over and put her arms around him, and all the newfound nervousness melted away like magic.

"I'll make you a deal. If you can guess the venue, I'll tell you everything. I'll even give you a hint—it's not Buckingham Palace," she said.

"That narrows it down. Is it bigger or smaller?"

"I'm not sure. Slightly smaller, I imagine. I've only been there once."

"I didn't know you'd been to Buckingham Palace," he said.

"Not *there*, silly. The county fair—"

Georgina clapped a hand over her mouth, and his mixed feelings collided. What was she thinking?

His stomach sank. Not even remotely what he'd expected.

"Why there?" he asked.

"Because we agreed it was the perfect venue for a wedding."

That was right. They had. The reminder of what he'd lost must have completely blocked it out.

"And because I want to replace the bad memory with a good one," she continued. "In fact, that should be our new rule."

"Like, never go to sleep angry at each other?" he asked.

"Definitely. And take turns walking Sundance, because once we're married, he'll be our baby, not just yours."

"Not the only one we'll have, I hope. *When* we decide to marry."

It wasn't even something he would have been able to articulate in the past without a stutter.

"I'm thinking two. Let me crack open my new planner to figure out the logistics. I'll pencil it in," she teased as she reached for the book. "Of course, that means we'll have to pick a date for the wedding. It will be one less thing we disagree on later. But I suppose that means we'll have to disagree on it now," she said, amused at her own cleverness.

He, however, wasn't laughing.

"We wouldn't have to," he said. "We have the tiebreaker right here."

She looked up. "You're serious."

"Very. Are you?"

She visibly gulped. Then nodded.

"Max, come here, please," Dylan said.

The little boy appeared at his side, a purple stuffed bull in his arms.

"Georgina and I need you to make one more important decision for us. We want you to pick our wedding date," he said.

She looked down at the planner and handed it to Max. "Select somewhere within these months. March or later." She then returned to Dylan's arms.

He pulled her closer and held her tight. All of a sudden, fatherhood seemed too far away. As did the wedding they'd now agreed to in advance, whose day was being determined by a six-year-old boy.

"I like this one!" Max practically shouted.

He and Georgina looked at each other and smiled.

She exhaled. "Me too. Max, grab a pencil, please, and draw a big heart in the square you chose."

"Put it in ink, Max," Dylan said. "I'll be there."

*I'm not going anywhere else. Not without Georgina.*

# *EPILOGUE*

*Four months later*

GEORGINA WASN'T SURE what Dylan was expecting, but this probably wasn't it.

His initial reaction to having the wedding in the county fairgrounds arena wasn't surprising. She'd had the same feelings when first considering it. This space held a painful memory for the two of them. She'd gone to the arena that day, so excited to share the plans she had for Rose and Monty's wedding and to show Dylan that his trust hadn't been misplaced.

Instead of even lukewarm support, he'd held up a mirror. And she was forced to look. Yet in doing so, she discovered what she really wanted, which was never all the embellishments but rather what was underneath.

After seeing how the whole ranch rodeo experience here had changed him in such a positive way—how it made him truly light up over this space and these people and this town, and even inspired him to shift the direction of his entire career—she was more determined than ever to reclaim that happiness for him.

For herself as well. No use pretending she was being completely selfless today. After all, he'd handed over complete control to put together the wedding of her dreams.

As she looked out to the arena from her temporary vantage point just inside one of the hallways, she was convinced she had accomplished that.

"You ready, sweetheart?" Vern asked as he approached.

The octogenarian had never looked so handsome. What a beautiful tuxedo he'd chosen. It had been in his closet for years, according to him.

She'd offered to drive him to her favorite place in Jackson Hole and rent a new tux—one that wasn't so tight around the midsection. But he'd held his ground. Said that forcing himself into this one would inspire him to get back to his "boyish figure" in time for his own formal ceremony in two months to the love of his life.

The man was beyond generous and hardworking. Not only by continuing to perform much of the work around his own ranch while bringing joy to others at Christmas without wanting an ounce of credit, but by escorting so many of Destiny Springs's fatherless brides down the aisle.

Today it was her turn to benefit from such a special gift.

"I'm more than ready, Santa."

He smiled and winked.

It was rather fun, sharing such a delicious secret with someone.

Dylan had tried to do that too. Furthermore, she would let him continue to think he'd gotten away with it. Actually, he could have, if she hadn't found it so suspicious that Max sided with her on everything, a little too eagerly. And how the little boy's room was mysteriously filled with new stuffed animals later that day—long after Santa had stopped delivering.

Her curiosity over who bought the toys was what inspired her to check the nanny cam on Becca's phone that evening. She'd reactivated it after the coast was clear and Vern could no longer be outed.

That evening, after she won every wedding plan negotiation, she looked at and listened to the recording, only to find Dylan and Max conspiring to let her have her way while she was upstairs, fetching her laptop.

Georgina had never met a man with a better heart. One who could speak the truth without words but wasn't afraid to resort to using them. That was how she knew he was being honest when he said he loved her and wanted to settle down in Destiny Springs and raise a family.

She'd accidently given away the venue before he could guess, and he made the decision that he'd rather be surprised as far as the rest of the details.

One thing that probably wouldn't surprise him was the royal-length train of her dress—ten feet from the waistline—even though any bride in her right mind wouldn't subject such a beautiful gown to a dirt aisle. Something that might surprise him, however, was that she was wearing her long blond hair down and wavy instead of in her usual French twist.

This was the dress of her dreams, minus the embellishments. Nothing but the best unadorned satin in the most flattering silhouette. Jess and Dorothy at Western Wear with Heart made it happen, even with a growing backlog of requests.

Georgina wasn't sure how she planned to repay Jess, but her partner, Dorothy, had heard about the vow-renewal ceremonies and wanted one for her and her ailing husband. Georgina insisted on reserving a date, in ink, in her planner. Yet another job she couldn't wait to start.

In fact, her own career had taken an unexpected turn. She was eager to add more vow renewals to her portfolio. She loved the simplicity, the lack of stress for everyone involved.

But today was *her* day.

She straightened her shoulders and gave Vern the nod to cue the band.

Pachelbel's Canon in D Major filled the arena. It had never sounded so lovely—and so untraditional. To be expected when the three violins were substituted with a bass, acoustic guitar and drums. The basso, however, was spot on. Montgomery Legend had the pipes for it. The entire Proud River band was sure doing the ceremony… *proud.*

With one hand gripping Vern's arm and another holding the single pink rose as her bouquet, she took the first steps toward the rest of her life. As she got closer to Dylan, she knew she'd made the right decision on every element of the wedding. His uncontained smile confirmed it. Sundance, Dylan's best man, must have concurred because his fluffy tail hadn't stopped wagging.

But now she was the one who was surprised. Dylan wasn't wearing the jeans and black jacket she'd specified. Instead, like Vern, he was also in a tuxedo. *Nothing like a man in a tux.* Oddly enough, it was the one thing she actually *did* want for this wedding but privately conceded during that final selection process, knowing he'd be more comfortable and less nervous if more casual. And it was the only thing—aside from the place and time—that she'd needed to fill him in on in advance.

He didn't listen. At least not to her words.

The band stopped playing, and Georgina and Dylan faced each other.

"You look beautiful," he said.

If he was nervous, she couldn't tell. By contrast, her hands were shaking ever so slightly as she set the rose on the ground, took his hands in hers and squeezed them tight.

"And you look so handsome. Thanks for not listening to me," she said.

"That's because I knew what you really wanted."

"Then you already knew that all I ever wanted was you."

The officiant proceeded to thank everyone for coming here today, then turned to Georgina first, at her request. She'd selected traditional vows but a nontraditional order.

She didn't need a prompt or a script. She'd recited these so many times in the imaginary weddings she'd held for her teddy bears, to dreams she'd had ever since she was a little girl.

Georgina took a deep breath, then looked into his eyes as she spoke.

"I, Georgina Hope Goodwin, take you, Dylan James Legend, to be my lawfully wedded husband. To have and to hold from this day forward.

For better, for worse, for richer, for poorer. In sickness and in health. To love and to cherish, until death do us part."

The officiant turned to Dylan and nodded for him to proceed.

"I… I've written my own vows, if that's okay," he said to the officiant and then to Georgina.

All of a sudden, she worried that this was too much stress and it was her fault. Too much pressure. Too many words.

"Of course that's okay," she said, squeezing his hands to reassure him.

He looked down and back up again.

"I, Dylan James Legend, promise you, Georgina Hope Goodwin, that I will encourage you, laugh with you and comfort you. Your dreams will be my dreams, and I will accompany you on any journey that calls for you. I promise to love you fully and without reservation today and every day, and to walk beside you, hand in hand, wherever life takes us together."

Tears welled in Georgina's eyes, which was never a part of the plan. She was *not* supposed to be a weeping bride. Then things turned even worse as a few tears streamed down her face, taking a little makeup with it. All the while, the officiant waited patiently for her to collect herself.

Dylan reached into his tuxedo pocket, pulled out a handkerchief and handed it to her.

She dabbed at her eyes, then dared to look back into his.

"How did you know I was going to need this?" she asked.

He smiled. "I didn't. I brought it for me."

When the time came for the ring exchange, Max, who had been so still and quiet, presented the simple platinum bands on an ivory satin pillow made for that purpose.

She and Dylan could barely contain a chuckle as he slid the ring on her finger to where it was flush against the pink sparkly plastic one that she would always consider her engagement ring.

They quickly moved to seal the kiss before the officiant could give the instructions. Another unspoken thing they obviously agreed on.

"I now pronounce you husband and wife. You may continue kissing the bride *after* I say one last thing," she said.

Georgina knew what was coming next, and she couldn't wait for everyone there to hear the words.

"Ladies and gentlemen, may I introduce Mr. and Mrs. Dylan James Legend."

The front row of a section of bleachers stood and clapped and cheered, creating a beautiful, symphonic beat that echoed throughout the otherwise empty stadium.

She and Dylan turned to face their families

and closest of friends. Georgina's sisters Hailey and Faye, along with their mom, were clapping the loudest. Becca was holding Alexandra, who hadn't let out a peep throughout the ceremony, until now. Both mother and daughter were crying. Cody, Nash, Parker and their newest Destiny Springs neighbor, Austin Cassidy, were trying to outdo each other with two-fingered whistles, while their wives took the more demure approach and simply clapped and lightly cheered.

By contrast, Rose and Monty shared some kisses of their own and probably thought no one was watching. Or perhaps they simply didn't care.

Dylan leaned in and whispered, "There is one decision you made that I wholeheartedly disagreed with."

Georgina looked at him and blinked. "What was it?"

"The guest list, of course. I wish we would've invited the whole world so that I could show you off, as my dad had said about Rose. That wouldn't have been practical, I know, but this arena does accommodate about two thousand."

He added a smile that told her he was serious about the sentiment but not about the complaint.

"Oh, but I did!" she insisted.

It seemed to take him several seconds to realize that what she'd said was true. She *had* invited the only world that mattered.

*Their world.*

\* \* \* \* \*

*Check out the previous books
in Susan Breeden's
Destiny Springs, Wyoming miniseries,
available now from Harlequin Heartwarming:*

The Bull Rider's Secret Son
Her Kind of Cowboy
The Cowboy's Rodeo Redemption
And Cowboy Makes Three

# Get up to 4 Free Books!

## We'll send you 2 free books from each series you try PLUS a free Mystery Gift.

FREE
Value Over
**$25**

Both the **Harlequin® Special Edition** and **Harlequin® Heartwarming™** series feature compelling novels filled with stories of love and strength where the bonds of friendship, family and community unite.

**YES!** Please send me 2 FREE novels from the Harlequin Special Edition or Harlequin Heartwarming series and my FREE Gift (gift is worth about $10 retail). After receiving them, if I don't wish to receive any more books, I can return the shipping statement marked "cancel." If I don't cancel, I will receive 6 brand-new Harlequin Special Edition books every month and be billed just $6.39 each in the U.S. or $7.19 each in Canada, or 4 brand-new Harlequin Heartwarming Larger-Print books every month and be billed just $7.19 each in the U.S. or $7.99 each in Canada, a savings of 20% off the cover price. It's quite a bargain! Shipping and handling is just 50¢ per book in the U.S. and $1.25 per book in Canada.* I understand that accepting the 2 free books and gift places me under no obligation to buy anything. I can always return a shipment and cancel at any time by calling the number below. The free books and gift are mine to keep no matter what I decide.

Choose one: ☐ **Harlequin**    ☐ **Harlequin**    ☐ **Or Try Both!**
            **Special Edition**    **Heartwarming**    (235/335 & 161/361 BPA G36Z)
            (235/335 BPA G36Y)    **Larger-Print**
                            (161/361 BPA G36Y)

Name (please print)

Address                                             Apt. #

City                       State/Province                 Zip/Postal Code

**Email:** Please check this box ☐ if you would like to receive newsletters and promotional emails from Harlequin Enterprises ULC and its affiliates. You can unsubscribe anytime.

### Mail to the Harlequin Reader Service:
**IN U.S.A.:** P.O. Box 1341, Buffalo, NY 14240-8531
**IN CANADA:** P.O. Box 603, Fort Erie, Ontario L2A 5X3

**Want to explore our other series or interested in ebooks? Visit www.ReaderService.com or call 1-800-873-8635.**

*Terms and prices subject to change without notice. Prices do not include sales taxes, which will be charged (if applicable) based on your state or country of residence. Canadian residents will be charged applicable taxes. Offer not valid in Quebec. This offer is limited to one order per household. Books received may not be as shown. Not valid for current subscribers to the Harlequin Special Edition or Harlequin Heartwarming series. All orders subject to approval. Credit or debit balances in a customer's account(s) may be offset by any other outstanding balance owed by or to the customer. Please allow 4 to 6 weeks for delivery. Offer available while quantities last.

**Your Privacy**—Your information is being collected by Harlequin Enterprises ULC, operating as Harlequin Reader Service. For a complete summary of the information we collect, how we use this information and to whom it is disclosed, please visit our privacy notice located at https://corporate.harlequin.com/privacy-notice. Notice to California Residents – Under California law, you have specific rights to control and access your data. For more information on these rights and how to exercise them, visit https://corporate.harlequin.com/california-privacy. For additional information for residents of other U.S. states that provide their residents with certain rights with respect to personal data, visit https://corporate.harlequin.com/other-state-residents-privacy-rights/.

HSEHW25